ALL IN TRILOGY

THE COMPLETE EDITION

LIZ MELDON

Copyright 2019 Liz Meldon
Published by Liz Meldon, Amazon Edition. All rights reserved.

License Notes
Thank you for downloading this ebook. This book remains the copyrighted property of the author and may not be redistributed to others for commercial or non-commercial purposes. Any unauthorized copies or distributions can be prosecuted to the fullest extent of the law.

This is a work of fiction. Any similarities to persons or situations is unintentional and coincidental. References or mention of trademarks are not intended to infringe on trademark status. Any trademarks referenced or used is done so with full acknowledgement of trademarked status and their respective owners. The use of any mentioned trademarks is not sponsored or authorized by the trademark owner.

Paperback ISBN: 978-0-9938943-5-0

CONTENTS

ALL IN TRILOGY: AFTER THE END

ACKNOWLEDGMENTS

Thank you to my fantastic beta reader Amanda, along with my phenomenal proofreader Phoenix, for catching my errors with poise and tact. As always, much love to my author besties group, my sun and stars, and my parents for being incredibly supportive of this journey. A huge shout out to the #bookstagram community for supporting this trilogy, from the first novella to the last. You guys are amazing. Last, and certainly not least, a great many thanks to my readers. Without you, there's nothing but me and my imagination.

Cover Art by Steamy Book Designs

FINN

Skye Summers: Museum Studies grad, yoga enthusiast, sushi fanatic, self-proclaimed cat lady...

Sugar baby hopelessly falling for her sugar daddy.

Unfortunately for Skye, internet security billionaire Cole Daniels, *professional* workaholic, has always been more like a best friend. When they were paired through an online sugar daddy service in Skye's most desperate hour, Cole rescued her from financial ruin and a stress-induced breakdown. In return, she has kept the press off his back by posing as his girlfriend for the last four years.

But Skye wants more. Not money or fame, but more of him. Cole: sweet, funny, and ceaselessly charming. At times, even he seems to crave a shift in their relationship to something a little messier--before swiftly pulling right back into the friend zone.

Things take a turn for the scandalous, however, when the latest gift from her sugar daddy arrives: a new dress. He's taking Skye to a swanky soiree that evening, and the accompanying note has a titillating aside:

PS: *Wear something underneath that makes you feel sexy.*

Thrilled, Skye obliges with her most daring lingerie. But when Cole's ulterior motives for the night surface, she's forced to swallow her disappointment and seek out her own fun--which arrives in the form of the sinfully handsome heir to a chocolate empire, Finn Rai.

1

DRESS SEXY

"So, if we could get a copy of your references, I think we're all done for today."

Skye Summers looked up from her interview notes, her heart dropping straight into her stomach. "My... Right. Uh."

Trying to hide her panic, she thumbed through the stack of extra résumés she kept in her interview binder. Résumé. Résumé. Résumé... No reference sheet. With the eyes of all three museum administrators boring holes into her forehead from across the table, she inhaled softly, then forced the most brilliant smile she could muster, given the circumstances.

"It seems I've left my reference list at home," she told them, doing her best to ignore the way Marvin from HR scribbled something on the corner of his questionnaire sheet. Her smile widened and trembled, starting to hurt her cheeks. "But I can email you a copy."

"Please do," Gretta, head of the art antiquities department Skye had been trying to get a position in, remarked. "It is a mandatory part of the hiring process. I believe it was on the application checklist."

"I apologize. I'll have it to you as soon as possible." That morning at another interview, Skye had been forced to give all four of the interviewers a printed copy of her references. She wasn't sure why they couldn't have just *shared* the one copy she had provided for them, but it didn't matter now. From the looks on the faces of the trio in front of her, the damage was done.

"Thank you for your time, Miss Summers. We'll be in touch."

Skye stood on shaky legs, hoping the cold sweat from the start of the interview had finally dried up as she shook each of their hands. *We'll be in touch.* It was a familiar song and dance. All those fake smiles. All the waning adrenaline. All the forced gratitude for them taking the time to even speak with her.

Job hunting sucked.

But at least she was getting called for interviews. She considered the idea as she made her way out of the small Etruscan Art and Pottery museum. Skye hadn't specialized in the area by any means, but having graduated a month ago with a degree in Museum Studies and Archival Organization, she had blitzed every museum in Coral Bay—and the rest of California—with an application for whatever positions they might have open. So far, three had called for interviews. One had outright rejected her an hour after she'd submitted her résumé. As stressful, and sometimes demoralizing, as pitching yourself to strangers could be, at least a few people were calling her. Skye knew plenty of former classmates who had been met with radio silence since firing off their applications.

So, really, she *actually* ought to be grateful for the fake smiles and the adrenaline spikes and the serious trauma her hair had endured lately with all the overzealous interview styling. But just because she knew she ought to be grateful didn't make the process any easier.

The first blast of salty, warm coastal air managed to wash the post-interview anxiety off her, and Skye stood on the front steps of the small museum sandwiched between a sushi bar and a vintage clothing boutique, breathing it all in. When she could finally take a step without her legs wobbling with nerves, she swapped her black pumps for teal flip-flops, shoving the heels into her huge pleather purse. Nothing felt better than taking off a painful pair of shoes and replacing them with comfort. Nothing. All her flip-flops were padded—none of this thin, zero-support nonsense for Skye—and she imagined this was exactly what it would feel like to walk on a cloud.

With tourist season kicking off in the sunny seaside town of Coral Bay, Skye opted to walk home instead of trying to flag down a cabbie, who'd only give her grief for being a local. They all wanted to cash in on out-of-towners who had no idea they were being driven the long way around. No thanks.

Halfway down the block she pulled her flaming red hair out of its severe ponytail, mussing out her waves with her fingers. One less uncomfortable thing to grapple with. Ten minutes later, by the time she reached her upscale apartment building—one that she had always thought was too good for her—the rings, bracelets, and earrings had come off too. Shuffling past the doorman, Skye felt more herself in that moment, wearing flip-flops and a pencil skirt that she had slightly unzipped and a flowy blouse that she had untucked, than she had all day. Two back-to-back hour-long interviews in a row wearing gorgeous, flattering, but ultimately not-her-style clothing had left her totally fried.

The interviews themselves drained her mentally, but the clothes sapped her physically.

One day it would be acceptable to wear yoga pants everywhere. If she were Queen of the Universe, it would be a mandate.

"How were the interviews, Miss Summers?"

She shot Ben, one of the three men who ran the twenty-four-seven lobby front desk, a sleepy smile and changed course, heading straight for him.

"Could have been better, I guess," she said with a huff, planting her elbows on the too-tall marble counter. "I don't think I'll be hearing from them, honestly."

The first interview, a museum at the north end of the city that specialized in men's fashion, hadn't left her feeling excited, and this second interview had ended on a sour note. Neither one was promising. The very first museum-focused interview she'd had had been a group interview where three other candidates monopolized all the talk time by screeching over everyone. Skye hadn't been able to get a word in—so, no History of Toilets tours for her. The loss had been devastating.

"Well, I'm sure you gave it your all," Ben mused, then ducked down behind the huge podium that hid the security monitors, among other tablet-shaped tech. "You have a package from Mr. Daniels. His assistant dropped it off an hour ago."

Her whole body warmed at the mention of that name, from the tip-top of her forehead, down along her curves, veering into her naughty bits, then to the tips of her painted toes. Cole Daniels. Internet security and tech guru, humble thirty-year-old *billionaire*...

Also Skye's sugar daddy of four years, and the only

reason she lived in a place with a lobby constructed of marble, granite, and silver.

"I didn't even know he was in town," she said in an effort to downplay her noticeable physical response to the man's name. Ben straightened moments later with a large rectangular box in hand: white, with a red silk bow on top—the only true splash of colour in the otherwise mutely decorated lobby. She accepted it with a grin, her insides twisting and turning. "Thanks."

"Anytime, Miss Summers. Just let me know if you need anything else today."

"You've always got my back."

She clutched the box to her as she hurried for the elevators, which Ben had already activated. Cole's gift was light and didn't rattle when she gave the package a little shake. Clothes, probably. She had told him a thousand times that he didn't have to buy her things—everything he did for her was more than enough already. Hell, paying her university tuition, the whole reason she had joined the sugar baby–sugar daddy service based out of LA, had been more than enough of a gift to last Skye the rest of her lifetime.

He never listened. Whenever he popped into town, usually in the summer months and around the new year, he came bearing gifts. Beautiful, thoughtful, expensive gifts that Skye didn't need, but never had the heart to turn down.

Kind of like her apartment. After financing her first year's tuition, Cole had handed her the keys to a swanky apartment and told her to use it for as long as she was in Coral Bay. When she'd protested, he had insisted that he needed her to house-sit the unit while he was away or else there would be insurance issues, a story Skye had never believed but used to validate her presence there whenever she was feeling guilty. After all, Cole never stayed with her when he was in town; he had a beach house on a huge private plot of land at the south end of the city. So, for the last four years, the apartment had been Skye's and Skye's alone.

After a smooth elevator ride up to the sixth floor, she hurried for her apartment, eager to rip into the box. As soon as she stuck the key in the lock, she was greeted by Oz's boisterous meows from the other side, a sound that always brought a smile to her face no matter what kind of day she'd had.

"My baby Ozzy," she cooed, slipping inside carefully—the little shit would bolt whenever the door was open wide enough—and scooping up the pampered ball of white fur. He purred noisily in response, rubbing his face along her cheek and chin, paws kneading the air in utter contentment.

Skye always considered tuition and the apartment to be the first gifts Cole had ever lavished her with, but really, Oz was number one on the list. The day before their first agency-arranged meet-up, the one couples used to figure out if they were a good fit, Skye's cat of eighteen and a half years had finally crossed over the rainbow bridge. Devastated, she'd called Cole in tears, asking to postpone the meeting for a few days while she dealt with the loss. At the time, rescheduling had been the last thing she wanted to do: her funds were drained, school seemed like a dream she'd never achieve, and Cole had been the first and only sugar daddy at the agency to request a meeting with her.

The whole thing had been her last resort to afford school after years of working constant part-time jobs, first to pay down her mom's debt after she died, then just to, you know, survive. Juggling multiple shifts while attempting to take the odd online class here and there, she had never gotten anywhere financially or academically. Back then, a friend had shared an article online about sugar daddy relationships, which led to a lot of research and internet sleuthing on her part. While Skye thought "sugar daddies" absurd in theory, one night, after downing a whole bottle of cheap wine, she had applied to the agency of her choosing when she was feeling particularly hopeless, overwhelmed, and exhausted.

Much to her surprise, the agency accepted her—for a fee. Most of her savings account, actually, with barely three months of rent left, plus a meager amount for food. The promise of a wealthy man covering her living expenses while she finally got her dream degree had forced her hand, and, for once in her life, the risk had paid off.

She had been fortunate that Cole stuck with her after their initial setback, considering how well they got along now and how smooth the whole process had been for her. That initial meeting, however, could have spiraled into disaster if he'd thought she was rejecting him—or whatever other reasons a fragile macho-male ego might have dreamt up.

Skye had quickly learned, thankfully, that Cole had the farthest thing from a fragile male ego.

After they had rescheduled for the following week, with Cole sounding super sympathetic on the phone, he had showed up at the outdoor café that they agreed to meet at bearing Oz in kitten form, a baby blue ribbon knotted into a bow around his neck, the colour matching his striking eyes.

Skye would never admit it, but since that moment, she'd been smitten—both with her precious Oz *and* Cole.

"What have you been up to?" she murmured as she pressed kisses to Oz's silky soft fur, kicking off her flip-flops and strolling into the sprawling apartment. The two-bedroom had an open concept area living/dining area and sandy-pink tile flooring. Seventy square feet of balcony space off the living room gave her a ton of space for breakfast outdoors and yoga in the sunshine, and the jacuzzi soaker tub in the master bath was to die for. Cole had furnished the apartment with the basics, though over the years she had added bits of herself to it in the form of abstract paintings, favored textbooks, and fresh floral arrangements—all cat-friendly, of course.

Settling on the edge of the couch, Skye placed Oz on her right and Cole's present on the coffee table, then hastily unwrapped the bow. She gave Oz the thick red ribbon to play with, wrapping it around his lithe figure—made larger by an insane amount of fur—and he immediately went into kill mode, flopping back on the cushions, mouth wide and back feet kicking. After a few moments of watching him play-kill, Skye lifted off the top part of the box and grabbed the note inside. As she suspected—upscale clothes of some kind, wrapped in tissue paper. At least the note was in Cole's handwriting; Skye had become quiet adept at differentiating between his scrawl and his assistant.

Consider the dress my apology for springing this on you last-minute. There's a gala tonight that I only just learned I need a plus-one to attend. I'll pick you up at eight.

x x Cole

Skye squirmed, heat flaring between her thighs, as she read

the words, Cole's gorgeous British accent dancing around her head.

Well. So much for her yoga class tonight. Skye had hoped all the stretching and deep breathing and socializing would help her forget the stress of post-grad interview season, but a fancy gala on the arm of a billionaire would probably work just as well.

"Ouch!" Oz had gone from murdering the ribbon a foot away to doing it directly against her thigh, and she pushed him back down the couch to avoid another clawing. Shaking her head, she flipped the small card over, then frowned when she spotted something on the back.

PS: Wear something underneath that makes you feel sexy.

x

Skye sat back on the couch, card falling to her lap, then ran her hands through her hair. Wear something sexy underneath? Like...sexy underwear? A flood of adrenaline pounded through her at the thought, a delicious spike of excited energy paired with repressed desire.

When she had first read about sugar daddies and their relationships with sugar babies—ugh, the term still made her cringe—Skye had just assumed all these women were glorified escorts, despite the agency she used vehemently denying the accusation. Skye had taken their word for it at the time, but she hadn't trusted it, not entirely, even after she signed her contracts to use the agency's services. After all, why would a rich, successful guy buy someone the world without expecting anything but companionship in return? That didn't make sense to her—until Cole. They had a clause in their personal contract that stipulated physical affection was not required under any circumstances unless expressly agreed to by both parties. It was not to be used as payment for gifts, and if it was used as an intimidation tactic, the contract was null and void—and the guilty party would have to make financial restitutions at an agreed upon amount.

Essentially, sex had been off the table from day one, just as Skye requested when she had applied to the agency. Once she had been paired with Cole Daniels, however, she regretted not thinking things through a little more carefully. Nowadays, since she had no desire to muddy their friendship, Skye hadn't acted on her underlying feelings. Not once in four years. In return, Cole hadn't done more than hold her hand, kiss her cheek, and give her a friendly hug.

Sure, at parties they ramped up the cuddling and touching for the benefit of others. After all, that was what Skye brought to the relationship: she appeared in public as his girlfriend. Cole traveled so much, worked so hard, that he had no time for a real relationship. Unfortunately, the press in the US and Britain had crucified one of their most eligible bachelors for appearing standoffish and uncomfortable with the dating scene. Like he was some weirdo for not having a model on his arm.

Skye had quickly learned that Cole wanted a genuine connection—he just didn't have space in his life to pursue anything romantic long-term. He wanted a close friend whom he could bring to parties and on vacations so the press would leave him alone. Apparently none of the women in his private life had fit the bill, so he'd gone with an outside hire. When Skye had heard his terms, she'd decided she could easily manage them, especially for a guy as sweet as Cole. In return, he supported her financially through school while she earned a degree at age twenty-nine that she could have had by age twenty-one but had never been able to afford.

But in her mind, it had never been *just* a friendship between them. To Skye, there had always been something more, some underlying tension, *heat*, that flared whenever they got together.

She had always just assumed it had to be one of two things when it came to Cole Daniels, sugar daddy and all around wonderful human being. One: he wasn't interested in her romantically. But if that was the case, he had a future in acting, given the way he treated her in public. Or two: he also didn't want to ruin what they had by complicating everything with sex. Skye had always hoped option two was the truth, but given how tight-lipped Cole was about his personal feelings, it could have easily been option one.

Lips pursed, she read the card over one more time, absently dragging the ribbon around to keep Oz busy. There *were* an awful lot of x-kisses here, even for Cole. And he had never asked her to dress *sexy* before. Generally, the term he used was *appropriate*, though he had always given her a rundown of the event beforehand so she could style herself accordingly.

Maybe it was finally happening.

Maybe he had decided to throw caution to the wind and cross the line they had both been dancing around for years.

Was she ready to take the plunge? Was she ready to make things messy, to complicate what had always been so clear-cut and easy?

Skye hoisted a purring Oz onto her lap, deciding she had about four hours to figure it out.

2

FLYING SOLO

There was something about sexy lingerie that could make any woman feel like a million bucks. For Skye, comfortable cotton—or, preferably, nothing at all—had been her go-to for just about any occasion. Given that she'd been so focused on school over the last few years, dates had been reserved for Cole, and none of those had resulted in her stripping down to anything more than a bikini. So, when he told her to wear something sexy under the mildly shapeless beige shift dress he'd bought for her, she went all out in a full black push-up bra and garter set that she'd purchased on a whim at a bachelorette party years ago.

As luck would have it, the getup still fit, and she paired it with a set of lacey panties to match, along with near sheer thigh-high black tights with a lace-inspired top to clip her garter belts to. Never had she dared to go quite so provocative, but if Cole was going to make a move tonight, then Skye wanted to be ready—in spades.

After polishing off leftover sushi for dinner, she showered, shaved, and moisturized whatever she could reach. She kept her makeup minimal, but paired her black and white ensemble with a bold red lip. It was a bit too matchy-matchy with the first pair of heels she chose, so those were downgraded to black wedges that didn't hurt her feet quite as much. Her coppery, sun-kissed hair rolled down her back in full Jessica Rabbit waves; it was the most work she'd put into her outfit in a long time. The last gala/cocktail party/snooty affair Cole had brought her to had been six months ago at a New Year's Eve gala in LA, and then he'd had a stylist, hairdresser, and makeup artist who did the work for her.

Tonight was all Skye, and as she strutted across the lobby, smiling at Ben when he flashed a ten out of ten with his fingers, she felt like she owned the world.

Funny how a little personal pampering and a killer outfit could make your mood do a complete one-eighty in just a few hours.

Her stomach somersaulted at the sight of Cole's usual black town car waiting for her outside the building. As she approached, her hands grew clammy, her ankles felt wobbly, and her sanity asked if she knew what she was doing. Given her choice of undergarments, Skye had made her decision: it was time for this relationship to get a little messy. If Cole made a move, if all signs pointed to liftoff, then Skye planned to give in wholeheartedly.

An unfamiliar driver stood waiting for her at the curb, and she smiled when he tipped his hat and opened the door. Skye slid in smoothly, pleased that she wouldn't have to fend off paparazzi today; they followed Cole *everywhere* when they figured out what country he was in.

"Hello, sweetheart."

Skye all but melted into the seat at his greeting—though it would have been more romantic if he'd actually looked up from his phone. At this point in their relationship, him clacking around on a screen didn't offend her: screens were his job, and his job was his life. Still... The note...

"Hi," she said, trying to keep her voice even as she leaned over and pressed a kiss to his cheek. "This is a fun surprise."

Dressed to the nines in a fitted tux, Cole was equal measures breathtaking and panty-dropping. While he was only a few inches taller than her, his trim yet muscular figure always filled out his impeccably tailored outfits perfectly. When he finally tucked his phone into his inner jacket pocket and looked up, the full force of those ocean-blue eyes hit her like a freight train, forcing Skye to fiddle with her clutch as her cheeks heated to a boil.

"Is it? I was worried I was pushing it a bit with the timing," he told her as the car peeled away from the curb, merging seamlessly with the late-night traffic. Coral Bay's size allotted most people the luxury of walking everywhere, but there must have been multiple events happening tonight, as the road was full of cabs. Skye tore her gaze from the window, then chuckled when she realized she had left a huge lipstick mark on Cole's cheek.

Scruffless today. She preferred him with a bit of brown-blond stubble, though the clean-shaven look highlighted that he'd been somewhere with a lot of sun recently, making his eyes pop—almost to the point where she couldn't meet them.

Or maybe she couldn't meet them because she was wearing the sexiest thing in her wardrobe under the loose-fitting, exquisitely soft dress.

"It's fine. I just had yoga tonight anyway," she insisted, rubbing the lipstick off with her thumb. Cole scowled and tried to twist out of reach, but she clamped down on his strong chin and held him in place. "Sit still and let me fix you."

He groaned. "*Mum*, you're embarrassing me."

Skye adored that side of him—the playful, silly, *real* side he so seldom let the public see. When they were alone, a bit of that upper-crust polish faded, hinting at the estuary accent he'd had since birth. Skye preferred that too.

With all the lipstick gone, Skye retreated to her side of the car, though she couldn't ignore the fact that their legs, both crossed, were touching.

"So, tell me about the interviews," he insisted as he stretched his arm out across the back of the seat. She swallowed hard, ignoring the way the heat of his slightly curled hand warmed the nape of her neck.

"All of them?"

"I haven't seen you in over two months," Cole said with a slight shake of his head. "Too long." His eyes dipped down to her body briefly before flickering back to her face. "Do you like the dress? I told Hunter to go for an off-white because of the, well..."

He gestured to her, struggling, and Skye's eyes narrowed.

"The *what*?"

"The ghost-pale speckled look," he said, which earned his leg a slap. He took it with a smirk. "What? You've said so yourself."

"Well, we can't all get our glamorous tans off the coast of some tropical paradise," Skye fired back. "You know I just burn, then go back to porcelain no matter what I try."

"My freckly queen—I'm *more* than aware."

Damn it. She bit her lip, cheeks hot again, and decided a change of subject was in order. So, she switched gears to her interviews, including the two from today and the one she'd had two weeks ago. Cole listened with an unflinching intensity that had unnerved her when they first met; now, she knew it was just Cole providing a rare moment of undivided attention, technology-free.

"Don't be ridiculous," he said, taking that I'm-a-sexy-professor-lecturing-you tone that always made her knees weak. "They'd be fools not to hire you."

"There are lots of qualified candidates locally because of the college. I don't know. I'm not too optimistic."

She noted the change in scenery behind him in the passing streetlamp light. They'd left Coral Bay proper about five minutes ago and were headed in the direction of the elite suburbs still within the city limits. Mansions, many of which backed directly onto the beach, dotted the coast. Ten-foot cement walls surrounded each gated community. Given that Cole's beach house was on the south end, not the north, she had never had a reason to do more than stare wistfully in passing at the homes poking through a forest of palm, oak, and cypress trees on the other side of the walls; another added measure to obstruct the plebeians' gaze. She could only assume the landscaping around the enormous manors would be even more impressive.

And it was. Given that Skye had had a sugar daddy relationship with a billionaire for a little over four years, she'd thought she would be used to opulence by now—not so. While Cole tapped around on his phone after flashing his ID to security at the gated front entrance, Skye spent the remainder of the ride all but pressed up against the car window, gawking at how big, beautiful, and lavish the houses were, each one bigger, more beautiful, and more lavish than the last.

They eventually stopped at the house to beat them all: a lone mansion at the end of the lane, surrounded by mangrove trees and blooming crape myrtles. After joining the queue in the circular driveway, Skye noted that a grand cement stairwell led up a slight incline to the main house, with impressive flourishing gardens on either side. Pod lights scattered across the lawn lit up the place, though one look at the house and you could tell there was a party in full swing inside.

"We won't be here long. Keep your phone on you for when I call," Cole told the driver before the man hopped out and hurried around to Skye's side of the car. She accepted his hand as he helped her out, trying not to ogle the house more than she already had. One of the things she had learned as Cole's sugar baby was not to appear as though she didn't belong. Blending in, acting bored, and feigning disinterest could all go on her résumé as special skills at this point.

Still. The house *was* pretty impressive. Like a Spanish manor in an era gone by, it sat atop a small hill overlooking its kingdom. Two stories, with a wrought iron balcony stretching the full length of the top floor, its exterior colouring reminded her of the inside of a seashell. It must have been breathtaking in the daylight. For now, she made do with the lights dotting the hillside gardens and the soft yellow glow of the veranda.

"Now, there are a few things I need to tell you about before we get in there." Cole threaded his fingers around hers as they climbed the stairs together in perfect unison.

"Okay."

"The party, it's..." He cleared his throat. "It's a sex party."

Skye stopped walking and tugged her hand away. It was a *what?*

"I know, I know, *totally* inappropriate for us," Cole

insisted, hands up somewhat apologetically. "There are a few people here who keep skirting my calls, intentionally giving me the runaround, and I really just need to corner them and sort things out. This was my best opportunity."

Skye opened and closed her dry mouth a few times, lost for words. His expression, his tone—none of it suggested he wanted to play tonight. Not with her, anyway, and not in the way she had hoped.

"When the organizer told me the theme this morning, I thought it'd be a bit unsettling if I showed up here without a date," he said, almost tentatively, like he was bracing for her response. "I'll only need an hour or so. There's a private poker game off-limits to everyone but a select few."

"And I take it you're one of the select few," Skye managed, her words a hoarse whisper until she cleared her throat. "And I also take it I'm *not* one of the select few. You know I don't know how to play poker."

When he nodded, she planted a hand on her hip and tried to ignore her racing heart. Clearly he hadn't brought her here for sex. It was the same story as always: Skye was here to smile for pictures, hang off his arm, and make it seem like he had an active romantic life so his social circles wouldn't think he was a total weirdo recluse outside the office.

So why the PS on his card? What was the point of her lingerie getup? Did he want her to fool around with other people? Her stomach knotted at the thought.

"Skye, please don't be cross—"

"I'm missing yoga for this," she hissed to divert her sudden rush of emotion, an uncomfortable blend of disappointment, frustration, and rejection.

"Yeah, but you said it was *just* yoga, remember?"

She pinched his arm, hard, when he offered what she

knew he thought was a cheeky grin, the one that always worked on her.

But not tonight.

"Skye, I'm sorry. I should have warned you sooner—"

"It's fine." She lifted her gaze to the house. Maybe this was for the best. Maybe they weren't meant to cross the line, to delve into the unexplored sensual side of their relationship. Maybe messy just wasn't for them. Skye swallowed hard, her mind jumping from them making it messy to them severing ties because they couldn't *handle* the messy, and the thought of losing Cole actually made her a little teary-eyed.

He noticed before she could brush the moisture away. "Skye? Is everything okay?"

"I just had a rough day," she admitted. "It's nothing. Seriously. Am I excited to spend the next hour by myself while you go bully some rich assholes? Not really, but it's fine. I'm fine."

"Oh, come now." He captured her hand again as another pair of couples made their way up the stairs around them. "You don't have to be by yourself. This is an excellent opportunity to network. I know for a fact several members of the arts and culture council will be here."

She arched an eyebrow. "Trolling for sex?"

"Well, probably." Cole smirked as they slowly resumed climbing the stairs. "I'm not saying you have to participate. Don't feel pressured to do anything you're not comfortable with." His voice seemed to catch as he spoke, like he wasn't entirely comfortable with the subject matter either. "Although it's my understanding these things don't heat up until midnight, so we have some time."

"What, you don't frequent sex parties?"

"Not without you," he stated, then begrudgingly dug out his phone when it chirped in his pocket.

And there it was. One of those *moments*, those instances where Skye had to wonder if she wasn't imagining things and Cole really did want her—or if she was losing it and that was just his sense of humor.

Whatever the case may be, she didn't have time to scrutinize it. Soon enough, she and Cole were inside, being welcomed by an army of party staff who explained the layout of the house, what was off-limits, and that swimming in the ocean while intoxicated was never a good idea. They were then escorted from the huge foyer with its crystal chandelier and gold trimmings to a large room positively brimming with people, a room that overlooked the backyard —and, by extension, the private hillside beach trailing down to the Pacific.

"See, plenty of people to butter up," Cole insisted. With the party tour guides gone, he stood slightly behind her, an arm around her waist and his hard body pressed flush against her back. Her skin prickled as his words rolled in soft, heated whispers across her ear, and she barely had the capacity to pay attention when he pointed out three city councilors, two museum benefactors, and one university department head. Then he kissed her cheek, the feel of his lips lingering long after they left, and gave her waist a little squeeze. "Go network, sweetheart. I'll be back before you know it."

She watched him go, skirting the crowd along the back wall and heading for a doorway with a black ribbon across it —one of those off-limits places, she assumed. However, as he neared, a waiter in head-to-toe navy pulled the rope aside and gestured for him to enter. Before he disappeared,

Cole met her eye and mouthed *I believe in you* from across the room.

Skye rolled her eyes, but couldn't keep a smile off her face. She adored that man, whether he wanted to take things to the next level or not. Her disappointment wasn't his concern; Skye had primed herself for something that would probably never happen. Whatever she felt in that moment was her problem and hers alone.

One she planned to drown in champagne as soon as possible. Squaring her shoulders, she ignored the way a cluster of men eyed her and flagged down a roving server. He almost glided away after she took one flute of golden bubbly, but Skye grabbed his sleeve and held him in place as she downed the entire thing, then took another.

"Okay," she muttered, tapping her finger against the crystal and scanning the crowd. "Network. I can network for an hour."

Zeroing in on a councilmember, a middle-aged woman whose dress got sheerer and sheerer as Skye approached, she mentally prepared her sell-yourself speech, then forced a bright smile and sidled into the conversation like she had been there the whole time.

3

RED WINE CASUALTY

So much for nothing wild happening before midnight.

Cole's one-hour mark had nearly come and gone, and the networking crowd had turned into a huge, convoluted orgy that spilled out onto the back patio in half that time. Feeling awkward and not the slightest bit interested in participating, Skye had slipped out of sight and decided to explore the huge mansion on her own. She had moved from champagne to a very rich red wine, which she had nursed throughout her unguided tour. So far, she had counted ten bedrooms, explored the lower level indoor pool with an enormous window that faced the beach, and had perused the owner's library, which also housed a fine art collection. Most of the works were abstract statues, with the occasional bit of seemingly authentic ancient pottery, but the real money was in the classic books. Whole bookcases were lined with them, all in mint condition, and Skye had examined each one while holding her red wine out as far as her arm would go in the opposite direction. No way could she afford to replace so much as a single floor tile in this place, never mind a whole antique book.

Although the greeters had gone into some detail about there being off-limits sections around the house, aside from a few black ropes over *open* doorways, there was nothing around to stop her from going wherever she damn well pleased. Every so often, Skye checked her phone to see if she had somehow missed Cole trying to reach her—and found nothing but her screen saver of a sleeping Oz staring back at her.

Any time she heard the sounds of fornication, drunken or otherwise, Skye shot off in the opposite direction, in no mood to deal with *that* particular nightmare.

She still couldn't believe Cole had brought her to a sex party with no intention of actually having sex with her. That bit stung the most. Well, no. The emotional, *feelings* side of things stung the most, but it was easier to pretend she was angry he didn't want to fuck her in her gorgeous lingerie.

Taking another sip of wine, so dark it might as well have been plum, she left the library behind and strolled down a hallway lit by a smattering of wall-mounted fixtures, styled to look like Victorian oil lamps. Her wedges clicked softly on the tile, off-white etched with streaks of grey, and she contemplated heading down to the beach to escape the whole thing. When Cole was ready to go, he could come find her, damn it.

Just as she rounded the corner, however, two bodies slammed into her—seemingly out of nowhere. She staggered back and tried desperately to hold her drink away from her dress, but the damage was done. Lukewarm liquid seeped through the fabric, right to her skin, dribbling down her neck, over her chest, and into her black lingerie.

The offenders, two female twenty-somethings with glazed eyes and flushed cheeks, skipped off in a fit of giggles, their hair the definition of bed head and their feet bare. And not an apology to be seen.

"What the *fuck*..." Skye stood there, half a glass of red wine staining Cole's gift, and couldn't decide whether to laugh or cry. Clearly the pair were drunk as skunks, but why hadn't she heard them coming? Had she been so lost in her own head, thinking about Cole, that her brain had ignored the impending danger? Worrying, if that was the case. Mouth pinched, she stared down at herself: she looked like a gunshot victim. "Fucking fuck *fuck*."

"If you just stand there staring and cursing like a sailor, it's going to set. If we act now, we can salvage it."

"W-What..." Skye whirled around to find a man charging down the hall toward her—the kind of man she assumed only lived on film and in romance novels. Tall, muscular, his olive skin paired with startlingly dark eyes, like he'd gone straight from the Mediterranean to the runway. He wore a fitted grey suit sans tie, bow or otherwise, the top of that white button-down popped open, black dress shoes that clicked curtly with every step—and an expression suggesting she had committed a cardinal sin in front of the Pope.

"I knew this would happen," he muttered in a rather posh English accent, the kind that made her toes curl in a way that Cole's didn't. "As soon as I saw the red wine, I knew there'd be a casualty tonight."

He strode right into her personal space and plucked the wine glass from her hand, then set it on top of a nearby wall lamp. Skye stiffened when he turned his attention to the soiled fabric of her dress, tsking under his breath as he picked at it, towering over her by a good half foot or so.

"Uh, okay, who the hell are you?" She took a few much-needed steps back, her heart racing for a myriad of reasons. Never in her life had desire slapped her so hard across the face within ten seconds of meeting a man. Sure, she could acknowledge gorgeous men—beach towns like Coral Bay in coastal California were full of them, and not just the rich kind like Cole—but this was unfamiliar territory. He'd stolen her breath away—and all he'd done was chastise her and complain about the host serving red wine.

What on earth was happening to her? Although she'd downed a few glasses of champagne and a bit of the red wine, she wasn't *that* drunk.

"Finn," he said curtly, like she ought to already know his name. "Come on. Let's try to save this while we can."

"Do you have some personal investment in my dress?" She tried not to sound snippy as he stalked away, but the presumption that she would just follow *him*, the guy lecturing her about red wine stains, blew her mind. He slowed as she added, "Did you design it or something?"

"I always think it's a shame to see beauty marred," he told her, marching back and snatching her hand. The physical contact sparked a blaze, one whose flames crept up Skye's arm and engulfed her body like a wildfire. As she grappled with the surge of desire, the instant connection, Finn half led, half tugged her down the hall, step by step, and over his shoulder, lips curved in a sinful smirk, said, "And when we've sorted out the dress, we'll see what we can do about cleaning up the rest of you."

Her eyebrows shot up, both impressed and surprised at his nerve, and she debated between yanking her hand free and storming off, just to teach him a lesson, and seeing where this bold, impulsive man would lead her.

In the end, Skye chose the latter after checking her phone and finding nothing from Cole.

Because she was covered in wine and had nothing else to do—so why not?

Finn guided her through the huge villa like he had intimate knowledge of the place, taking her down halls, up stairs, and across balconies, finally stopping in a bathroom with one of those rainstorm showers where the spray came from above. Oh, and a jacuzzi tub, *and* a set of double sinks sunk down in sparkling granite countertop. Given how ostentatious every other room in the house appeared, it shouldn't surprise her that the bathroom would be first-rate too.

"Dress off," he ordered briskly, crouching down and opening one of the little doors under the sink. Slowly, hesitantly, Skye complied with the request, then held the garment out to him. When he straightened up, his eyes flickered down to her chest, then southward, his lips slightly parted. A soft clearing of her throat brought him back to her face, though the pinched look of annoyance was gone, replaced instead with a flush of dark desire splayed plainly across his features.

Well done, lingerie. It'd had the intended effect—just on the wrong man.

Or maybe not. Given that Cole had never looked at her like he wanted to eat her up—or out—maybe Finn was the *exact* person she was supposed to use this getup on, especially after her confidence faceplant with tonight's earlier letdown.

"Take this," Finn told her, voice gruff as he shoved a white towel in her direction. "Then blot out the wine while I get the rest of what we need."

She hastily shuffled out of the way as he brushed by her

—and shot straight out the door like someone had a gun to his head. The towel he had given her was *way* too luxurious to be used on wine mopping, but everything in the spotless bathroom was too good for cleaning, so Skye worked with what she had.

Frowning, she laid her dress out on the counter and tried to soak up what she could. A quick glance in the mirror showed her heaving cleavage, made spectacular by the lacey black push-up with a cute little satin bow between her full breasts. Her coppery red waves fell over one shoulder, and while still clearly styled, they appeared feathered now, like someone had combed their fingers through them. Her brown eyes wandered lower, pleased with the way the garter belt cinched snug around her high waist, the straps that connected down to her stockings pressing just enough into her skin that there would be a faint mark. Her panties, thank goodness, hadn't been bunched when Finn gave her that sensual once-over.

All in all, she looked positively fuckable.

Given her near nonexistent romantic life over the last sugar daddy'd years, it was about damn time she looked this good. Skye threw her shoulders back, ruby-red lips twisted into a coy smile, and continued to rub at the red wine stain —which didn't seem to want to disappear anytime soon.

"Blot!" Finn's thunderous proclamation from the doorway made her jump, and he rushed forward with the rest of his supplies in hand like a doctor beelining for a crashing patient. "You have to *blot*, not rub! Are you insane?"

"No," she said slowly, stepping aside with crossed arms when he snatched the towel away from her, "but I'm starting to think you are."

He chuckled, the sound skittering across her skin and

shooting straight to her sex, as he dabbed the towel across the dress. "Flatterer."

Skye watched, perched on the edge of the bathroom counter, what could very well be a lunatic dab, dab, dab at her dress until the towel had soaked up a good deal of the wine. He then grabbed an empty glass bowl and set the faintly pink fabric across it, pulled it taut, and coated every inch of stain with salt. After, he ducked out of the bathroom, only to return moments later with a kettle—the same electric kettle she had at home, actually.

"Okay, this is getting ridiculous," she said, biting back laughter. "Who does this?"

"A man who was once a very, very, *very* messy boy," Finn told her as he poured steaming hot water over the dress. Moments later, the salt was gone—as was most of the stain. When he straightened, a triumphant grin on his lips, she offered a round of genteel applause, tapping her fingertips together.

"Bravo. Looks just like new."

"Nearly." Setting his equipment aside, he wrung out the dress—gently, with more care than she had ever seen a man handle an article of clothing with before—and then passed it off to the loitering woman in a maid's costume in the doorway. Skye blushed; she hadn't even realized they weren't alone.

"Uh, hold on—"

"We'll get it washed and dried before you leave. One hour, at the most," Finn told her, closing the door after thanking the other woman. And like that, her dress was gone, disappearing in the arms of a stranger—just as Skye had.

"You didn't have to do any of this, you know." She bit

her lower lip as his wandering gaze burned a trail of intense interest across her skin. Leaning against the wall, arms crossed, Finn shrugged.

"What can I say? I'm a giver." He chuckled again, and she felt herself clench—that husky voice paired with that accent. *Ugh*. Exquisite.

"Well, thank you. You've saved me a hefty dry-cleaning bill."

"I aim to please. Now..." Finn's gaze wandered the bathroom before landing on her with the focus of a predatory cat's. "Whatever shall we do to keep ourselves occupied in the meantime?"

Skye pursed her lips as she sat on the rim of the bathtub, the cool porcelain paired with his lusty stare igniting a rush of goosebumps just about everywhere.

"I'm not going back out there like this."

"No?" He tsked again. "But you're so dressed for the occasion. You'd be a hit, I'm sure."

"No thank you." The thought of touching *any* of those people in the orgy downstairs also made her shiver—with distaste. Finn, on the other hand... Skye could most definitely touch Finn.

"Then I suppose it will be my honor to keep you entertained right down to the last second." He crossed the bathroom and sat a few feet from her on the edge of the tub, his dark stare holding hers unflinchingly. "Can I tell you what *I'd* like to do?"

Skye almost laughed; it didn't take a rocket scientist to figure that one out.

"Shoot."

"I'd like to lick every last drop of red wine off that ivory skin of yours," he rumbled, leaning in slightly as her heartbeat quickened. "I'd like to trace every freckle. Explore every curve." Finn caught her chin between thumb and forefinger, edging her toward him. "And I'd like to see if you taste as divine as I think you will..."

4

EMOTIONAL OOMPH

In that moment, all Skye wanted was to croon something sexy back at him in an equally seductive tone. Hell, she was dressed for this production—she looked the part, and now she just had to say the lines.

A horrific sort of barking laugh crawled up her throat and exploded in his face instead. Mortified, Skye pulled away and pressed her hands to her steadily reddening cheeks.

"I'm so sorry."

"Don't be," Finn said, clearing his throat. He might have seemed put-together, but there was a flicker of faltering confidence—shown in the slight twitch of his cheek—that told Skye her rejection had stung. "Clearly I read the room wrong."

"No, no, it's not that," she insisted, surprised at herself. "It's just... Men don't ever really talk to me like that. I didn't know how to respond. I didn't... Yeah."

She braced for a snide comment and a storm out, but instead found Finn studying her with a renewed interest, and while he didn't inch toward her, something in his eyes had gone back to drawing her in.

"Well, men *should* say things like that to you." He grinned. "Because you're stunning..." Dark lashes fluttered as he blinked rapidly, as if thrown off by something. "And I now realize I don't even know your name."

"Would it matter if you did?"

"Not ordinarily," he replied smoothly, "but in this particular instance, I think yes. In this instance, I very much want to know your name."

"Well, how fucking blessed am I?" Clearly a playboy. Clearly used to getting his way. She couldn't fathom why he wasn't downstairs being King of the Orgy.

"Look, no, I'm sorry," Finn scrambled when she stood up. Although Skye had no intention of storming out, she liked seeing him squirm a little. He waited until she sat back down, her arms crossed, then sighed. "Let's start over." He held out his hand. "Hi, my name's Finn and I'd like to lick wine off your body."

She snorted, and, after a brief hesitation, grasped his hand. "Skye."

"Beautiful."

She shrugged. "Sometimes."

"Now, let's talk facts," Finn said, crossing one leg over the other and resting his elbow on his knee, chin on his fist. "First, you are at a sex party. Second, you are dressed like a Christmas present I want to unwrap. Third, I'm charming as the day is long—"

"Not as charming as you think." She raised an eyebrow at him, enjoying the challenge. "Just because I'm dressed a certain way doesn't mean you can make assumptions about me."

"No, I suppose not. I'd still like to ravish you, if I could."

"And if I say no? Will I never see my dress again?"

"Of course you'll see it again. I don't take hostages."

"Will I get kicked out of this den of sin?"

"Not by me."

"Will you stomp out of here and call me a bitch?"

"*Never.*" He paired his response with an appropriately disgusted look, one that Skye read as genuine. "Tell me your reservations. Is it me? Do I not stoke the embers of your burning loins?"

"Gross," she said, laughing.

"Are you here with someone?" She faltered, and Finn leaned back with a knowing nod. "I should have guessed someone so striking would already be taken."

"We're not..." She licked her lips. How could she categorize her relationship with Cole? She and her sugar daddy had never been romantic, even if the feelings, for her, were there. They were friends with mutual, nonsexual benefits. Skye swallowed hard. "It's complicated."

"Ah." Finn's eyes narrowed slightly, like a psychologist assessing her from the other side of the couch. "And would you rather he and I switch places, with he the one wanting to taste you all over?" Her cheeks warmed again, almost to the point of pain, and Finn chuckled. "I'll take that as a yes."

Even if that was true, Skye didn't hate the fact that Finn was here either. "How does that make you feel?"

"A bit wounded." He placed a hand to his heart. "But I'm a big boy. I can take care of myself."

"Then maybe that's my advice to you. Take *care* of yourself."

He inhaled sharply, lips twisting into a wicked smile. "Oh, I like you, Miss Skye. Very much."

There it was again—that fire. It crackled across her skin,

leaving her hot and flushed and desperate to fan herself down. Instead, she folded her hands together and tried to maintain this unexpected air of cocky nonchalance.

"You know, even if I *were* interested in your offer," she started, adding a one-shouldered shrug for effect, "and I'm not one hundred percent saying I'm not—but if I were, I'd need a little more from you."

"Saving your dress wasn't enough?"

"I need a backstory," she told him. "I need to feel invested in you as a character. I need a bit of *oomph* to get going."

"Emotional oomph?"

"Emotional oomph." She gestured between them. "I need to feel like I kind of know you, at least. Just a little bit of connection."

"Mental oomph too, then."

"I guess you could call it that."

"You drive a hard bargain, Skye."

She tried to come up with a quip on the fly using the word *hard*, but couldn't. Instead, she just shrugged again and offered a demure fluttering of her lashes. "I guess so. Those are my terms."

"I can't just be a man in a good suit who wants to fuck you?"

While longing throbbed through her entire body, Skye managed to shake her head. "What happened to just wanting a taste? You've really upped the ante here."

"What can I say? Witty banter does it for me."

She looked away, lips pressed together, not wanting him to see just how much of an effect he had on her. Witty banter apparently did it for her too.

All these years with a sugar daddy, she had been too busy getting on with her life finally, too busy taking care of herself at last, to consider dating or sleeping with anyone. For the most part, Cole kept her busy enough that her emotional needs were met—even if they didn't see each other in person as often as Skye would have liked, they spoke on the phone or through video chat at minimum once a week—but she had suppressed her physical needs for a long time now. There was nothing in their contract that said she *couldn't* be intimate with another man; she just couldn't parade him around in front of the press afterward. Nor should she choose someone who might sell their dirty secret to the highest bidder the next morning. Skye did a quick scan of the man in front of her. For some reason, she felt like she could trust him.

Maybe Finn was just the man to quench her thirst, to break the dry spell—to make her scream.

A chill sprinted down her body, reverberating across her sex and settling on her sensitive bud, eager for the caress of those strong hands.

Why not?

It was just sex.

"Okay, backstory," she said a little breathlessly. "Name. Age. Height. Some fun facts. Go."

Any other guy would have hightailed it out of there by now. Actually, any other guy would have offered a vaguely sympathetic "that sucks" at the sight of her covered in wine, then darted after the two drunk, scantily clad women who had almost ruined her night.

Finn, meanwhile, inhaled deeply, his broad chest expanding and deflating—tantalizing, hypnotic. She wondered just how hard it would be if she poked at it. The tailoring certainly highlighted a toned figure underneath.

"Right. Here we go then." Finn clapped his hands together, snapping her back to the conversation. "My name is Finn Rai. Thirty-five. Six-three. Oldest of five. My parents own a chocolate company—"

"Rai's Sweets?" Her eyebrows shot up. "As in... You're..."

He nodded, seeming almost embarrassed she had figured it out so fast. "That's me."

"You're a Rai. From Rai's Sweets." The revelation knocked the wind right out of her sails. She'd been playfully tormenting a billionaire. Rai's Sweets competed with the best of them—and they made her favourite milk-chocolate salted caramel bites. "I...I always buy your salted caramels at the gym."

Finn snorted. "Probably the worst place for us to sell them."

"Or the best. We're all hungry at the gym." Okay. The fact that he was heir to a billion-dollar candy empire shouldn't throw her off. Cole was a billionaire. She met men and women who basically hemorrhaged cash at every event he took her to. Finn Rai was just another man—a man who wanted to fuck her.

Skye rolled her shoulders back to bolster her courage, noting the way Finn's eyes dipped down her chest briefly before jumping back to her face. She had played with rich men and their ilk for four years now, with and without Cole there to back her up. This was manageable.

Still, though. It was almost like she had just met a celebrity she'd never known she idolized until that second. Those salted-caramel-chocolate pieces of paradise rocked her world at least twice a week.

"Let's see, what else..." While his brow furrowed, as though deep in thought, the too-obvious smirk suggested he thought he was in the clear. He wasn't wrong. "I play squash every Saturday with my niece and nephew in Santa

Barbara. If I could, I'd run a wildcat sanctuary, but apparently that doesn't look great on a portfolio. I hate mustard. Relish is also questionable. My father was born in Mumbai but emigrated to London in—"

He stopped abruptly when she placed a hand on his knee. Warmth radiated up her arm.

"I think I'm good."

"Yeah?"

"Yeah."

"Well, Miss Skye," Finn said, standing and buttoning his jacket—like they'd just concluded a multimillion-dollar deal of some kind. "I think you've made a very wise decision. One that I hope will be more than satisfactory for all parties involved..."

Before Skye could get a word in edgewise, Finn grasped her chin firmly and claimed her lips. White-hot excitement twisted through her, and a moan escaped unexpectedly as she let herself be taken. A swift nip at her lower lip encouraged her to open her mouth to him, his tongue sweeping over hers, encouraging it to play—but with grace, with poise. A strange thing to consider, a tongue being graceful, but she'd had too many inexperienced men shoving their tongues to the back of her throat in her day; Finn was a welcome change of pace.

Her hands shot up, clutching at his jacket, eager to feel that body against hers, and an arm around her lower back eased her to her feet. He tasted like mint and smelled like heaven, the faint hint of scruff across his cheeks and chin adding a sharp edge to the kiss. Just as she'd suspected, Finn was a man who took care of himself physically, the grooves of his body firm beneath the hurried exploration of her greedy hands. Unable to help herself, Skye popped his jacket buttons open, then slid up his torso and pushed said jacket off his muscular shoulders. Their lips parted, but only just, still hovering near enough that she felt each hot breath, her nerves on fire.

"Straight to business then?" he asked as his jacket fell to the floor, and she answered with a desperate kiss of her own. He had claimed her—she thought it fair to return the favor. Her fingers wove through his thick head of hair, tongue brushing over his and retracting before he could retaliate. She moaned again when he pulled her to him, hard, dipped her backward, and kissed her like he wanted to devour her.

Skye had never been devoured before.

And it was about damn time, honestly.

What thrilled her the most was that Finn had no qualms in taking what he wanted. The force behind his kiss, the way his hands roamed her body—he made his desires known, then acted on them. After all the years of questions, of analyzing every touch, every look shared between her and Cole, Skye couldn't have asked for a better, or more needed, one-night stand companion.

An embarrassing squeak slipped out of her mouth when Finn hoisted her up and deposited her on the bathroom counter. The combination of cool marble on the backs of her thighs and Finn's searing gaze blazing down her front sent a shiver down her spine, her skin erupting with little bumps. A throb of need pounded through her system with each touch, and when he slipped his hands under her knees and dragged her to the edge of the counter, she could feel a slickness between her thighs, her sex wet and wanting, that made her cheeks flame.

"You blush beautifully," he murmured, tracing the red from her cheek, down her chin, then to the valley between her breasts. "Makes me want to eat you right up."

"Isn't that what you promised?"

"I did indeed."

"I just want to make sure I'm getting what was offered."

"Oh, you will." Lust pooled deep within his gaze as it darted up to meet hers. "That and more."

"Big talk. Let's see if you can back it up..." Her voice hitched when he ran his tongue along her jawline to her ear, tracing the shell before nibbling at her lobe. She arched beneath him, a hand digging into his shoulder as he quested lower. Each kiss alternated between firm and soft, chaste and filthy, until he paused where her neck and shoulder met to suck—hard. Her eyes widened and her hips bucked like they had a mind of their own. "*Oh!*"

Rather than sliding over the edge of the counter, she straddled Finn's waist, his belt buckle biting into the tender skin of her inner thigh. Her soft hiss made him reposition himself, and in place of metal, Skye found a very solid, almost worryingly thick cock pressed against her. She bit her lip, deciding right then and there to just surrender to the ride.

After all, if she really wanted to, she could always get off—in more ways than one, probably.

Finn ended his love bite with a flash of teeth; her toes curled in response, her back arching further and forcing her up against him. Just as he'd promised, he spent enough time on her wine-drenched skin to leave her a tormented mess, a symphony of soft moans tumbling from her lips while she ground her hips against him. This was what happened when you went on a four-year dry spell waiting for a man who clearly had no interest in you—just a little affection, a touch of physical intimacy, and Skye was gone.

While she wanted him to devote the same time and attention to her nipples, which had hardened to stiff peaks beneath her lacey bra, Finn continued his journey downward—though not without kissing each along the way.

"It seems a shame to ruin your outfit," he murmured against her skin, and at that point Skye didn't care if he just ripped it all off and had his way with her, though she would appreciate his care for expensive lingerie when this was over.

Slowly, Finn eased down her body, pressing kisses and licks here and there, catching the garter belt around her waist with his teeth. He snapped it, the sharp sting against her skin making her squirm. He paused, however, when he reached her panties.

"This... is a complicated contraption," he mused, hands skimming over the undergarment—pleasure spasmed through her when he grazed her sex—and down to her stockings, then to the ties that connected the stockings to the belt at her waist.

"I can just—"

"Ah, ah," he chided, batting her hands away with a smirk. "Allow me."

Skye sat back on her elbows, head resting against the mirror, and watched as he navigated her complex lingerie getup with all the precision and care of an archival technician handling a delicate artifact. Each brush of his fingers over her skin sent a rush of excitement fluttering through her body before eventually settling in her core. Even the slightest of movements now reminded her she was wet, positively dripping with need.

Carefully, as if wanting to preserve Skye exactly as she was, Finn unbuckled each belt, one at a time, and slid her panties down until they reached mid-thigh. Free from the constraints of straps, he was able to pull them off completely, but only after buckling her back in—and snapping each garter, just to watch her writhe. He then folded the damp lacey material in half and set it aside on the counter, though for a moment it looked like he wanted to tuck it away in his pocket.

Skye couldn't decide if she'd let him get away with it or not, but she wanted to see him try.

"Now, come forward," he urged softly with a crooked finger. Biting the insides of her cheeks, Skye complied, slowly scooting to the edge of the counter again, though he kept prompting her until she was about to fall off.

"But—"

"And give me those beautiful legs." Finn sounded comfortable issuing directions, and, besides a quick flick of his gaze to hers, had no problem following through when she hesitated. He lifted each leg over one shoulder, and colour flooded Skye's cheeks when she realized she was straddling his face—sans panties. His tongue darted quickly across his lower lip as he took in the view, as if admiring a work of art. "Perfect."

Although she wanted to watch him appreciate her, she just couldn't. Instead, Skye made herself comfortable on her elbows and let her head fall back, losing herself in the gentle nips he peppered up her thighs. Alternating between each side, the sensations grew sharper, more defined, the closer he got to his destination, and by the time she felt his breath on her wet slit, her body shook, having had enough of the teasing, the torment—desperate for it to end.

Desperate for that *moment*.

"Oh, *fuck*!" she cried when his mouth finally closed over her swollen clit, tongue flicking at the sensitive bud. So primed for pleasure that each sweep of his tongue, each suckle of his lips, nearly sent her crashing over the edge. Her ankles locked behind him as his hands kneaded her backside, massaging each cheek as his relentless mouth ravaged her. At one point, when it became too much, too much pleasure, too much *everything*, Skye tried to wriggle out of his grip, but Finn held tight, renewing his blissful torment with a wild look in his eye, tongue thrusting in and out of her briefly before returning to her clit.

What she would have done for a finger or two...

Only she didn't need it. Before long, she pitched over the edge between sanity and ecstasy, gasping his name like a proclamation of worship, when a climax hammered her every which way. Finn held her twitching body tight, offering no relief from his talented tongue, not until she tugged at his hair and uttered a pitiful, "Please, *god...*"

Her orgasm prickled through her, and rather than extinguishing the blaze Finn's touch set across her skin, it only made it worse—fuel to the fire. As he set her on the counter, her back against the mirror, the tension in her muscles eased away, but not completely as it always had after a stellar climax. Instead, she found herself hungry for more, desperate to douse the flames any way she could.

Finn had already moved away from her, headed for one of the sinks to rinse his mouth. When their gazes met, however, it was clear the fervor burning within him was far from extinguished too.

The thought thrilled her. Excited her. Worried her—but not enough to send her running. So, Skye reached for him, ignoring the slight shake in her fingers, and waited. The blaze snapped and spat and hissed behind his eyes; and within the span of a few tense, controlled breaths, the fire brought him back to her.

5

MY FAVOURITE THINGS

Finn came for her like she was his only source of oxygen—of life itself. Skye threaded her fingers through his hair, lips slightly parted as he claimed them for his own again. Desire, strong as ever, oozed through her body as the memory of her recent climax faded, replaced by a need she had never felt before. She squealed softly when Finn yanked her back to the edge of the counter, hands roaming her figure at his leisure before they slipped beneath her, cupped her backside, and lifted her up to him. Arms wrapped around his neck, she caught his lower lip with her teeth, reveling in the warning growl that rumbled deep within his chest.

There was something primal about him. Something animalistic in the way he looked at her, in the way he handled her. At first glance, Skye never would have guessed that was the case. While breathtakingly handsome, Finn had also appeared uptight, wealthy, and unwilling to wrinkle his suit. But his jacket had been on the floor ever since she yanked it off his body, there to be stepped on and kicked around. In her eagerness to explore his muscular planes, she had ripped a button right off his pressed dress shirt—and he hadn't batted an eye.

For the first time in a long time, Skye had a man's complete and utter attention. No distractions. No half-focus. It was very clear in the way he touched her, kissed her, bucked against her, that in that moment, she and he were the only ones in the whole world.

She shivered at the thought, at the idea of being the object of a man's lust from top to bottom. It was a feeling she could certainly get used to.

Before she had a chance to wrap her legs around his hips, eager to rub herself against his still *very* present erection, Finn broke the kiss and in one swift motion flipped her around and bent her over the counter. Her hands snapped to the mirror to steady herself, eyes fluttering shut as he ran his lips along her neck, hands closing around her breasts.

"Do you know my favourite thing about fucking?" he asked huskily in her ear. As one hand slipped beneath her bra to finally pluck at her almost painfully hard nipple, the other wandered lower, two fingers testing the sensitive bundle at the crest of her sex. Skye uttered a breathy cry at the first caress, so gentle and so light—yet it sent a tremor of white-hot pleasure licking up her body. He murmured her name, as if to remind her he'd asked her a question, and her eyes shot open to see their reflections in the mirror.

It was then she noted their size difference, that he had at least a half foot on her, his solid frame making her feel petite—dainty even—in his arms. In her mind, Skye was far from dainty. Average. Toned from yoga and the gym. Attractive enough to pass as Cole's fake girlfriend. But not petite.

Yet Finn made her feel that way: safe, but in his control, in his very capable hands.

"W-What?" she managed as he continued to massage her slick sex, occasionally slipping a finger between her folds before returning to her clit. "What's your favourite thing?"

"Well..." He tweaked a nipple, eyes darting to hers when they widened in surprise. A twinge of pain intermingled with the steady stream of pleasure rolling out from her core—like the ocean lapping at the shore. "I suppose there are *two* things I enjoy more than anything else. Can't you guess?"

"I always assumed men just like fucking," she said, her voice catching when he rolled her nipple between his fingers, "period."

"Uncultured men, sure."

She watched as he removed his hand from her bra, leaving one nipple woefully unattended, while he continued to drive her closer to that precipice again below. Somehow he managed to torment her without hurting her, perhaps guessing how sensitive she'd be after that last orgasm. "There's nothing *I* like more than watching a woman come undone. To experience pure bliss while I watch..."

The noise he made, the one that caught in his throat like a possessive snarl, as he grazed his teeth along her neck—it was almost her undoing. Skye trembled, fingers curling over the mirror, no longer interested in their reflections.

The light glinting off the foil square in his hand caught her interest instead, and she watched, her body sagging in the absence of his hand between her thighs, as he ripped it open—then resumed his gentle torture, rubbing and caressing and coaxing her quivering body closer to yet another climax.

"My second favourite is perhaps the less important of the two," he murmured. Behind her, Skye felt him maneuvering himself out of his trousers, his hardness dropping against her lower back momentarily before he sheathed it in the condom. He pressed a kiss to her shoulder. "Widen your stance, Miss Skye."

A request. An order. A polite command. Whatever it was, she complied willingly, opening herself to him, and bending further over the countertop.

"You see, my second favourite thing..." His hand smoothed up her back while the other gripped her hip. "Are you ready for it?"

"Stop being an ass—"

He thrust into her, filling her slick channel, and she gasped, a sound that evolved into a moan when his hips collided with her backside. His eyes... She caught them in the mirror. Not once did they leave her face, not until she ducked her head and groaned, temporarily overwhelmed by the whole affair, her cheeks hot.

"It's that moment," Finn whispered, bending over her, leaving a string of kisses between her shoulder blades, up her neck, as she adjusted to him. Trailing his tongue along the shell of her ear, he chuckled. "The first time I take a woman... Watching her. The surprise. The pleasure. The excitement. There's nothing more beautiful."

Her only response was an incoherent jumble of words that even Skye didn't understand. His mouth moved down from her ear, slowly working along her jaw, her cheek, until he clasped her chin and turned her head so his lips could claim hers. While thrown by the feeling of fullness, by the pleasure pulsing out from where they joined, Skye kissed him back with equal fervor. She wasn't a passive participant in this, and she made it clear when she wrapped an arm around his neck and sucked on his tongue, catching the lingering taste of herself there and moaning.

Finn's hand grazed her bare stomach, slowly questing upward to slip between her breasts. His palm's slight pressure eased her upward, just enough so she felt the heat of his torso on her back, her body framed by the hard confines of his. At first she was too shy to look at herself in the mirror, but as he started to thrust into her, slowly, firmly, she found her courage.

And it truly was a sight to behold. Skye could never watch other people fuck—*maybe* porn, if she was in the mood—but there was something uniquely thrilling about watching herself being taken by an almost stranger. A man so stunning that she still wondered why her—why all the effort? There were plenty of women here who would have been less of a challenge.

But all her worries, her thoughts, melted away as he slid in and out of her. Never completely. They were always in contact, one way or another. Be it the caress of his lips along her ear, the thickness of his cock filling her sex, or the fiery hold of his gaze when their eyes met in the mirror; contact was essential. With one hand pressed to the mirror for support, she twined her other through his hair, reaching behind, arching herself for him, noting the groan he made when she did. While his pace quickened somewhat, it was always steady. Rhythmic and constant. Ever-present. Like the pounding of her heart. No longer racing, it seemed to beat in time with their lovemaking...

Or was it fucking?

Skye didn't mind either term; they both suited Finn Rai. The way he pursued her, the way he pleasured her—that was fucking. The way he looked at her, kissed her, toyed with her clit—that was lovemaking. There was room for both.

"To me," he whispered, mouth trailing along her jawline as his pace quickened, skilled fingers dragging her to the edge —and Skye was more than willing to take the plunge, "there's nothing sexier than watching a woman enjoy herself. Nothing I like more than tasting her pleasure, watching it unfurl..."

"From women everywhere, I s-salute you," she said, her words breathier than she would have liked. The bite had vanished. The bark too. All Skye had left was surrender—and god damn did she bask in it.

Her hand tore from his hair, which earned her a kiss from the gorgeous man behind her, and Skye braced it against the mirror as he thrust harder, faster, his fingers working her into a desperate frenzy—until the floodgates parted, until the levies broke, until the sky opened and drowned the earth. She came with a soft cry this time, eyes screwed shut as she rode out wave after wave of pleasure. Finn cursed when she clenched hard around him, and before she knew it, he was dragging her away from the granite countertop and pressing her back against the wall.

It happened so fast she almost had to pinch herself, so lost in her climax that the movements of her body felt foreign—like they weren't hers, like she was merely watching someone else, but from their point of view.

Finn's kiss revived her. Reality slammed back into her in time with his lips—kissing her as though he feared he might lose her. Still tingling with pleasure and heat, Skye cupped his face and kissed him back. She didn't have to fear she'd lose him. Skye had him. And in that moment, she really didn't want to let him go.

Finn hiked her legs up, wrapping them around his waist, then slipped himself back into her. She winced, straddling the line between pleasure and pain as he filled her. He gave her a moment, gliding his fingers over her hips and the gentle swell of her breasts.

"Are you okay?" he murmured thickly. Skye nodded. "You sure?"

"Just peachy," she told him. "Seriously. I can take what you dish out—"

Another kiss, this time to swallow her words. Skye wrapped her arms around him, gulping down air when Finn buried his face against her neck—and finally just *fucked* her. There were no words. No teasing philosophies about women and their pleasure whispered against her skin. They were just a man and a woman, locked in each other's arms, as Finn pounded into her. Searching for his own pleasure, one he had certainly earned at this point. Skye hung on for the ride, easing away from the sharpness of each thrust, steadily filled with a gentle, more subdued pleasure. She gripped his hair, tugging ever so slightly when he nipped at her shoulder.

He took her hard and fast. Roughly. Savagely. But it was still lovemaking.

At least, that was how Skye saw it. Because when he kissed her, his pace stuttering off and his face flushed, there was no mistaking what this was.

Finn came with a soft groan, their mouths barely touching, open to one another in an almost-kiss. His whole body stiffened, then slowly relaxed against her, with Skye twirling his hair around her fingers rather than pulling at it. Combing it. Scratching his scalp as he sighed contentedly, his forehead resting on her shoulder.

"That was..." He exhaled a soft chuckle, shaking his head. No words. Skye grinned, totally on the same page.

"Fucking awesome?"

"You Americans," he muttered as he slowly eased out of her, then patiently waited for her to straighten herself out before backing away. "So brash."

She smirked, ignoring the tremors skittering through her body, the hot and ever-present flush spreading from her cheeks to the hilt of her sex. "But honest?"

"Sometimes." Finn appeared a little unsteady as he stumbled back and plopped down on the edge of the jacuzzi tub. "In this instance, I certainly hope so."

While she had the sudden urge to climb onto his lap and just hug him, Skye resisted. Instead, she wobbled over to the sinks, turning her head away as he disposed of the condom, and hopped onto the cold countertop.

"I'll let you figure that one out for yourself," she told him, which made his eyes narrow slightly, his smile unsure.

"I can always try to prove my worth—"

She held up her hands, laughing. "No, you've proved your worth. I can't go again."

Finn's smile brightened as he stretched his long legs out, his brown skin covered in a scant smattering of black hairs. She found the way he rolled out his ankles oddly endearing, like they were both passengers on a long-haul flight.

"I'll take that as a compliment," he said.

"You should."

They watched one another, just as before, but this time it was Finn who reached out for Skye. He did so with a casual toss of his head and a twitch of his lips, and soon enough, she left the countertop behind, colliding in a sweet kiss that, for the first time, didn't steal her breath or her words—but a little piece of her heart.

6

LOVEMAFUCKING HAS CONSEQUENCES

A knock at the door a half hour later jolted them from their conversation. Skye and Finn had been sitting opposite one another in the jacuzzi, sans water, and chatting—which, to be fair, was the last thing Skye had thought a man like Finn would want to do post-sex. She'd figured he'd be out of there like a shot, and she wouldn't have faulted him for that. Amazing fucking—or, whatever, *lovemaking*—at a sex party didn't exactly lend itself to cuddling afterward. Skye assumed it would be onto the next conquest, but there they were, talking about chocolate empires and shitty job interviews like they'd been friends for years.

"Just a moment," Finn muttered, hopping out of the tub and crossing the bathroom with a few quick strides of those long legs. He'd slipped his black briefs on a while ago after complaining the tub was too cold to sit in totally nude, but Skye found it just the right antidote to her sore nether regions. Four years of nothing and then, out of nowhere, ravenous lovemafucking? Yeah. She'd definitely be feeling it tomorrow.

He returned a few moments later with her dress hanging over his arm—clean. Her eyebrows shot up, and she set aside the glass of water she'd been nursing.

"Is that...?"

"As promised," he announced, unfurling it and shaking it out. "Not perfect, but better than if I'd left you to your own devices."

Sure enough, most of the red wine stain had totally vanished. She only noticed a faint pink outline if she squinted hard enough. Impressive.

"Hey, I could have..." She laughed when he cocked his head to the side, waiting. "Okay, no, I would have totally ruined the dress. Thank you."

"Of course." Finn handed it back to her, and she resisted the urge to rub the just-out-of-the-dryer warmth against her cheek. "Listen, I don't know how long you intended to be here tonight—"

"An hour, tops," she said, Cole's words a distant memory. Thinking about him plucked at the guilt strings within her, unseen fingers twanging each one and watching them vibrate. Cole. Where the hell was Cole?

"Well, if you're leaving, then perhaps—"

"But I've been here more than an hour already," Skye told him. "So, what's up?"

His expression shifted from its cautious optimism to something a little giddier, which she appreciated. All these moguls, Cole included, were so tight-lipped about their emotions. Finn was a breath of fresh air in more ways than one.

"I need to fetch a few things, but why don't you get dressed?" He grabbed his shirt off the ground, but didn't button it up, then slipped into his trousers. "I'll take you on a tour of the back gardens, maybe we can go down to the beach?"

Her eyes flickered to her purse, long abandoned on the bathroom counter. She hadn't heard her phone go off once since she'd arrived. Cole hadn't asked after her. Was he still playing poker, or had he found a girl he *actually* wanted to take to bed? Skye swallowed hard.

"Sure. Why not? I bet the view's beautiful this time of night."

"Clear skies," Finn noted. "We can probably see Jupiter from here."

He winked, then darted out of the room, leaving her grinning like an idiot—a grin that faded in his absence, those invisible fingers plucking at the guilt strings even harder.

No. Stop that. She didn't deserve to feel guilty. Cole had made it perfectly clear that he wanted to maintain their friendship, the kind of bond she had with no one else in her life, so why force something that might ruin it? The contract had only said she couldn't have any public relationships. Sex was mentioned in reference to Skye and Cole, not Skye and gorgeous strangers at swanky parties.

It wasn't like she'd *cheated.* She and Cole weren't in a personal, intimate relationship. Well, not a romantic one, anyway. In public, sure. Skye dragged the dress Cole had purchased over her head, catching her furrowed brow in the mirror. She and Cole were friends. Maybe more. But maybe not. Not officially. He hadn't insisted she be celibate for the last four years—it was a decision she had made all on her own.

She squared her shoulders, then climbed out of the tub and stood in front of the mirror.

"You didn't do anything wrong," she said firmly, then

ruffled her hair. No matter how many times she repeated those words, the guilt didn't go away.

And that wasn't fair. Not to her, not to Finn, and probably not to Cole.

Cole didn't *want* her.

"Shake it off, girl." She leaned in and did what she could to fix her smudged makeup. "It's just for tonight."

Swallowing whatever weird mishmash of emotion that stilted her movements and muddied her thoughts, Skye primped, checked out the quality of her laundered dress, and sat around twiddling her thumbs. Eventually, she moved on to playing with her phone, something she did so rarely that she had no idea what to even *do* on there. After a quick email check—no job offers—she added her underwear to her intricate lingerie get-up, one that she couldn't wait to take off now, and left the bathroom for the first time in what felt like hours.

No Finn.

Frowning, she retraced her steps back to where this had all begun: that fateful corner where two drunk girls had made her spill red wine all over herself. Still no Finn. The enormous house had quieted down in her absence, but a glance out the windows overlooking the back gardens and beach suggested most of the party had just moved outside, with and without their clothes.

Skye drummed her fingers on the ledge, breathing in the warm night air as an ocean-side breeze billowed across the property. Had Finn bailed on her? Had she misread him *completely*?

"Skye?"

She whirled around, heart leaping into her throat, as Cole's voice echoed down the sparsely furnished corridor. He strode toward her with a familiar smile on his face, the kind that always affected her from head to toe. It still did, but in that moment, prickly guilt struck her, not flirtatious affection.

"Hey," she managed when he kissed her cheek. "Where've you been?"

"The game went on *much* longer than I'd anticipated," he said with a huff. "And by game, I don't mean poker."

She forced a laugh. "I figured as much."

"I hope you weren't too bored." He dug out his phone when it chirped in his pocket, brow puckering slightly as he tapped around on the screen. "Are you ready to go? It's a fucking madhouse in here."

"Yeah... All those...sexual deviants." Why did she feel like this? Cole didn't want her like she wanted him. He'd made it perfectly clear over the last four years. She *shouldn't* feel guilty. Being with Finn had been like coming up for air after living on the edge of drowning. Not that Cole had ever dragged her below the water's surface, but maybe it was just the situation.

Cole slipped his phone away before appraising her. "You all right? You look a little..." Those bright eyes swept over her, assessing her with the attention to detail he was known for. "Flushed."

"I've had a few to drink," she told him, which wasn't a lie. She was just more drunk on Finn Rai than she was on alcohol. "We can go if you're finished."

His head bobbed in agreement, though Skye didn't miss the slight clench of his jaw. A flicker. A twitch of the muscle. It was a tic he'd never been able to hide whenever something bothered him.

"Yes, let's get out of this den of lust," he said, his chuckle sounding just as forced as hers had, "before we see something that neither of us will be able to forget."

Skye folded her arms over her chest. "Agreed."

They set out together, Cole seeming to know his way around the mansion better than her, but not ten steps down the hall did Skye hear her name bouncing off the walls again. Finn. She tensed at the sound of thundering footsteps, as though he were running. When he flew around the corner, he came to a sudden stop, eyes darting swiftly between her and Cole—a bottle of champagne in hand.

"Finn!" Cole greeted, his tone suggesting a connection between them that Skye had never heard of before. "How're you, man? I'd hoped I'd see the host before we left. It's been, what, five years since you were actually living in this country? I'd thought you had just rented the place out, not that you were throwing this soiree yourself..."

The two moved toward each other, hands extended and grasped. All the while Finn appeared to be trying very hard not to look at her.

"I thought you didn't show," Finn told him. "Did you get everything you needed? Bernard give you any trouble? I swear to God, that fucking greasy little prick—"

"No, I got him. It's all settled."

Skye fiddled with her dress, unsure where she fit in this unexpected turn of events. Of course, she assumed those who ran in Cole and Finn's elite circles knew each other, but the way the pair spoke to one another, the way their body language read, suggested this was more than a casual acquaintanceship. This was friendship. She tried and failed to swallow the lump growing in her throat.

"Listen, are you two, er, heading out?" Finn rustled the bottle of Pinot Noir suggestively while Cole shook his head.

"No, no, I dragged this one out here with the promise that we'd be gone in an hour," he insisted, holding a hand out to Skye with a breezy smile. "I think we'd best be off."

Stiff legs carried her to him, and she slid her hand into his, noting the way Finn's gaze followed the movement.

"Do you two know each other?" Cole asked, motioning between them. Skye almost lied and said no, but then she remembered Finn had been shouting her name as he hunted her down, face full of giddy mischief.

"We just met tonight," Skye told him. "Finn was going to give me a tour of the beach."

There it was again: the jaw flicker. A brief clench. The gesture noted by both she and Finn, who had tucked the champagne behind his back. His eyes narrowed slightly as he looked between her and Cole, and moments later, a frightening look of awareness, like he knew her most intimate secret, surfaced.

"Wait, Cole, is Skye your—"

"Listen, thanks for hosting," Cole said curtly, "and, you know, for telling me Bernard would be here. He's been annoyingly difficult to track down, even for me."

"Yeah..." Finn sounded distracted, still studying her and Cole with a startling sharpness that made the man holding her hand fidget. "Sure. Of course." Finn cleared his throat, suddenly more present. "I know how long you've been gunning for him. I figured it was time to end your silly cat-and-mouse charade before it got boring, right?"

"I appreciate it." Cole let go of her hand in order to shake Finn's, this time with a noticeable sense of finality. "Again, thank you. I'm sure it was a lovely party, but we've got to be going."

"Of course. Get your assistant to pencil something in with mine before you jet off again."

"Sure. We'll do lunch. I've got this fantastic new personal chef at the house... The things he can do with raw fish will astound you."

Skye just stood there, waiting for it all to end. The way something had seemed to *click* in Finn's eyes when he looked between them—did he know the true nature of her and Cole's relationship? Were they close enough that Cole would actually share that with him? Perhaps not her name, but maybe...

"It was a pleasure to meet you, Skye."

She snapped out of her thoughts, smiling brightly as she always did at these sorts of things when someone actually paid attention to her. "Yes. It was really nice to meet you, Mr. Rai."

Fuck. He seemed almost disappointed with her, but the look was gone before she could confirm it. Cole snagged her hand again, and, after a few more pleasantries, they were off. Neither said a word, not even as they descended that enormous stairwell down the hilly front lawn of the house.

Finn's house.

Cole had said he was the host.

Over the pounding of her heart, she was finally able to dissect that conversation, her face in a permanent state of blush. Cole had made two references that Finn either owned the house, or, at the very least, was responsible for the orgy happening in its living room. Why hadn't Finn said anything?

"Skye!"

Both she and Cole paused a few feet from their awaiting car, only to find Finn jogging down the stairs after them, her purse in hand.

"You left this in the..." He caught himself as Skye took the clutch back, Cole's eyes burning holes into the side of her head. "Veranda. On the veranda. I didn't want you to forget it."

"Thank you," she murmured, then turned away as

quickly as she could. Cole already had the car door open for her, and she heard them exchanging stiff, albeit friendly, banter before Cole climbed in after her. Skye didn't glance back as the car pulled away, but she knew by the way the hairs on her neck stood that Finn was at the curb, watching them go.

"Shall I take you home?" Cole asked.

"Please."

"No pizza pick-up on the way?"

"I'm just tired," she told him. Physically. Emotionally. She needed to crash and process her thoughts—and maybe her feelings too. Still, she managed a smile. "Thank you."

He nodded. "Of course."

About halfway home, she found the courage to ask the question she needed an answer to before they parted ways.

"How do you know Finn?"

"We've known each other for about ten years," Cole admitted as he tapped around on his phone, not looking up at her. "We met just at the start of my first company taking off. A lot of people wanted things from me, but Finn just wanted...me, I guess. My friendship. He's been making sure I don't make a total fuck-up of myself ever since. It's been a long time since we've even been in the same country. Seeing him was a pleasant surprise."

"Oh." She stared back out the window, watching the brief stretch of coastal highway turn back into the outer suburbs of Coral Bay. "That's nice."

"He's a good man."

"So are you," she said without thinking. Out of the corner of her eye, she noticed Cole look up sharply—but when he spoke next, it was like she hadn't said it at all.

"I've got something for you."

When she tore her gaze from the window, she found

him holding out a black envelope to her, which she accepted with a slight frown.

"What is it?"

"My poker winnings," he said with a shrug, a hint of his easy smile returning. Her stomach did its usual somersault in response, the butterflies fluttering back to life. However, that all came crashing to a halt when she saw the amount inside the envelope. At first she thought it was a huge envelope of one-dollar bills—but billionaires don't play poker with one-dollar bills.

"Cole, I can't." She tried to shove the envelope into his hands, but he pulled away, chuckling.

"Take it. I won it for you."

"How much is this?" Skye demanded, a strange, unwelcome sense of panic making her chest tight.

"About ten thousand—"

"Cole!" They seldom discussed money, but she always refused to take anything that wasn't related to rent, groceries, or tuition. That was probably why he showered her in expensive gifts whenever he breezed into town; she wouldn't take cash. Skye didn't *want* cash. Especially not when it felt like he was paying her for attending an orgy tonight—where she'd subsequently had sex with the host. "Take it back."

"No, I don't want it."

"Cole."

His expression fell slightly when her eyes watered, and he stopped fighting her when she all but threw the envelope at him. Flustered, Skye sat back in her seat and brushed her hair out of her face. "It's not that I don't appreciate the gesture. I just don't want it. Donate it somewhere instead."

Cautiously, Cole slid the envelope back into his jacket

pocket. “Skye... I didn’t mean to... I hope I didn’t insult you. That wasn’t my intention.”

“You didn’t.”

“It sort of seems like I did.”

“I just...” She knew she ought to tell him what had happened, but not here. Not where someone could overhear —no matter how hard the driver pretended to be focused on the road. “It’s been a weird night. I’m sorry.”

He appraised her for a moment. “Are you okay?”

“Yeah,” Skye said quickly.

“You sure?”

“I’m totally fine...” She flashed a smile. “I promise.”

He looked like he believed her.

Skye almost did too.

7

IDIOTS. IDIOTS EVERYWHERE

"Can I ask you something?"

"Hmm." Cole closed the car door behind her, having just told the driver to wait inside. Her apartment building towered overhead, quiet and familiar, beckoning her in. But Skye couldn't just go. She couldn't do their usual cheek-kiss thing and walk away like tonight hadn't happened.

"Why did you tell me to wear something sexy under this?" When Cole's eyebrows creased, she clarified. "On the note. On the back... You said—"

"We were going to a sex party," he said briskly, hands sliding into his pockets. "I didn't want you to feel like a fish out of water."

"By wearing lingerie?"

"Sure."

"Because I'd be, what, showing off my underwear or something?"

Colour flooded his cheeks. "Well. You know. I don't... If you wanted to, I figured I'd give you the option."

"Oh." Adrenaline made her hands clammy and her

body tremble. Given they were on the cusp of summer, she couldn't blame it on the weather, either. "Is that all? No other reason that I should wear something sexy under the dress you bought me?"

"No." He pulled out his phone, but this time he just stared at it, not even bothering to poke at the black screen. A beat passed before his bright, gorgeous eyes darted up to hers. "Should there have been a reason?"

His words steadily proved her suspicions correct—that he *wasn't* interested—but his eyes told another story entirely. She waited, gripping her clutch so tight in both hands that she would be surprised if anything inside remained in one piece. The early-morning sounds of laughter, drunk tourists leaving bars, and taxis whizzing through the near-vacant streets trickled into the space between them, and still she waited. Nothing.

Fine.

"No." She shook her head and half turned toward her building. "No, I guess not. Never mind."

"Skye..." Cole took a few steps toward her, lips parted slightly. However, he seemed to lose his nerve the second she gave him her full attention. "Thanks for coming with me tonight. I really appreciate it. I appreciate your time."

She bit the insides of her cheeks, wishing he would appreciate something more about her—but all things considered, time was a valuable commodity, especially in his world. Cole's appreciation of it... It was sweet. She swallowed hard, closing her eyes briefly when he leaned in, his cologne engulfing her senses, and kissed her cheek. Skye drifted toward him when he lingered, then cleared her throat and stepped away, needing the space.

"Goodnight," she said, slowly making her way toward the lobby. "I'll see you around?"

"I'll be in Coral Bay for a few weeks. Most of the summer, actually," he told her. "I'm sure there will be plenty of other sex parties to crash."

Skye grinned. As much as she wanted him to want her, now there was this desperation for things to just go back to the way they were—before it felt awkward. Jokes were a good way to start.

A quick wave earned her a smile, and she hurried across the lobby to an awaiting elevator, then disappeared inside. It was hard to remember she'd had the best sex of her life tonight—because that was *definitely* what it was—with all the Cole drama mulling around her brain, but she let it all go when Oz greeted her at the door with a characteristically exuberant yowl and a shower of purrs.

"My love," she whispered, scooping him up and nuzzling his soft fur after locking the door. "I missed you."

He kneaded her arm in response, little claws pulsing in and out of her skin as he smothered her in his scent. Classic guy move. Kicking off her heels, she headed in, turning on lights as she went, and plopped down on the couch with Oz. Once he'd had enough of her smothering, he headed for the fridge, meowing incessantly, as if to remind her he needed to be fed before she went to bed.

"I'm coming, I'm coming..."

After she checked her phone. Maybe there'd be a latent message from a certain someone.

However, as soon as she opened her clutch, fresh rose petals spilled out of it.

"What the hell?" Dozens of them. A few in slightly less than perfect condition, like someone had torn them straight off the flower. No wonder her clutch had felt bulkier; she had been too wrapped up in Cole to notice at first.

Beneath the petals was a business card, and she needn't

have a PhD to figure out who it was from. Her lips twitched into a smile at the sight of Finn's name—and the smile grew when she read the note on the back.

Thanks for tonight. These kinds of things are always so dull.

~~*We should connect again soon. Lots to discuss, I think.*~~

~~*Not in a blackmaily sort of way.*~~

~~*Sorry.*~~

~~*I'm not writing this note again.*~~

~~*It's the only business card I can find and you're about two seconds away from leaving.*~~

Let's have brunch.

xx

Finn

"Fuck me," Skye muttered, holding the card to her lips for a moment before setting it on the coffee table. Suddenly finding herself energized, she shot up and started to pace her apartment, eventually ending up in front of the window that overlooked the street below. Her heart skipped a beat: there was Cole, leaning against his car with a cigarette in hand, jacket off and bowtie gone.

She had only ever seen him smoke when he tanked a business deal.

And she'd thought all his back-alley dealings tonight had gone well.

So why the cigarette?

He looked up in the direction of her apartment, expression unreadable from the sixth floor.

"Fuck *me,*" she whispered again. Pushing away from the window, she shot straight to her shower. What she needed was some hot water, some soothing scents, and a night to sleep on everything that had happened.

Because things were always better in the morning. Clearer. Easier to sift through. More manageable.

Right?

COLE

Skye Summers: Gainfully employed university grad, cat servant, leftover sushi connoisseur...

Sugar baby falling hard and fast for two men.

Still reeling from her steamy encounter with Finn, Skye has a tidal wave of feelings to decode when the snarky billionaire shows up on her doorstep with a bouquet of chocolate roses. Oh, and a declaration that if she and Cole aren't a real couple outside of their sugar daddy contract, then Finn is coming after her heart--hard.

And, honestly, Skye doesn't hate his enthusiasm. In fact, she finds Finn and his wit rather charming.

Her suppressed feelings for sugar daddy Cole, however, refuse to quit. Even if they left things a little awkward after Finn's party, four years of blossoming love aren't easy to forget.

But when Cole waltzes into her usual Wednesday evening yoga class, looking gorgeous as ever, Skye finally learns that her feelings might not be so one-sided...

8

A SWEET SURPRISE

"Now, we would be interested in meeting with you sometime in the next week for a more in-depth interview."

Skye Summers did an embarrassing little dance around her living room, thrilled that she had passed the phone portion of her interview.

"Perfect," she said, hoping she didn't *sound* like she was bouncing around her apartment at the thought. If anything, weren't you supposed to sound like you didn't need the job in question, that the arduous, soul-crushing postgrad job hunt was just something you did in your spare time —for fun?

"Does Wednesday at three work?" Her interviewer Hans Timmons, an older gent with a kind voice who had managed to make Skye feel comfortable for the first time *ever* during an over-the-phone interrogation, ran the only sex museum for miles. While he insisted that it was more of a gallery for nude artworks, Skye knew better. And she didn't care. The history of human sexuality was just as important as exhibits dedicated to Roman gladiators—*more* important, given how prudish society in general was these days.

While it hadn't been her area of study—at all—in college, she was willing to take whatever job she could if it meant she had a paid museum position to add to her bleak résumé. Sure, the thing was loaded with the dozens of customer service jobs she'd toiled away at before she met her sugar daddy Cole, but those could only get her so far in this new world of museum grunt positions. Even though she would be at the bottom of the ladder in all the spots she had applied for—*assistant* implied she'd have zero creative power, only a step above intern—she was required to have a ridiculous amount of work experience, despite having just graduated. Apparently her cover letter had been doing her good since she'd completed her degree a little over a month ago: she'd had six interviews since May, and as June crawled by, she hoped to have a few more before the true Californian summer hit her ocean-side town of Coral Bay.

"Three o'clock sounds perfect," she insisted, voice quivering just slightly as she penciled the appointment into her day planner. "Would you like me to bring anything beyond my résumé and references?"

"No, that'll be all. I look forward to chatting more with you, Miss Summers."

"You as well, Mr. Timmons."

They played the who-has-the-last-word game for about ten seconds longer before he hung up, and Skye tossed the phone on her couch, threw her arms up, and squee'd. Every in-person interview was a victory. Sure, it'd be nice to get the job, but every time someone read her cover letter, scrutinized her résumé, and deigned her worthy of a phone call, it meant she was doing something right. Some of her college friends still hadn't landed an interview yet.

Skye just needed one to *stick*. And she had a good feeling about this one. She could chat about sex all day. Sure, her cheeks would be permanently pink for about three months when she first started, but it would all be old hat after a while.

Oz, her ball of pure white feline fluff, sleepily cracked open one blue eye from the other end of the couch, clearly unimpressed that his afternoon nap had been interrupted—again. She grinned, creeping across the cushions toward him, then laughed when he rolled onto his back, belly up for rubs.

"I'm not falling for that," she cooed in a voice strictly reserved for cat cuddling. Knowing better than to stick her hand in the bear trap, she went for his cute little face instead, smooshing it between both hands and showering him with kisses. His only protest was a pitiful meow, and while his paws pressed to her face, his claws remained sheathed.

She loved him for that.

And she adored Cole—despite their recent weirdness at Finn Rai's...sexual event—for giving her this little bundle of kitten joy four years prior. Life was somehow easier with her Oz man around.

Purrs intensified, the cat gave in to her affections, but just as Skye was about to scoop him into her arms, someone knocked at her apartment's door. She straightened with a frown; the front desk hadn't called to let her know someone had stopped by to see her. Since the bash at Finn's house, she had nothing scheduled with Cole either. None of her friends were likely to make random house calls.

Another knock, this time louder. Untangling herself from Ozzy, she strode over, tugging her little booty shorts down—it was too warm for yoga pants, too cold with the AC blasting, so she opted for less clothes and open windows to strike a happy medium. She did a quick T-shirt check to make sure it wasn't see-through, then peered through the peephole.

Roses peered back.

Slowly, toeing the line between caution and curiosity, Skye undid the various locks, then opened the door just a few inches—and found Finn Rai smirking on the other side of that bouquet.

"Finn..." Her first instinct was to shut the door and pretend she wasn't home. She hadn't taken him up on the tantalizing offer of brunch suggested on the card he had slipped into her purse last week—though not because she didn't *want* to. Skye just hadn't decided what would be healthiest for her relationship with Cole yet, but that hadn't kept the deliriously sexy Finn Rai, heir to the Rai's Sweets chocolate empire in Britain, out of her dreams.

"Skye..." With a voice like velvet, his head tipped to one side as that smirk shifted into a grin. "Are you indecent?"

"No." She hesitated a few moments longer before opening the door, then popped a hand onto her cocked hip, ignoring the bouquet that was clearly meant for wooing her. "Just wondering how you got my address. Pretty sure I didn't give it to you."

He was even more handsome in daylight: tall, with the broad shoulders of a swimmer, brown skin a tad more sun-kissed than she remembered, and a devilishly handsome smile. He wore a pair of knee-length green shorts, stopping at the right length for her to admire marvelously toned calves, and a beige tee with a slight V-neck—just enough for her to catch a glance at the muscular chest she knew lay beneath. Flip-flops replaced the leather dress shoes of their last encounter, and she decided right then and there he was one of the few men who looked equally scrumptious in formal attire and casual loungewear. Still, the slightly styled cowlick of his jet black hair, the dark hue mirrored in his eyes, suggested he had put some effort into his appearance.

The butterflies in her stomach fluttered to life at the thought.

"Well, you see, I have *eyes* everywhere," he teased. The delectable rumble of that sultry baritone, wrapped in a posh English accent—oh, it was positively swoon-worthy. Skye leaned on the door for support, hoping Finn wouldn't notice, and narrowed her eyes.

He waited, as if expecting a response, then cleared his throat and straightened, lowering the bouquet. "Actually, Cole gave it to me."

"*What?*"

"I said I was sending thank-you cards," Finn admitted with an impish shrug. "These are for you."

Skye bit her lower lip before letting her gaze drop to the roses. They really were quite lovely, though there was something strange about their color. Darker than standard roses... Thicker, too. Finn held the bouquet out for her, and when she finally accepted it with a long, drawn-out sigh, Skye caught a whiff of one of her favourite scents.

"They're chocolate?" She went for one of the leaves, laughing softly when it popped off and started to melt between her fingers. Finn slipped his hands in his pockets and rocked back and forth onto the balls of his feet, his pleasure at her surprise obvious.

"Any old idiot can get actual flowers," he mused.

She popped the leaf in her mouth and briefly closed her eyes, savoring the exquisite taste. Rai's Sweets really did make the best chocolates, and from the look on his face, Finn knew it.

"I had it commissioned for you at the shop in LA. It arrived this morning." He watched her break off another leaf and pop it in her mouth, smiling. "I'm actually in charge of rolling out this new service in the US... We can pretty much make anything out of chocolate."

"It tastes delicious," she murmured, swallowing a moan.

"And, as I recall, so do you." Finn pursed his lips when she looked up sharply, cheeks on fire, and appeared to be trying not to laugh. "Can I come in? Just to talk... Or more, if you want. I'm game either way."

Skye contemplated slamming the door in his smug face, just to knock him down a few pegs, but couldn't bring herself to do it. Instead, she sighed again and stepped aside.

"Just to talk," she insisted, fighting the urge to dreamily float along behind him in his cologne cloud as he breezed by. Sandalwood. Cedar. Woodsy yet refined—the scent brought forth images of Finn hiking through towering red pines to a cabin. Said cabin would be stocked with every amenity a billionaire could need, and he'd sip bourbon on a deck while Skye padded toward him, wearing his discarded shirt over her naked, glowing, totally satisfied body, post-orgasm...

She blinked and slammed the door harder than necessary.

Whoa.

This...was not good. Did the cologne companies know their product had such insane effects on women?

Or was it all Finn? Maybe he just enhanced something that was already mind-altering...

Focus, Skye.

Shaking her head, she crossed the spacious, sparsely furnished apartment and set the bouquet of chocolate roses on the kitchen island. Finn had already made himself comfortable on the couch, and as she turned back, deciding to hover there at the island to keep some distance between them, she found him lifting a limp, sleepy Oz onto his lap. The cat appeared mildly disgruntled to be manhandled by a stranger, but soon closed his eyes, purring, as Finn massaged his neck.

Skye knew just how talented those fingers could be...

Another headshake to refocus. "What are you doing here?"

"Straight the point today, I see," he mused, his attention on Oz. Skye folded her arms over her chest.

"Well, we left things kind of awkward, and now you're here, so..."

"I just wanted to talk," Finn told her. He finally looked up from Oz, perfectly businesslike, and stretched his arm along the back of the couch. "Are you romantically involved with Cole Daniels?"

Anxiety skittered through her in prickling waves.

"How is that any of your business?"

"I've made it my business." Finn's eyes narrowed slightly. "I'm many things in this life, Skye. Some pleasant, others not. I know that. However, one thing I'm not is a man who fucks his friend's girlfriend. I've never been that man, nor do I have any intention of becoming that man. So," he scooped Oz up to his chest, then inched to the edge of the couch and leaned forward, meeting her eye, "I need to know the truth."

To anyone else, Skye would have told her usual lie, that she and Cole had been dating for *years*, right away. However, knowing that Finn had met Cole long before she even started telling said lie, she couldn't deceive him. She couldn't let him walk away thinking he had screwed over one of the nicest men Skye had the privilege of associating with. And, given how firmly he spoke, his tone suggesting an instant shift from playful to no-nonsense, she had a feeling Finn felt the same way about Cole as she did.

Well. Maybe not completely. Even though she had come to terms with the fact that Cole probably, maybe, *potentially* wasn't interested in pushing the boundaries of their relationship, she still had feelings for him. Ones she had been trying to bury by throwing herself into her workouts, her day trips to the beach, her Friday night sushi gab-fests with her friends, and her soul-crushing job hunt. Skye liked to keep busy, but in the week that had followed her run-in with Finn and her weird goodbye with Cole, she had been living on overdrive. Hell, she was due at the cat sanctuary in an hour so she could voluntarily clean cages and litterboxes, immediately followed by a paint-and-wine-night thing with her girl Brynn and a few friends downtown.

"Skye." She leapt out of her wandering thoughts at the sharp way Finn said her name.

"It's complicated," was the best answer she could give him.

He did a great job at maintaining his steely demeanor while Oz, now wide awake, sniffed and rubbed his fuzzy cheeks against Finn's stubbly cheek. "Why?"

"Because..." She threw her hands up. "Because it just is."

"I am privy to some information regarding his use of that *agency*." The way his face pinched with distaste sent her hackles up. She recrossed her arms, scowling as he struggled to say it aloud—something Skye had grappled with at first too. "The... The... Well... I know that he has a, er..." He gestured to her, floundering. "You know."

"Sugar baby?" she offered, after which Finn settled back on the couch, Oz still cuddled to his chest, and scoffed.

"Yes, *that*. What a ridiculous title."

"I'm not arguing with you there."

"He's told me some details of the arrangement," Finn continued without missing a beat. "I'm surprised we've never run into each other at events, but Cole and I have been a bit opposite with schedules in the last five years, and for my own sanity I don't follow the tabloids. But from what I've gathered, he's very fond of his...sugar... Oh, don't make me say it."

While it was tempting to draw out his torment, the subject matter was a little too dangerous for Skye to hem and haw around.

"Look, I can't confirm or deny anything that you're saying," she told him, reaching back and snagging another chocolate leaf, "as per my contract."

She popped it in her mouth quickly, though she didn't taste the chocolate as strongly this time. The silence that followed weighed her down, smothering her taste buds, drying out her throat. Finn was back to massaging Oz, his brow slightly furrowed.

"Right." He cleared his throat. "I see."

Panic started to make its presence known as a wave of nausea struck her. "You can't say anything to anyone—"

"Like I would do that to Cole." Another scoff. He retracted his hands when Oz took a swipe at him, and they both watched the fluffy white creature toddle off his lap and settle one cushion away. The cat stared at Finn for a moment, then began furiously grooming himself, as if to clean off all that scrumptious man smell. Finn chuckled, then folded his hands on his lap with a soft sigh. "Cole and I are friends. Not *society* friends, actual friends. *Good* friends. His reasons for using the agency's services have always made sense to me. Before you arrived, the press, particularly back home, was ruthless when it came to his love life. I wouldn't ever bring that on him again."

Relief left her unsteady, and Skye grabbed another leaf before joining him on the couch, keeping Oz between them as a buffer.

"Thank you," she said softly, breaking the leaf in half and offering him some, which he accepted with a small smile.

"Of course. I don't want either of you to get into any legal trouble. You don't have to tell me anything about your relationship." He studied the leaf, the green shimmer catching in the sunlight streaming through the enormous windows at the far end of the couch. "Cole has always spoken of you, without naming you, rather affectionately. I assumed there was a sort of familial-like bond between him and his...person."

Great. Skye chomped on her half of the leaf, catching the bits that crumbled onto her shirt. So, Cole talked about her like she was, what, a little sister? He had always been protective over her; he'd spared no expense on security for the apartment, installed all the right apps on her phone and laptop to keep her data safe, and insisted on her being escorted home after night outings, usually by his assistant if he couldn't do it personally—even when his assistant wasn't technically on the clock. She was a year younger; it made some sense that he would describe her as a sister to someone like Finn.

But just because it made sense didn't make it feel good.

"Judging from your expression, that isn't welcome news," Finn mused. Heat flooded her cheeks and she looked away quickly, wishing he couldn't read her quite so well. After all, he didn't know her; they'd just had sex.

"It's fine," she said, ignoring how stiff her words sounded. "Cole and I are friends too. I mean, outside of all the, you know, sugar daddy stuff, I actually think he's one of my best friends. It doesn't bother me that he'd talk about me like that."

"Funny how I don't believe you."

"Well, I guess that's your problem, isn't it?" She picked at her nails, waiting. If Finn had worn a suit, he might have stood and buttoned up his jacket. Instead, he merely drummed his fingers along the back of the couch, smirking, and then tapped Oz lightly on the head. The cat rolled over, paws poised for destruction.

"I'm not here to waste anyone's time, Miss Summers," he said, a shiver running down her spine at the use of her last name—something else she hadn't given him. "Least of all my own."

Her gaze followed him as he stood. "Because you're a very busy man?"

"Precisely."

"Most of you are."

"Hmm. I suppose." He pursed his lips, as if unimpressed with her implication. "So, let me be perfectly frank. Are you in love with Cole?"

Her whole body seemed to spontaneously ignite at the question, her cheeks on fire, the heat spreading down her neck and under the scoop neck of her slouchy tee. "I... I... No."

Skye had never asked herself the question before, not seriously anyway, but it worried her that she stuttered over her answer. Even if she *did* love Cole, what was the point? Nothing was ever going to happen—why pine over a man who adored you like a sister, and whose friendship you might never be able to live without?

"Right," Finn said briskly, running a hand down the front of his T-shirt like he was smoothing the creases from a four-hundred-dollar button-down. "If there's romantic love between you two, I'll bow out. I'll withdraw my name from consideration. I have no interest in mangling either of your hearts."

She sniffed, her heart pounding. "How noble of you."

"But since you're not in love with him"—he looked down at her for confirmation, and she hastily shook her head—"then I'm all in."

"But—"

"Not in public, of course," Finn insisted, quieting her with his hands as one might soothe a startled horse. "I understand there are contractual obligations between you and Cole regarding your public personas, and I'm not here to sully that. But in private, I'm coming after you." He all but smoldered down at her and Skye's stupid stomach butterflies were positively beside themselves. "*Hard.*"

"Why?" Skye couldn't think of anything else to say in response to that. Never in her life had someone stated their active intention to pursue her. Even before Cole and the whole sugar daddy business, her dating life had been stunted because she worked all the time. Dates were more like one-night stands, and long-term relationships were usually just friends-with-benefits hook-ups that usually included food after.

Finn studied her for a moment, his expression softening. "Do you believe in love at first sight?"

She snorted. "No."

"Me neither. Worth a shot though." He flashed a smirk before swooping down and kissing her firmly, a hand on the back of the couch while the other cupped her face. The butterflies turned to fireworks, and she let out a tattered, ragged moan, her eyes dropping closed as her body arched up toward him of its own accord, desperate to be closer. Finn pulled away abruptly, ending the kiss just as quickly as it began, and her lips tingled pleasantly in his absence. When she pressed her hands to her furiously burning cheeks, her eyes wide, he laughed and headed for the door.

"Now, put my number from the business card into your phone," he instructed, pointing to the abandoned black rectangle on the couch, "and text me so I have a better means of reaching you. Otherwise I'm just going to keep showing up here at inopportune times to kiss you."

"What a nightmare," she said, pleased that her voice wasn't a breathless mess. "Whatever's a girl to do?"

"Call me." He flashed one last gorgeous grin before leaving, the most graceful, suave exit her front door had ever experienced.

Alone again, Skye sank down into the couch and groaned, hands pressing harder to her cheeks.

In her peripherals, over her fingertips, she caught Ozzy staring at her.

"Oh, don't judge me," she snapped. "You were all over him too."

The cat offered a slow blink in response before resuming his noisy grooming session.

What the hell had just happened? Was this real life? She wasn't dreaming, passed out in delirious excitement after landing an interview?

She let out a laugh born from adrenaline, anxiety, and flattery before heading for the chocolate roses on her kitchen island. Skye broke the head off one and shoved it in her mouth, then let herself moan as loudly as she had wanted to initially. Rai's Sweets made the best chocolate in the entire world—fact. Unable to resist, Skye pulled out a barstool and dug in, deciding that gorging herself was easier —and more fun—than thinking about Finn Rai's proposal.

And his burning question: was she in love with Cole?

She shook her head. No. That was a question she could save for another day. For now—twelve long-stemmed roses made entirely of chocolate were begging to be eaten in a single sitting.

Who was Skye to refuse them?

9

DOWNWARD DOG

"We have five other candidates to interview before the week is up, but I think you'd be a fine addition to the staff here."

Skye forced herself to sit still and swallow that maniacal cackle climbing up her throat at the thought of being able to end her job hunting for good. Hans Timmons, her interviewer at Gallery Sens, the sex museum disguised as a fine arts gallery for nudes to throw off fickle outsiders, had seemed thrilled with all her answers. Over the course of her nearly two-hour-long interview, they had chatted about her Museum Studies degree, her old customer service jobs, her cat—pretty much everything under the sun.

Not only did he appear to like talking to her, but he hadn't stopped smiling since Skye walked in, and she knew it hadn't anything to do with her slim-fit green pencil skirt or the snug beige blouse she wore with it; all the Pride flags, pins, and law-reform-themed newspaper clippings suggested he went to bat for a different team altogether. Which she preferred. Skye had experienced one too many gross, leering interviewers in her day. None in the museum sector so far, but those fast food managers had liked to play just as fast and loose as their burgers.

"Well, thank you for a fantastic interview," she said, offering her hand over the desk and smiling when he took it with a surprisingly firm grip. Given the frail figure and the skin so tanned it could be a decent leather handbag knock-off, she had expected the same wimpy little fingertip-grab she'd endured at other museum interviews. Not so. It was clear that Hans Timmons had a zest for life and had found his calling. She could only hope to feel the same one day.

"I'll be in touch after the weekend, whether you get the position or not."

"I appreciate it."

After getting sucked into a quick chat about weekend plans, which so far consisted of a tentatively scheduled beach day with her friends, Skye excused herself, ignored the other buttoned-up candidate waiting outside the office door, and practically skipped outside. The museum was a comfortable twenty-minute walk from home; it would be less comfortable as the summer dragged on and the heat got worse, but she really dug the guy running things. Now, if only everyone else could tank their interviews, then the coveted position of curator's assistant—to the *whole* museum—would be hers.

Rather than wearing the exhaustion of a two-hour conversation like a second skin, Skye walked out of Gallery Sens with a giddy spring in her step. While she'd planned to pick up food on the way home and crash on the couch with Ozzy, right now she had the energy to make her usual Wednesday night yoga class.

So, she hurried home, changing out of her sweaty—both from the nerves *and* the late-afternoon heat—interview attire and into her standard yoga gear: bright purple knee-length leggings, a cute new sports bra, and a big slouchy tee. This T-shirt in particular had a photo of kitten-aged Oz on it; her friend Brynn had made it to celebrate her main man's first birthday three years ago. Throw in her comfiest flip-flops, a dollop of sunscreen for the walk, and her vintage aviators—another gift from Cole—and Skye was ready to party.

She paused only briefly, leaning against the kitchen island to respond to Finn's text asking how her interview went. When she gave him the good news, he texted back a slew of heart-eyed emojis, which made her laugh, followed by an invitation to celebratory drinks at a bar up the street. Grinning, Skye shot him down as politely as she could, which he gracefully accepted a few moments later by asking if they were still team-watching a reality cooking show together that night instead. Last week, they had realized they both watched the same show every Wednesday night, and then spent the whole episode texting about the dramatic contestants and the awful judges—and now apparently it was their new weekly thing. Skye's butterflies did somersaults at the thought, and she agreed, promising to have her snark ready for eight-o'clock sharp.

After, she stuffed her phone and a little post-yoga sundress into her cat-themed tote bag, showered Oz with kisses, and zipped out the door.

Fifteen minutes later, Skye had her things in a locker, her favourite studio mat—the teal one with a neon-green palm tree pattern always made her feel good—tucked under her arm, and was strolling from the locker rooms through the main reception hall of the studio. While the front desk attendants were all *namaste* and bowing and serene smiles for class attendees, Skye merely offered her usual friendly nod and tried not to engage. It wasn't that she didn't believe in the spiritual side of yoga; she knew it was there and what it could do for people. It was just that she felt a bit...silly pretending when she was really just there for the awesome workout.

Never had her balance, core strength, or flexibility been better than when she'd started doing yoga. Adding it to her weekly gym routine, a requirement from the sugar daddy agency contract to keep in relatively good shape, had done wonders for her overall health. She just couldn't get behind the flow of energies and chakras and the power of the mind rhetoric. Still, those who *did* go for that kind of mindset made the classes really peaceful, and it was the only place she was able to work out without feeling even slightly self-conscious.

Her eyes darted to the smoothie bar when one of the blenders whirred to life. There was no namaste-fake-smiles nonsense over there—ever. All that mattered to the folks behind the counter was upselling, and while the product was expensive, damn was it good. Skye already had plans to grab something to slurp on the way home after her session.

Now, would it be a Berry Blaster or a Greenie Energy Booster today? She scanned the menu board as she followed the herd toward the studio doorway, a few minutes to spare to find her place somewhere toward the back and get comfortable. However, in her moment of distraction, mentally debating whether to add protein or wheat grass to her smoothie, she hadn't realized that not everyone was moving with the flow of foot traffic—and walked right into a very, *very* solid body.

"Oh my god, I'm so..." Skye's mouth fell open when she found herself staring up at a decidedly dressed-down Cole Daniels. Heat rushed to her cheeks. This was their first face-to-face run-in since Finn's party. "Hi."

"Hey," he greeted, swiping a hand through his sun-kissed brown-blond hair, the motion followed by an easy sort of grin that made her knees weak. "Fancy meeting you here."

Yeah, fancy that. She had only attended this class once a week for the last two years—which he knew about, since his credit card got the bill. Skye shifted the rolled mat under her arm, then planted her free hand on her hip. While she and Cole may not have physically seen much of each other since that awkward goodbye, they had exchanged a few equally awkward text messages over the last two weeks.

Maybe this was Cole's attempt to smooth things over. Dressed in a deliciously form-fitting white T-shirt and a pair of loose black shorts, the kind that didn't show *everything* but managed to highlight enough, he had clearly stepped out of his comfort zone and into hers. Just because they had had similar childhoods, similar family struggles, including frequent brushes with the poverty line and unstable parental figures, didn't mean Cole slummed it often these days. His suits, his cars, his various beach homes, his ridiculous number of technological devices—he did what he could to distance himself from anything even *remotely* casual.

Her gaze darted down to his feet. Sandals. Cole Daniels. Wearing *sandals*. Hell might have frozen over.

"Yeah," she said slowly. "Fancy meeting you here." Her lips quirked. "What, the home gym getting a bit boring?"

"My private yoga guy's a pretentious twat," he replied with a shrug. "You always speak so highly of this place... Thought I'd give it a go."

"Huh." Why hadn't he told her? He'd known she'd be here on a Wednesday night, usually around this time. Cole's eye twitched, and when he chuckled, she caught a glint of playfulness in those ocean-blues.

"What? Don't believe me?"

"You should have told me." Skye shrugged, and a quick glance toward the door sent the pair across the now-empty reception area at a good clip. "We could have made it a date."

"I've already sprung one outing on you this trip," he said, his voice dropping as they crossed the threshold into the studio. Incense burned on either side of the door, the vanilla clashing with the lavender. She glanced up and bit back a smile: Cole hated both scents, though he downplayed his disgust well. Only a slight flicker of contempt skittered across his scruffy cheeks, like he was trying to be on his best behaviour.

For her?

Maybe.

"Today can be off the clock, if you want," he told her as they hurried to the far left corner, snagging the only two spots available. Skye took the last row, while Cole settled one row up, one spot over. She knew he was joking, but the comment didn't sit all that well with her as she unrolled her mat. When she looked up, she found him studying her, one hand fisted, the other clicking his nails together furiously. As their eyes met, he cleared his throat and stilled. "I just mean... We're two friends doing yoga together, that's all."

Her unease softened, and Skye managed a genuine smile, her chest tight with affection. "Yeah. Of course we are."

He exhaled softly, hands loosening, and stepped onto his mat as the instructor floated into the room in a burlap dress *thing* that looked itchy as all hell.

As Tash, who Skye knew for a fact only adopted the air

of mysticism when she taught classes, welcomed everyone to that night's session, Skye tried to ignore the hurricane of *feeling* roiling in her gut at Cole's sudden appearance. After all, she and Finn had been texting and chatting over the phone relentlessly since he dropped by her place last week. Skye had shot down all invitations for a date, preferring just to talk about their days and whatever else came to mind—safe options. She wasn't opposed to dinner or anything; she just hadn't decided if she wanted to go through with it—if she wanted to go somewhere public with another man, pretending just to be friends as he literally charmed her pants off.

And now, seeing Cole, all that flirtatious energy she had reserved for Finn, all the excitement he brought out of her just at the sight of his name on her call display, turned to a lead weight that she couldn't shake. Skye knew she shouldn't feel like that. Cole had confirmed, yet again, that they were just friends—with contracted benefits, none of which were the kind Skye wanted. Yet there she was, dropping down for a brief stint of cat-cow, feeling guilty for what had transpired over the last week.

Because she had texted the boy she had a new, thrilling crush on.

And now here she was staring at the ridiculously sculpted ass of the *other* boy she had very real feelings for. Maybe love. Maybe something in the murky middle between love and best friend. A man who, as he lifted that sculpted ass up into a long downward dog, still made her feel awkward after the way they'd left things...

If only Skye put some stock in all the Zen chatter Tash spouted from the front of the room. Maybe things would have been easier. As it was, Skye's mind had started to race, and no amount of deep, concentrated nostril inhales or sharp, punctuated mouth exhales could stop it.

In fact, as she lay in flat back position, breathing in time with the rest of the class, Skye decided that today's class had been a bit of a wash. No matter how hard she tried, she had constantly found herself distracted by Cole—by the corded muscle along his arms in every warrior pose, or by the ripple of strength up his back and across his shoulder during a plank. Of course, the physically scrumptious distractions were just a bonus. Cole himself was her mind's primary target, and every single one of Tash's reminders to focus, to empty her mind, to live in the now, fell on deaf ears. He had totally thrown her off her game, and by the time everyone was rolling up their mats and bowing to the front of the room, Skye was more tense than when she'd arrived.

"Hey." Cole went straight for her, barring her escape route with his slightly perspiring figure. Skye, meanwhile, positively *glowed*. Perfect.

"How'd you find it?" she asked, trying as subtly as she could to wipe the sweat from her neck, forehead, and cheeks. "Good?"

"I can see why you like it so much," he insisted warmly. "Do you..." His ocean-blues wandered down, fixating on her shirt. "Is that...Oz?"

"Yeah." Her cheeks coloured when he chuckled, and she drew in a soft breath as he snagged the front of her shirt —delicately, pinched between two fingers on each hand— and pulled it taut to get a better look. The blush spread to the rest of her body, heating her core more than yoga class had during the last hour. "A friend made it for me."

"I love it." He studied the picture for a moment, head cocked to one side, his tone noticeably affectionate. "I always forget how small he was."

"Pretty sure he's still a runt, but the floof more than makes up for it."

"And that attitude."

Skye laughed, relieved when Cole let her damp shirt fall back against her body. No one wanted a gorgeous man touching sweat-drenched clothing. "Yeah, that too."

"Listen, Skye..." Cole cleared his throat and ushered her aside as the next class started to filter into the room—yoga for seniors. He dropped his voice when he spoke next, forcing her to lean in. "Do you want to grab a drink or something? I feel like we left things a bit...weird, and I don't like it."

"*Yes.*" She swallowed hard, hoping that hadn't sounded too eager. "I mean, are you finally admitting that you came to this class to see me, or are we still going with the story from earlier?"

"I think we both know the real reason," he told her, a faint hint of colour rising to his cheeks. "Any place in particular you want to go?"

She knew he expected her to list one of the dozen uber-expensive bars in the area that catered to the men who ran in his social circle, but Skye had a better idea in mind.

"Smoothie from the juice bar, then a walk along the beach?"

Cole's handsome features brightened. "Sounds perfect."

"I, er..." She tucked a sweaty bit of hair behind her ear. "I need to freshen up first, though. Do you mind?"

"Not at all."

"I'll see you in ten?"

"Let's make it twenty," Cole remarked as they headed for the door. He winked when she glanced up. "I know how you enjoy your luxurious showers."

Knowing her response would be the least eloquent

thing imaginable, Skye merely shot him a grin and hurried to the change rooms. Before running into Cole, she had just planned to towel off, change, then head home. Now she had to shift gears completely, racing for one of the three shower stalls at the back of the women's changing area, beating out a few others who had cocktail attire and heels in their open lockers.

Cole was right, of course. Skye loved taking long, hot, steamy showers. She loved indulging herself with bubble baths and pampering her skin with every pricey lotion known to man. It stemmed from the fact that until she met her sugar daddy, Skye had *never* treated herself—unless treating herself consisted of a small vanilla ice cream cone from a street vendor between shifts at two different, equally exhausting jobs. Now, however, she hadn't the time to be indulgent.

Cole was waiting for her.

He wanted to patch things up. He had actually *acknowledged* the weirdness.

Which was *huge*. He had always been the kind of guy to pretend everything with her was fine, to ignore tension and bow to her whims. Skye knew he was a shark in business, but personal issues? He was a pussycat, which, honestly, kept the dramatics down—but all those years of sweeping issues under the rug were finally coming to a head. She knew it. Apparently Cole knew it. And she wasn't going to lose this momentum by wasting time under the yoga studio's gloriously powerful water pressure.

So, Skye was in and out in twelve minutes flat, a personal best these days. Hair chucked up in a bun on top of her head, she had scrubbed, exfoliated, and shaved whatever she could as fast as she could. Once out, she blitzed back to her locker, dried off in a flurry of fluffy towel movements, and changed into her sundress, which had a built-in bra that did wonders for her chest. New underwear. Hair down and finger-combed. A spritz of the floral-scented perfume that lived in her tote bag year-round. A quick time-check told her she hadn't left time for makeup, but her skin had lost its post-workout redness and there wasn't a pimple in sight—good enough.

By the time she hurried out into the lobby, her twenty minutes had *just* expired, and she found herself slightly breathless. Bit embarrassing, really. With a herd of fit seniors milling about between the entrance and the doors to the studio, she took a second for one last primp in the mirror behind the buddha statue, did the most refreshing inhale-exhale combo all day, then scanned the reception area for Cole.

She found him at the juice bar, paying, and before she could rush over to stop him—he paid for enough in her life, and she wasn't exactly on a paparazzi assignment tonight—he thanked the barista behind the counter and scanned the room for her. A shiver raced down her spine when their eyes met, and she pressed her lips together to hide the shy smile that surfaced as he made his way over.

"Berry Blaster with protein," he said as he handed over an almost too large smoothie, "for my little, er, raspberry."

Skye's eyebrows crept up as he cleared his throat.

"Sorry, that was awful."

"I'll strike it from the record," she insisted coyly. "What'd you get?"

"Mint lemon."

Yikes. She schooled her features. "Verdict?"

He took a long, labored sip, then studied the bright pink straw. "Thick."

"Just how I like it." She hastily shoved her own bright

pink straw in her mouth, flushed, and then nodded to the door in a *shall we?* sort of way. Cole led the charge, and Skye chugged along behind him, kicking herself. Normally their innuendos were flirty—not uncomfortable.

Although the yoga studio wasn't far from the beach, Cole insisted on driving them over, not wanting to leave his classic 1958 baby blue Impala parked, top up, on the street for long. *Clearly* he hadn't intended to stay for the session if Skye hadn't shown up. So, after the two-minute drive, during which Skye let her hair free and focused on not getting any smoothie or lingering body lotion on the luxuriously wide seat, they parked in a relatively empty public lot. Leaving her things in the trunk, Skye headed for the beach, her pace casual, like they had nowhere else in the world to be. Halfway down the boardwalk, she perched on the edge of the hip-high stone wall, legs crossed at the ankles.

Cole stood before her and faced the water, one hand in his pocket as he nursed his smoothie, cheeks gaunt for a moment under the strain. Skye had always loved the beach, and while she despised stereotypes, others might describe her as a typical seaside Cali girl. Yoga lover. Sushi aficionado. Sock-free unless absolutely necessary. Go with the flow. Bonfire on the beach expert. Mermaid without the fin and seashell bra. Cole's Coral Bay beach house sat on the edge of a cliff with a path directly down to private sand and surf; every party he hosted there was an epic tease, a test of her will to play her role flawlessly. If she'd had less restraint, she would have blown off the exquisite caviar and tedious conversations to spend the night with waves lapping at her toes.

Somehow, today didn't feel like the day to ditch her flip-flops and stroll along the surf. From Cole's expression, he seemed to be in the same mindset.

Had Finn told him about what had happened that night? Did Cole know she and one of his best friends had been exchanging flirty text messages and phone calls ever since? Would he even care, or was he more concerned about the impact on their contracted relationship?

She bit her lip, watching him for a moment, before turning her gaze outward and letting it wander the clear blue expanse of the Pacific. It really was beautiful—and she'd give anything to be neck-deep in it right now, laughing and frolicking with Cole as though nothing had changed. But that clearly wasn't the case. Sighing, she stood and dusted off the back of her yellow strapless sundress. Without her heels on, she was a few generous inches shorter than him.

"Cole," she touched his shoulder gently, "I think we need to talk about—"

Before she could get it out, Cole whirled around and grabbed her, his hand curving across her lower back and his face stopping within a breath of hers. They stared at one another in a moment of stunned silence, blood pounding in her ears, and Skye found herself distracted by the soft parting of his lips. Heat and adrenaline prickled through her. Seconds slowed to *years*, until there was nothing but Cole and Skye, standing on the brink, on the precipice of what she had desired from the moment she first met him. She angled her face up slightly, bringing their mouths so exquisitely close that she could feel the hum of his lips in hers.

And then he kissed her.

Finally.

While tentative and tender, a mere brush of his lips

against hers, it was most *definitely* a kiss. Her eyes widened, her body stiffened, and Skye nearly dropped her smoothie. A surge of warmth raced from her mouth down to the peak of her thighs, and it lingered, her heart racing, when Cole pulled away.

"I... What...?" she babbled, her whole body on fire. "Cole, you..."

"Skye." He cupped her face, thumbing the sensitized skin of her lower lip. "I don't know, but it's happening."

Her eyes closed this time as he swooped down, smoothie falling to the ground when he took her mouth fiercely, passionately. Their lips parted in an instant, his tongue sweeping over hers, and Skye wrapped her arms around his neck and stood up on her tip-toes.

If she'd thought that last kiss had set her on fire, this one had turned her into a blazing inferno.

The rock-hard planes of his body melded perfectly with the soft curves of hers, and she moaned weakly as his fingers twined through her loose red waves, the other hand scooping her up by her backside. Any hint of space between them, any distance, disappeared. The rest of the world faded away. The crashing waves fell silent. The cries of circling seagulls vanished. It was just her and Cole, holding each other tighter than Skye had ever been held in her life—like their very survival depended on that kiss, and if they broke apart, even for a moment, the world would end.

That was how she'd always felt. Sure, Cole traveled most of the time, but she had still considered him a primary figure in her life. If he disappeared, for whatever reason, her world *would* end. It would just stop spinning. Crops would die. The oceans would rise. All that doomsday stuff—it would come true for her.

And for the last four years, Skye had assumed she was

the only one who felt that way, that his world would keep on spinning no matter what. He'd find a new sugar baby. Maybe he'd arrange a business-savvy marriage. *Something.* But from the way he kissed her, like he was dying of thirst and Skye was his own personal oasis, and the way he held her, possessively, like she was untouchable to every other soul out there...

Well, it hadn't all been in her head.

Skye hadn't imagined the spark, the chemistry, the affectionate glances.

When she pulled away, fearing she might suffocate, Skye's eyes were watery as they fluttered open. Her lips tingled in a way she never wanted to stop.

"I... think we need to talk," Cole admitted, sounding just as breathless as she felt. His cheeks bore a flush of desire, and his eyes, normally bright blue and clear like her beloved Pacific, reminded her more of the Atlantic—in the middle of a cyclone.

"Yeah, there are some things to say," she managed. "Clearly."

"And maybe here isn't the best place," he said. Then, he ducked down and grabbed her fallen smoothie, tossing it in the nearby garbage bin. When he faced her again, he wore a hopeful, though slightly guarded expression. It wasn't one she knew all that well, yet it still managed to make her heart skip a beat. Skye brushed a hand through her hair, then nodded in the general direction of his car.

"My place or yours?"

10

FINALLY

"Skye, I have to apologize," Cole said as they drove the long bend along the shoreline leading up to his secluded villa. "I didn't know there were photographers at the beach. I was hoping they hadn't realized I was even *in* Coral Bay."

She bit the insides of her cheeks to keep from snapping at him. As they had headed back to the car after that life-changing kiss, she and Cole had been swarmed by paparazzi. Most of the questions were shouted at him, as they always were, and Skye couldn't help wondering if that kiss had been for *their* benefit, not hers. After all, no one had ever been able to get a snap of such a passionate, candid embrace between them. It'd be all over tomorrow's tabloids. Was it all for show?

Her heart said no, but her mind wasn't quite so convinced.

"Really. I honestly didn't know. If I did, I wouldn't have kissed you. You know I hate giving those bastards a story." Cole slowed the car as they approached his front gate. What Skye loved most about his villa was that it was the only one in the area. He had bought the land surrounding it and refused to sell an inch to developers hungry to build condos or hotels. In fact, last year he had put in an application to have the land protected by law, citing conservation efforts and the like. The deal still hadn't gone through, but in the meantime, Skye got to enjoy the view—green forest and hills to her left, the ocean, cliffs, and pristine sandy beaches to her right—unencumbered. It almost helped her forget what had just happened with the photographers.

"It's fine," she managed as he punched in the gate code. Moments later, a series of mechanisms unlocked noisily before the wrought iron barrier swung open. "I believe you."

Sort of. Cole had never pulled publicity stunts in the past. He wasn't hurting for press, his companies were doing great, and Skye's appearance at most public functions had quelled rumors that he was some weirdo perma-bachelor. Still, the whole ordeal had put a dampener on things.

The car came to a gentle stop in front of the closed two-door garage, and when Cole cut the engine, Skye immediately heard the roar of the waves from somewhere below. From the street view, Cole's beach house appeared to be a standard bungalow, but it backed onto a small cliff overlooking the ocean. The lower level extended down the side of the cliff, and a somewhat unwieldy set of stairs carved into the landscape took you down to the water. Or, for the non-daredevils, Skye included, you could exit the door off the kitchen and just follow the path down a much gentler slope to the private beach.

She loved this house. Whenever Cole brought her there, it was like she had her own remote island paradise. He'd considered selling it a few years ago, but she was glad he hung onto it. Something about him having a home in Coral Bay, near her, was always comforting.

She fiddled with the hem of her sundress, acutely aware that they had been silently sitting in the car for at least two minutes while she admired the house. After all, she hadn't visited since last year—but that was more of an excuse, really, so she could justify not speaking first.

Just as she was about to comment on how lovely the gardens looked, a blend of cactus and seasonal florals on either side of the stone walkway leading up to the front door, Cole unbuckled his seatbelt and faced her.

"Skye."

"Cole," she said, more out of habit than anything, and clicked her seatbelt free. Now was when the talking should happen, but knowing Cole, he would probably ask what she wanted to drink, if she was hungry, comment on the weather. She met his gaze hesitantly, lower lip caught between her teeth, and arched an eyebrow. A challenge. *Do something. I dare you.*

Much to her surprise, he complied—in spades.

Cole cupped her cheek, fingers brushing along her skin to the back of her neck as he dragged her into a breathtaking kiss. A wave of desire crashed into her and she clutched at his wrist as their mouths opened to one another. His tongue swept over hers, faintly, tentatively, and she sighed against him. Unable to contain herself, Skye clambered across the car, never once breaking contact, and straddled him. Cole hastily pushed his seat back, the sudden shift jostling them together. Her hands slipped to his shoulders, firm and muscular, as his wandered down her back, and, much to her surprise, cupped her backside.

She gasped, eyes fluttering to meet his, and within them she still saw the ocean—only there were no calm waters today. No endless stretches of pristine blue-green that she wanted to dip her toes in and ripple. Today, storms raged once more. Sea and foam and waves and molten grey sky—she saw it all. Threading her fingers through his hair, she arched up against him, pressing him into the seat as the kiss deepened. Cole's groan sent delight skittering through her body, pooling in her already damp sex. The little bundle of pleasure-seeking nerves at the crest of her thighs pulsed with need, and she ground down over Cole's steadily hardening erection. Tendrils of pleasure coursed through her body in response—so she did it again, smiling against his mouth at the sound of yet another groan, this time its timbre deepening to a growl.

Cole responded by lifting the back of her dress and spanking what her bikini-cut panties left exposed. Skye's eyes shot open at the sharp sting of pain, paired neatly with another wave of pleasure shooting out from her core. The jolt broke their kiss, but Cole merely watched her with those stormy blues, not once offering the bumbling apology she half expected. Instead, he rubbed a hand over the delicate skin of her backside, taking away some of the bite—only to smack her again, grinning faintly when she squeaked. Skye drew in a few shaky breaths, both pleased and surprised at this rather daring side of him. It was...unexpected.

And, quite frankly, more of a turn on than she would have thought. Kissing Cole, period, had practically flooded her panties. After this, there'd be no hope for saving them.

With one hand still cradling her stinging behind, Cole threaded the other up and into her hair, which he wrapped around his fist and tugged. Not harshly. Just enough to force her chin up, and Skye's fingers bit into his shoulders when he placed kiss after kiss along her jaw, under her chin, and down her neck. When she felt teeth graze her collarbone, Skye shivered and moaned his name softly. His response came in a harsh rush of hot breath against her skin, and he straightened suddenly, gripping the bodice of her sundress and yanking it down her body. Her sex clenched, an exquisite *need* coming to full bloom within, and she sat back, giving him a moment to appreciate her.

And appreciate he did. His gaze explored every inch of her exposed skin, and her nipples hardened to stiff peaks.

"God, you're perfect," he murmured as his hand crept up her stomach and cupped one breast. He then snagged her nipple between his thumb and forefinger, and she whimpered when he rolled it, her body quivering at the delicious blend of pain and pleasure.

"Cole..." She had no idea what she wanted to say, but his name, rolling off her tongue... It only seemed to excite them both. He ducked down, capturing the nipple in his hot mouth, flicking it with his tongue, teasing it with the gentle scrape of teeth. Desperate for some sort of release from the steadily mounting tension, Skye ground down against his tented pants, fingers weaving through his hair as she rocked against him. Cole enveloped her other pert nipple with his mouth, groaning as her hand tightened in his hair. Each time she bucked her hips, his hardness brushed over her swollen clit, dragging a desperate mewl out of her. All Skye wanted was him—it was all she'd ever wanted.

"Fuck *me*," he hissed when he finally came up for air.

"Gladly," she whimpered back when he trailed his tongue between her breasts, then darted down and lightly nipped at her side. The hint of teeth made her squeal, but when she tried to squirm away, Cole held her in place with a hand slipping between them to cup her.

"You've no idea what you do to me," he whispered huskily. "You're so *wet*..."

"Because that's what *you* do to *me*."

Without warning, he pushed her soaked panties aside and plunged two fingers into her. Both slid in without resistance, filling her—but not as much as she would have liked. Almost. Desperately close.

Cole grabbed the back of her head and dragged her in for a searing kiss, fingers thrusting in and out of her, torturously slow and steady. He managed to rub both her clit and her inner wall, the combined pleasure of both a monstrous distraction, so much so that she could barely concentrate on kissing him. He chuckled against her mouth, clearly enjoying her dilemma, then nipped at her bottom lip.

"C-Cole..." She clenched her eyes shut, gasping, on the edge of a climax. "I can't... You..."

"Are you all right?" His fingers stopped, and she caught a flicker of concern breaking through his lust-ridden features.

The brief reprieve from his relentless pace provided the moment of clarity she needed—to ensure her fingers were working. She hastily unbuckled his belt and unzipped his pants, quickly freeing his confined cock—which was bigger than she'd expected. Smoothing the glistening liquid at the tip down to the base, she grinned when Cole's head tipped back, his lips slightly parted as she dragged a loose fist up and down. If she had more patience, she might have taken her time; after all, he had reveled in her torment long enough. Skye ought to return the favor.

But when it came to Cole, she was an impatient hussy with no shame. So, Skye lifted her hips, panties pushed to one side, and dragged his hard tip between her slick folds, back and forth, enjoying the way Cole twitched beneath her, then slid down his full length.

She had never had metaphorical fireworks go off before, but when their eyes met, it was the biggest, grandest display the world had ever seen. Cole cupped her face and steered her down, their lips colliding as the colorful explosions danced across her mind's eye. Her sex tightened around him, adjusting to the size, and she embraced the fleeting moment of calm, the eye of the storm, to lose herself in their kiss.

She had imagined it over and over again, sometimes using that fantasy to reach a blissful climax before bed. The real thing was so much better.

Pulling back, she gasped down a few breaths, her forehead resting against his. Slowly, she started to move, testing the waters, her hips swirling and bucking as he watched her, utterly transfixed. Eventually her pace quickened, helped along by his hands splayed over her backside. Each time he filled her, Skye lost hold of a piece of her sanity, careening closer and closer to the edge of ecstasy. She didn't try to contain her cries, her moans, her whimpers, and soon Cole's harsh breaths intermingled with them, forming the sweetest chorus she had ever heard—the kind she'd hear again in her dreams tonight.

Suddenly, the seat fell back, clicking into place, and she giggled as they fell with it. With more room to move, Cole locked his arm around her waist, trapping her in place against his hard, lean body. With a hand woven through her hair, he pulled her head back, tongue leaving a wet hot trail up her neck, before thrusting into her so hard that her teeth chattered. Pleasure bloomed, washing over her in steady waves as he finally set his own pace. Hard. Fast. Pounding in and out of her, Cole held her in place. Unable to move, unable to kiss him—all she could do was moan and give in to wild abandon.

"Are you going to come for me?" he demanded, the authority in his tone nearly pushing her over the edge. She whimpered her response, barely coherent, which earned her a swift smack on the bottom, its sting biting through the pleasurable haze. "Use your words, sweetheart."

"Y-yes," she cried, fingers digging so hard into the leather seat that she swore she heard something rip. "God, *yes*!"

He let go of her hair as a stunning climax tore through her, and Skye bowed against him, shaking. Her mind's fireworks had gone postal, exploding as one while sweet heat rocked her body. She collapsed against him, his vigorous pace prolonging the blissful torture of an orgasm that left her momentarily blind, deaf, and dumb. Skye floated back to reality, only just, when Cole's arm clamped down around her, making it a little hard to breathe, and he hissed her name against her skin. Tensed, Cole spilled himself into her, then slowly sagged into the seat.

With a hand gently clasping the back of her neck, he guided her back to him for one last kiss.

The kind of kiss that could last forever.

Skye had never seen the inside of Cole's bedroom.

The thought only just occurred to her as she stood at the foot of his bed, staring out two floor-to-ceiling glass walls that overlooked the Pacific. If she had stayed overnight in the past, there was a guest bedroom with her name on it. There was also an awesome home theater setup that she and Cole made use of from time to time, streaming marathons and ingesting *way* too much popcorn.

Mind you, the kitchen wasn't bad either. Stainless steel appliances. Black granite countertops. An island the size of a small country. Double-door fridge always stocked with her favourite munchies. The kitchen was Skye's retreat on the rare occasion that Cole hosted something with people she couldn't stand. She'd spend at least a collective hour hiding out with the chef and his team, sampling everything before it went out, hoping no one would notice her missing.

But the bedroom had always been off-limits—in both a literal sense, as Cole kept the door closed when he hosted company, and in the metaphorical sense, as Skye tried to wrangle her feelings and preserve a friendship she valued more than anything. Yet here she was. Wrapped in an ankle-length teal swimsuit cover-up, one she had left behind sometime last year, otherwise still naked beneath, she crossed her arms over her chest and stared out across the water. Perfect surf waves rolled toward the shoreline, their white tips surging forward and crashing against the sand. She bit her lip. Crashing. Were she and Cole crashing? Were they about to?

Sex always made things complicated.

It had all seemed pretty uncomplicated, of course, when he carried her into the house, down the stairs, and into the master suite, where he undressed her and dragged her into a shower that rivaled the size of her entire bathroom. It had seemed uncomplicated when he nudged her under the spray, combed his fingers through her hair, and attended to every inch of her with a sudsy loofah.

And it certainly hadn't *felt* complicated when he kissed her, when he marched her back against the slate grey tile, hoisted her up, and fucked her through two more earthshattering climaxes.

But in the quiet after the storm, things were complicated. As she watched the ocean, clear blue to match the sky, Skye felt complications creep up her body and gnaw away at her resolve.

This was what she had always wanted...

So why had panic sunk its claws into her and refused to let go?

"Sushi order placed," Cole announced as he strode back into the bedroom, shoving his phone in his pants pocket. "I got your usual... Is that all right?"

"Fine," she told him, her voice catching. His brow furrowed—he'd noticed—and she cleared her throat. "Sounds great, actually."

"In the meantime..." He tossed a packet of something onto the bed. "A sweet for my sweet."

The chocolate stuffed with ooey-gooey salted caramel.

A Rai's Sweets staple. Panic sunk its claws deeper.

"I had a few packets in the fridge for you," he told her. Just the way she liked her chocolate. Cool. Crunchy. The caramel less likely to ooze all over her fingers.

"Cole..." She settled on the edge of the bed. At first, she'd wanted to refuse the chocolates, knowing that this was a serious conversation they needed to have, but she couldn't help herself. They really were her favourite. So, she snatched the packet and ripped it open, then offered some to him as he sat stiffly on the other side. His polite refusal made her sigh, and she brought one cool ball of deliciousness to her mouth; but her hand fell to her lap seconds later, chocolate slowly melting onto her fingertips.

"Do you regret it?" He asked it so softly that she almost missed it.

"*No*," she insisted. "Not for a second."

He exhaled sharply, his hand flexing in and out of a fist. "Good."

"Do you?"

"No."

To anyone else, it might have sounded like they were on the same page, but Skye knew Cole better than that. So, she took a slow, measured breath, and set her chocolates aside.

"But," she started, fully aware that this would kill their post-sex-pre-sushi pleasantness, "it complicates things."

Cole's phone buzzed, and her eyes narrowed when he started to reach for it. Slowly, he threaded his hands together and set them on his lap.

"It doesn't have to."

"No, of course it doesn't." She couldn't fault him there, but that was wishful thinking. "But you know it does."

"Skye..." He shook his head and stood, strolling for the window-wall, his eyes lifted to the horizon. "We can just carry on the way things have always been. Nothing needs to change."

Her shoulders slumped, the panic giving way to hurt. Didn't he want them to change? Hadn't what just happened *meant* something to him? She started fiddling with the fabric of her cover-up.

"I don't want to do that." Finally. It was out there. Skye swallowed hard and caught Cole frowning as he pulled one hand out of his pocket and curled it into a fist. Curled. Uncurled. Pumping in and out—his thinking tick. She'd always thought it an anxious habit, but could never prove it. A smile flashed across his face, one so brilliant she couldn't miss it. But within seconds, it was gone. Restrained. Hidden away, same as always. The hurt melted to frustration, hedging on anger.

"Really?" Cole asked, his gaze still on the water—faraway, beyond what Skye could reach.

"Is that such a fucking shock to you?" she snapped, and he turned back sharply, his frown deepening. She waited for him to say something, to counter her accusation. Her eyebrows shot up the longer they stared at one another. "Seriously?"

He opened and closed his mouth, words failing, before posing the question she'd always dreaded. "Do... Do you want to end our contract?"

"*No.*" Ending the contract could potentially mean Cole stepping out of her life—for good. She didn't want that either, but she couldn't stand the thought of things fizzling out, all because neither of them had the courage to say what they really felt.

She ought to just tell him. *Feelings*—she had them bad. Maybe love. Probably love. But she couldn't slice herself open and spill her soul for a man with the emotional capacity of a thumbtack. He had always been so adept at pretending, and the thought of him doing it with her... Well, she couldn't stand it. If he didn't feel the same way, if he hadn't the audacity to say it, then why should she?

And she knew that was pathetic. Childish. Two teenagers pretending not to understand the effect they had on one another. It was petty, too.

"Skye, I don't want to end it either," he muttered, crossing the room and taking a seat beside her. The bed jostled slightly, and she looked briefly at the water before pinning her stare on her hands.

"I'm sorry, Cole, but I just..." She gulped. "I need more from you."

"I... I've been trying to give more, but you just won't take it." Cole exhaled, the sound rife with frustration. "You keep telling me you don't want the money, but I don't have much else to gi—"

"I'm not talking about *money*!" Was he being purposefully obtuse? From the furrowed brow and the slightly distracted way he kept glancing at his pocket whenever his phone buzzed, Skye wasn't so sure. A rush of heat spread from her cheeks down to her chest, and he swallowed hard at the sight. Obviously he was aware he'd said the wrong thing, but when he made no effort to fix it, she shook her head and stood. "I can't... I have to go."

"Skye." He snagged her hand before she could stalk out, his touch electric. Why had she said anything at all? A hint of physical contact and her body responded—she should have just mounted him after he gave her chocolate and spent the rest of the night in blissful fucking ignorance. Maybe if they had spoken tomorrow, taken some time to digest, things would be different. But here they were. She had broken the seal. There was no going back now.

So, she waited. She met his stare, she squeezed his hand, and she waited. Her heart leapt at the faint sound of *something* on the tip of his tongue, but disappointment hit hard when he said nothing instead. Fine.

"I'm glad today happened," she said as firmly as she could, "but, Cole, I need more. Not an end to anything. I just need more."

And with that, she tugged her hand free and made her way through the house. She paused, briefly, to change from one dress to another in the hall, grabbing her tote along the way. With her mind a clouded mess, her feet did most of the work, following familiar paths taken many times over until she was standing in the front driveway, staring at the car she and Cole had christened less than an hour earlier.

Within minutes, a town car rolled up. Skye glanced

back, waiting for one last attempt, for Cole to come running out after her and demand that she stay, that they talk more. All he'd have to do was kiss her. That was all it would take.

Nothing.

Swallowing her hurt, she climbed into the car on shaky legs—and left.

11

NEW POV

"I'm sorry…" Skye pressed a hand to her forehead, heart pounding so hard that she could barely hear Hans Timmons, owner of Gallery Sens, through her phone. "You're going to have to repeat that."

He chuckled kindly. "I said, I'd like to offer you a *job*. J. O. B. Does that sound appealing to you, Miss Summers?"

"*Yes*," she all but squealed. How embarrassing—you'd think she was fifteen and getting hired at her first job *ever*. But to have a museum contact her regarding employment, it kind of was her first job—career-wise, anyway.

"Now, I know you applied to assist the curator," Hans remarked, and Skye had to amp her phone's volume to hear the old man's gentle voice. "Unfortunately, I've decided to fill that position with someone who has more experience."

Just like that, her excitement faceplanted. "Oh?"

"I think you'll get there," he assured her, "but you need a little hands-on work outside of your classes. Now, the position I have isn't glamorous—"

"I didn't get into this field for the glamor."

He laughed again. "Well, good! You'll find none of it here. The position I had in mind is ticket seller. You'll essentially man the front desk. Answer phones. Sell admissions. Educate curious lookie-loos and the like."

Glorified receptionist. Skye swallowed hard. She could do that. It didn't sound all that difficult, though she knew the museum got a little busier when Coral Bay's college resumed classes in the fall. First-year students were told to visit Gallery Sens after their Sex Ed and Consent lecture during orientation week. It was like a rite of passage. Everyone went in thinking it would be a porn shop, and then they left feeling cultured. Being a local, Skye hadn't participated, but she had heard all the stories.

"I know it isn't what you want," Hans continued softly, "but I think you'll gain a lot of experience learning how everything works. You'll be hands-on during opening and closing, and you'll assist when we have shows and functions to attend. What do you say? Would you like some time to think on it?"

"No," she told him. "I mean. I know I *should* take the time, but I think this sounds like a wonderful opportunity to learn."

And no one else had called her for follow-up interviews —or an interview in general. She had been fortunate to land the few she had.

"Does that mean you're accepting?"

"Yes, it certainly does."

"Splendid!"

They chatted about a few minor details; the offer would be made official when she came down to cross her Ts and dot her Is. After a few more minutes of her thanking him and Hans expressing his excitement for her to start, and both engaging in the who says goodbye first game again, Skye hung up and flopped down on the couch. Oz gave a sleepy meow in protest when the cushion bounced, and she reached over to ruffle his fur. Unimpressed, the cat got up, stretched, and sauntered down to the armrest to continue his late afternoon snoozefest uninterrupted.

As she took a few contemplative moments to herself to process what had just happened, an enormous smile crossed her lips. Apparently her life didn't have to be consumed by boy drama and stress. She could, on her own merit, land a job in a shitty economy. With a steady paycheck coming in, she might even be able to stop taking an allowance from Cole...

And possibly end their sugar daddy/baby relationship altogether.

Just like that, the smile was gone, and her stomachache, the one that had been tailing her ever since she left Cole's the other week, sidled back into place. Once again, they hadn't spoken much since *it* happened. Skye had wanted the time to think, unencumbered by her heart's desire to be close to Cole no matter what, and she had let his phone calls go unanswered. Of course, every voicemail he left was listened to, scrutinized, and relayed in cryptic summary to her friend Brynn.

The pair had met in college, both at least six years older than everyone else in their classes, and had been friends ever since. Brynn had started working at a coffee shop up the street while she hunted for museum work, and had been in New York visiting family since graduation. Her recent return meant Skye could rant about her "boyfriend," though she had to be careful about how far she went and selective in the details offered. Being in a secret sugar daddy relationship with a contract kind of put a damper on girl talk, but Skye made do with what she had.

Unfortunately, the meat of the issue was that Cole couldn't communicate with her. He wouldn't confirm or deny any feelings for her, despite Skye giving him the opportunity. Brynn thought they were already dating, so Skye had been forced to play up the communication struggles they'd had lately instead.

All things considered, Skye was almost equally at fault. Sure, she had told him she wanted more, but she could have elaborated. She could have specified. She could have just spilled her guts and told him she had feelings for him. But she hadn't. And he hadn't said anything either. So, there they were, a week later and awkward.

A sharp knock at the door sent her shuffling across the living room. Through the peephole she saw yet another bouquet of chocolate roses, but this time no Finn. She accepted them with a smile, offering the delivery guy a taste —which he turned down—before locking herself in and falling back against the door.

And then there was Finn.

Finn, who hadn't stopped calling and texting her. Finn, who greeted her each morning with a cute message. Finn, who couldn't seem to *stop* talking about how interested he was in her. Finn, who had stolen a little piece of her heart—over the freakin' phone.

Ugh. She dug the card out of the bouquet, her smile returning as she read it.

You still owe me lunch, you minx.

Hope this is a suitable substitute. Don't eat it all at once.

Or do. Who am I to judge?

xx Finn

"Fuck me," she muttered before chomping off a rose head, whole hog, and chewing a mouthful of delicious, perfectly tempered chocolate. Seconds later, her phone buzzed from where she had left it on the coffee table. Cole. Again. She looked down at the bouquet. She looked back at her phone.

Not ready to address either, she ignored the call, set the bouquet in the fridge, and opted for TV and Oz cuddles instead. Somehow, it had felt like the universe was setting her up to *choose* between Cole and Finn, and Skye just couldn't do that. Not right now, anyway. It was hardly an even playing field—for either of them. She had known Cole longer. She adored him. They had an established emotional connection, an easy friendship. Being with him had just felt *right.* But none of that negated the fact that they were currently in an official stalemate.

Finn made her heart happy. He was upfront about his romantic interest in her. He knew the details of her sugar daddy relationship with Cole and *still* wanted to pursue her. Intimacy with Finn had also felt right, in its own way. But he wasn't a safe bet. Not yet. She just didn't know him well enough. Internet sleuthing listed him as a playboy, but most of those articles were at least a few years old. Could she take a chance on puppy love with a guy as smooth as Finn?

She zoned out, staring at the TV screen, absently gnawing her lower lip—feeling like the worst person *ever.* How could she even entertain the idea of Finn, the magnificent creature that he was, when she felt such strong, deep-seated feelings for Cole?

Were those feelings even real if she was so easily taken with Finn?

Groaning, Skye snatched her remote and switched to a reality show, hoping it might cheer her up. It was always nice to see that there were bigger screw-ups out there in the romance department than Skye Eloise Summers.

Mercifully, reality TV proved to be just what she needed. A half hour blitzed by with only a few panicky thoughts, and when she finally grabbed her phone, ready to check the voicemail she knew Cole had left, she found a text from Brynn instead.

Work was dead so I got sent home early. Drinks tonight? Karen and Jazz are in town.

Skye brightened at the thought. Karen and Jazz were two college pals who had fled the Coral Bay coop after graduation. It'd be nice to see them—but it would be even nicer to have a distraction from all her boy drama, which had totally eclipsed her job-offer-high. So, she fired a quick message back, thumbs flying over her screen.

Was just offered gainful employment. Count me in!

Finn Rai needed to find more entertaining dinner companions in Coral Bay. Three hours and a five-course meal at a brilliant penthouse restaurant downtown had resulted in him wanting to either fall asleep or blow his brains out at least twice, respectively. It was the usual Coral Bay crowd, which made matters worse; he should enjoy his usual crowd if he kept hanging around them. However, sometimes it felt like they only did all this—dinners, drinks, dancing, galas, gallery openings, fashion shows, charity auctions—because they were the local elite. Like they *had* to see each other once a week because their tax bracket demanded it.

Maybe he needed to host another sex party. Finn frowned. No. Even those had grown dull with this crowd, and there was only one woman these days he was interested in stripping down and worshipping—and she didn't technically run with the local elite. Not in any official capacity, anyway.

He should have forced Cole to come tonight. At least he could have endured the torture of dry conversation and predictable drunken antics with a friend, a friend who was so seldom on the same continent as Finn that it was a fucking crime. Alas, the bastard had to work. As usual. It was his standard excuse, the one that got him out of everything scot-free. He buried himself in it, his excuse. On purpose, too, though Finn could never understand for the life of him *why*. Cole had never been in it for the money, not really.

Whatever the reason, Cole had backed out at the last minute. Finn had sat through veritable hell all by his lonesome—*again*—and barely managed to escape with his patience intact. But that was behind him. The night ahead. He shifted gears and his sleek little grey corvette whizzed around the taxi slowing in front of a nightclub, mindful to keep an eye out for inebriated tourists.

His eyes widened at a familiar figure.

Apparently, he needed to keep an eye out for redheaded minxes too.

Finn did a double take when he swore he spotted a Miss Skye Summers strolling away from the club all by her lonesome. Shoes in hand, she wore a short green dress so sinfully tight it was probably a hazard for him to keep driving. He slowed instantly, pissing off the driver behind him—who then raced around, flipping Finn off as he went. The chocolate prince paid him no mind, waving absently as he stared down the gorgeous, teetering sidewalk creature, trying to determine if she was, in fact, the very woman who had captured and held his interest longer than any woman had.

He'd spent much of his adult years philandering around, never staying in one bed long enough for it to get cold. But there was something about her. A flicker of light. A spark that ignited something inside him, the fire spreading, swallowing him whole for the first time in, well, ever.

Of course, it was too soon for him to croon love songs and hold a boom box up outside her window, but he was damn interested. And it wasn't because she kept fending off his advances, either. He wasn't a man who desired something *more* when it was denied to him, although that had been part of the fun these last few weeks.

Finn couldn't put his finger on it. He grappled with it daily, his curious infatuation with Skye, but at this point he had just decided to *go* with it and see where the interest would take him. Something in the way she made his heart happy told him the chase would be worth it in the end.

And, for once, that didn't scare him.

Another careful study of that lithe body, firm and toned,

thighs exposed where her dress cut off just under her perfect backside, confirmed his suspicions. This was, in fact, Miss Summers, and she appeared to be a little drunk. What kind of man would he be if he let her walk *anywhere* by herself?

A fool. That's what he'd be.

Grinning, Finn zipped into the opening between two parked cars a few spots ahead of her, then rolled down the window, knowing she wouldn't be able to see through the dark tint.

"And what's this?" he called out when she stumbled by, jumping nearly a foot in the air at the sound of his voice. "Doth the lady require transportation?"

Skye stared at him for a moment, her eyes narrowed, then cautiously approached. Her features brightened with recognition, and Finn patted the passenger seat.

"Get in, you ridiculous creature," he ordered. "I can't stand the thought of what the sidewalk must be doing to those perfect little feet of yours."

"What, are you stalking me now?" she asked, the purr of her voice doing terribly wonderful things to his cock. Finn cleared his throat and shifted in place, only mildly annoyed that he turned into a teenager who'd never seen a pair of tits before whenever he was around her.

"Hardly. On my way home from dinner," he told her. "Thought I'd do something charitable. Get in."

She pursed her pink lips into a sumptuous pout, then clambered in with a little less grace than she perhaps intended. Her cheeks flushed as she drew the seatbelt across her body, and Finn's gaze lingered on the way it cut between her breasts. Memories of his tongue sweeping between those two perfect mounds... Oh, this wasn't helping. He sent his dark stare up to her face instead, noting the constellation of freckles over her nose and cheeks. Minimal makeup. A little sweaty, honestly. As if reading his mind, she swept her long red locks up into a messy bun on the top of her head, snagging a hair elastic off her wrist.

"Nice car," she noted as she took the two-seater in.

"It does its job."

"One of many, I'm sure." She shot him a saucy little smirk, one he wanted to kiss right off her face. However, Finn knew he had been forward enough. He didn't want to send her running by being too aggressive with his advances, even if Skye seemed to enjoy them. So, he flicked on his turning signal and checked that the way was clear.

"Where to, my lady?" he asked as he pulled out. "Mi chariot es su chariot."

"Home," she said with a long, tired sigh. In his peripheral view, he caught her rubbing her eyes, smearing what little makeup she had there.

"Did you really intend to walk the whole way?" She lived closer to the center of town. The club was in the north, and while not a terribly long way—Coral Bay's core was quite walkable—Finn couldn't imagine it'd be an enjoyable stroll with no shoes on. Although he would have liked to see her wearing those heels. Black. Deliciously high. They probably made her long legs and pert bottom look spectacular.

"I gave the last of my cash to my friends," she admitted with a shrug. "Brynn... My friend threw up in the bathroom, so the bouncers kicked her out, which meant our night was over too. My other friends are taking her home and there was no room in the cab. Weather's nice. Thought I'd walk."

Finn chuckled. "Well, aren't you a giver."

"I aim to please."

"I can attest that you succeed."

He heard the leather seat groan as she shifted onto her side, facing him. Finn, to his credit, kept his eyes on the road. While it wasn't exactly busy this time of night, summers in Coral Bay were known for tourists who thought themselves untouchable. Finn had no interest in hitting some idiot who figured nothing mattered because they were on vacation.

He would have preferred to be staring elsewhere, of course. The exposed soft skin of her thighs. The sweet neckline of her dress, barely concealing a perfect pair beneath. Her eyes... Hazel. Beautiful. The kind he could stare into all night if she let him.

"Hey," she said softly, "look, I'm sorry I haven't followed up on the lunch plans yet."

"It's fine." And it really was. Finn could be patient if it meant getting precisely what he wanted. "I'm ready when you are."

"It's not that I don't want to, but—"

"It's complicated?" he offered. Yeah, he'd heard that one before. If he were a smarter man, he would wash his hands of complicated, but here he was, riding out the storm. Skye sighed, fidgeting with the heels of her shoes. He glanced at her quickly, and the silence extended until they reached a light that had just turned red, even though there was no one else at the intersection.

"I had sex with Cole last week," she admitted quietly. Finn ceased drumming his fingers on the steering wheel, the news like a punch to the gut.

Cole had been at the back of his mind ever since he had realized, and confirmed, that Skye was the woman his friend supported. He had always spoken fondly of her, but when Finn pressed for more details, slyly hinting around to find out if it was a love connection, Cole shut down. Buried himself in work. Changed the subject. For a while, Finn had assumed that was answer enough. Maybe there were genuine feelings, or maybe his friend was just embarrassed to have a fake girlfriend on his payroll.

When he had asked Skye if she loved Cole, he'd needed to know for certain he wasn't stepping on any toes. He could *never* do that to Cole, a man who had entered his life almost a decade ago as a pet project. Finn had been in the midst of his transition away from playboy, party boy, and tabloid darling for the sake of his family's reputation. He had needed a man like Cole, so obsessively dedicated to his work, to keep him on track with his own career aspirations. In turn, Finn had seen a bit of himself in the young, up-and-coming millionaire, new to the scene and noticeably struggling. Under Finn's guidance, he had worked with Cole, an uncouth former programmer thrust into a social circle he wasn't ready for, on social etiquette and style.

Beyond that, Finn had wanted to keep Cole from making the same mistakes he had when he was a twenty-year-old blessed with an ungodly amount of money to his name.

And here they were, years later, closer than ever despite the physical distance these last few years—and now, apparently, sharing a woman. It wasn't the first time, though before, the women had always been one-night stands. Something to do on the rare occasion they were both feeling adventurous in a new city. Just a bit of fun, really. With Skye, things were different. She was fun, but she wasn't *for* fun.

The light changed to green, but the conversation didn't

resume. Skye repositioned herself to face forward again, her head bowed and her hands still. The silence carried on until they reached her apartment, and Finn parked at the end of the street. Even with the tinted windows, he thought she might want some privacy from the doorman.

"When I asked if there was anything going on between you, I really meant what I said," he told her, cutting the engine and unfastening his seatbelt. "I'm not a man who fucks my friend's girl. I'm just not, Skye."

"I know," she said, her voice quivering in the sort of way one does before they start crying. Finn closed his eyes for a moment. It hadn't been his intention to make her cry, but he needed to be clear on this.

"Skye—"

"And I wasn't trying to lead you on or trick you," she insisted with a sniffle. When her gaze met his, it watered. "Really, I just liked talking to you. I kind of... I'm feeling things I know I shouldn't, because I really do care for Cole, and I..." She opened and closed her mouth a few times, then stared down at her hands. "I don't know what I'm doing."

Fuck.

"What does Cole have to say about all this?" was the best Finn could do on the spot. There were a thousand other things he would have rather said instead. That he had enjoyed speaking with her too. That she was the first thing he thought of when he woke up in the mornings, and that she was quickly becoming the last to cross his mind before he fell asleep. But that wouldn't help the situation. Not now, anyway.

"I don't know," she muttered miserably. "I tried to give him a chance to say something, but he didn't. It's like he wants things to stay the same. Maybe... Maybe pretend it hadn't happened at all."

"Rather typical of him, I'm afraid." Finn smoothed a hand over his hair, sighing. "He's never been very adept at expressing himself."

"Yeah, that isn't news to me." She gave what sounded like a forced laugh, one that didn't reach her eyes, and then set a hand on his arm. A pulse of energy, of gravity, raced through him, and Finn found himself leaning toward her.

"I don't know what's happening with him, and honestly, I hate feeling like this," Skye told him, gripping his arm gently before pulling away. Finn yearned to follow, but he held firm as she carried on. "But I don't want to call it quits on us either. I... I can't imagine not waking up to a message from you, and I'm so sorry for that. Really. I'm sorry for all of this. It's all my fault."

Tears rolled down her cheeks. With a hand half covering her face, she tried to excuse herself, but Finn reached out for her, the brush of his fingers along her back stopping her.

"Hey, hey, it's all right," he murmured. "Shit happens, Skye. That's life. I'm not...angry with you, if that helps."

He always felt so helpless when women cried, because all it took was one wrong word, a slip of the tongue, for everything to go from bad to worse. If they weren't in the car, he would have wrapped her in a hug and not let go until the tears stopped. Given their current situation, however, that didn't seem possible, so he made do with what he could. Finn rubbed a hand up and down Skye's back, stopping it at the nape of her neck.

"Hey," he whispered, catching her chin and steering her back to him. "It's not the end of the world."

"Sometimes it feels that way," she told him, tears flecked with mascara streaking down her face. Finn smiled and brushed the damp trails away with his thumb.

"I know. Love has a habit of doing that to you, the merciless bitch."

Skye laughed, a real one this time, and set her hand on his knee. "Thank you."

"Anytime." He caught the way her eyelashes fluttered, wet and sticking together, when she looked from his eyes to his lips, lingering there. Finn knew he ought to dissuade her, to say something else to make her laugh, to break the tension —but he didn't. He waited. He stroked the back of her neck and leaned just a breath closer, if only to catch a hint of her natural scent again.

That was all it took. Eyes fluttering closed, Skye closed the gap between them, pressing her lips to his. There it was again—that *feeling*. He'd had it the first time he saw her, standing there covered in wine and cursing up a storm. Affection. A warming in his gut, a tightening in his chest.

Before he could deepen the kiss as he wanted, eager to explore every inch of her, she pulled back.

"I'm sorry," she whispered, her eyes wide. "I shouldn't have done that. I..."

"Yes," he cupped her face and dragged it back to his, "you should have."

Finn cherished the little gasp that escaped her before he reclaimed her mouth. Her hands wandered along the length of his forearms, the tender caress of her fingertips igniting a fire within that he knew would be damn near impossible to extinguish. So, Finn savored her while he had the chance. The taste of her tongue—she'd recently enjoyed a mojito— as he stroked it with his own, the kiss deep and desperate and verging on unhinged. The feel of her in his arms again, her body quivering at the touch of his hands, exploring at will, determined to commit every dip and curve to memory —until she started to pull away, a groan caught in her throat.

Finn knew he could have held her tighter, dragged her across the seats, albeit a bit awkwardly, and planted her squarely in his lap. She'd feel his hardness against her, and perhaps it would encourage her...

He sighed softly and opted for restraint instead. Tonight wasn't the night for that. Not when she was drunk. And had been crying about all this. He couldn't do that to her in good conscience. Besides, Finn wanted *her* to remember and savor every perfect moment of it too. If their previous fucking suggested anything, it was that Skye Summers was just as eager as him to indulge her sexual appetite.

She withdrew gasping, as though breaching the water's surface after the tsunami struck, cheeks flushed, her eyes wild with desire. Finn recognized that look. He'd seen it before, staring back at him in the mirror when he'd worshipped her lovely body for the first time. Only tonight, he knew the look wouldn't last.

"I should..." Skye tucked loose red strays behind her ear. "I should go."

"I know."

"I'm sorry."

"Stop saying that." He stole one last nibble of her supple lips before easing back in his seat. "I mean it."

With a nod and a little half smile, she climbed out of the car and scurried back to her building. He watched her go in the mirror, and once she was inside, Finn slumped forward and sighed.

It was time to get this sorted, and he knew precisely where to start. Unlike a certain someone, Finn had no problems putting his feelings on the table. Taking his phone out of his jacket pocket, he tapped around until he reached Cole's profile, then pressed the call button.

Cole answered on the second ring.

"Lunch," Finn ordered before his friend could get a word in beyond hello, "tomorrow. Put your work aside for a half hour, you tit. There's something we need to talk about...urgently."

12

A GENTLEMEN'S AGREEMENT

Finn tapped a finger twice on the brim of his glass, eyes narrowed at Cole as he wove through the patio seating, a hostess at his heels. When his friend was finally within hearing distance, Finn nodded to the seat across from him.

"Sorry I'm late—"

"Sit," Finn ordered. "Now. And turn your phones off, for goodness sake."

The hostess batted her fake lashes as she looked between them, then set a menu down in front of Cole and scuttled off. Pleased that his friend was merely fifteen minutes late rather than the standard half hour, Finn took a quick sip of his rum and coke, ice rattling against the glass, and then uncrossed his long legs and straightened. He had specified *this* particular table to his assistant when she made the reservation, knowing it was the farthest from the kitchen and closest to the water. A white wood fence enclosed the outdoor dining area, and, given the time of day, post-lunch-rush, it was about half full of quietly chatting patrons. The Pacific crashed against the shore some ten feet away, a soothing accompaniment to what was bound to be an awkward conversation.

"I feel like I'm being scolded," Cole remarked, grinning ever so slightly as he shut off both of his phones and set each on the table between them as proof. When Finn didn't reply, his eyebrows shot up. "*Am* I being scolded?"

"Possibly." Finn shook his head when Cole started to open the menu booklet. "I've already ordered for us."

"Typical." Cole let the weighted cover drop shut. "So, what have I done now? I haven't had one of these little talks in years."

"Perhaps I let it go on for too long, then."

"Finn." Cole cocked his head to the side. "Fuck off."

They smirked at each other when the waitress arrived, setting a water down in front of each and rattling off the specials for Cole's benefit on the off chance that he would change his mind. But Finn knew him better than that. Cole had fish and chips every time they dined at The Crest, Coral Bay's exclusive harborside yacht club. Every bloody time. Fish and chips, like he was a caricature of English stereotypes. Finn had opted for an eel roll and a seaweed salad positively laden with sashimi.

The white linens strewn over the table fluttered in the seaside breeze, and Finn watched his friend take a quick sip of water after the waitress disappeared. No alcohol. Never. Caffeine? Always. Perhaps Finn should have ordered him a coffee too, judging by the bags under his eyes.

"We need to talk about Skye Summers," Finn stated, noting the way Cole instantly stiffened, his grip tightening around the bulbous water glass in hand. "Is she the woman you've been..." Lips pursed, Finn refused to use the appropriate terminology—because it made him nauseous to even think it. "...financially supporting for the last few years?"

Cole swallowed hard before setting the glass back on the table. Carefully. Precisely. Cautiously. Three adjectives that had always suited him best.

"Did she tell you?"

Finn fiddled with the silverware, knowing someone would be around shortly to replace his fork with chopsticks. "In a way. I guessed the moment I saw you two together at my soiree the other night."

Cole's expression turned incredulous. "Soiree? Really?"

"Orgy," Finn clarified, grinning at the plum-colored blush blossoming across his friend's face, "is that better?"

Jaw clenched, Cole turned his attention outward, his gaze on the ocean. "Sure."

"She's rather smitten with you," Finn told him, as if he didn't already know. How could he not? "However, I think, recently, she's become just a little smitten with me."

"Is that why you called me here? To stake your claim?"

"Hardly. I appreciate that you think so little of me."

Their eyes met and held for a moment before Cole let out a long, tired sigh, his shoulders slumping. "Sorry. I know you wouldn't...but..."

"*But*," Finn chose his words carefully, "we appear to have found ourselves in a *situation*, one that seems to have left Miss Summers a bit flustered herself. I thought it best we discuss it before anything happens."

"Have you two...?"

"I think you already know the answer to that." Finn spied their waitress approaching, food in hand. "Just as I know that you two have recently...furthered your relationship."

"And here we have the fish and chips," the waitress

trilled. She set the plate down in front of Cole, who looked as though he'd just smelled something ghastly, before expertly maneuvering Finn's rather large plate into the small space before him. "Is there anything else I can get you?"

"We're fine," Finn told her with a quick smile. "Thank you."

The silence that followed was one of a handful of awkward pauses he had ever experienced with Cole. He had hoped to be frank and matter-of-fact about all this. After all, they were two logical, reasonable men. This was an issue that affected them both, and if they didn't sort it out now, their future with Skye was in jeopardy. However, Finn hadn't factored in that matters of the heart were not logical or reasonable. If he played his cards poorly, he might end up losing both Cole and Skye—which would be a devastating loss indeed.

"Do you love her?" he asked, watching Cole pick up a fry, then set it back down, then pick it up again. At no point during that little dance did the damn thing end up anywhere near his mouth.

"I don't have time to love her." Cole grabbed the ketchup bottle and shook it over his plate. When nothing came out, he smacked the bottom. When that yielded no results, he set it back down on the table, slamming it harder than necessary.

"That isn't a no," Finn told him. In the following silence, he unwrapped his chopsticks and started eating. Cole had always been a man who was quick and decisive in business. Tech was his game and had been long before the rest of the industry caught up. Where he faltered, however, was just about every other category of his life. He forgot birthdays, and, on the off chance that he did remember, he always chose an inappropriate gift. He was infamously terrible at punctuality and struck many in their social circles as awkward. He couldn't flirt worth a damn—and Finn had *tried* to teach him many times over; Skye was something special if she managed to bring out the charming side of him. Other women Finn had attempted to set him up with the past hadn't been quite so fortunate.

Finn had been able to look past all of that years ago, spying a socially inept diamond that just needed a polishing. His friend had certainly changed over the last decade, all for the better, but his near-absolute dedication to his job, to his company, and to the thousands and thousands of people he employed had not.

Yet to Finn, it was clear that Cole's inability to separate, to step away from the job, hindered him. It was also obvious that when it came to Skye Summers, it pained him, too.

"You know I would never do anything to ruin our friendship," Finn said softly as Cole added a liberal amount of salt to his beer-battered cod. A head bob told him the man acknowledged, understood, and agreed. Finn knew him that well. "So, let's sort this out, then. If you could be with her, would you?"

"I don't entertain the thought because I can't," Cole said hoarsely, stabbing his fork into his lunch with thinly veiled anger. "My work is my life, and sometimes that makes it difficult, but you know I could never step back and sign everything away to a board of trustees."

"Even if you chose them yourself?"

"I want to make sure my people are taken care of," Cole muttered. "At every level, down to the person sweeping the floors at our factories. How can I promise them they'll be looked after if I'm not steering the ship?" He dunked his fish in tartar sauce. "Skye... Sometimes I wish I didn't care."

"About her?"

"About the job," he stated, frowning. "I wish I could just walk away. I wish I could pull myself out. I'm not in it for the money. I could sign on the dotted line now and never have to work a day in my life again. I wish... I'd give anything to be that man, but I'm not."

Finn wouldn't have admired, respected, or enjoyed Cole as much as he did if he were that man.

Halfway through his eel rolls already, Finn set the chopsticks down. "Cole... If you could be with her, would you?"

"Yes," Cole whispered, then cleared his throat, his voice louder—and his hand flexing in and out of a fist, signaling a spike in stress, "but I've fucked it all up. I've been a complete twat, and she's going to cut and run."

Straight to you. Cole didn't utter the sentiment aloud, but Finn could read it plain as day in his eyes. He exhaled softly and took another sip of his drink. At that point, one of the ice cubes had melted completely. Not that he minded. It was barely noon, for goodness sake. No need to delve into the hard stuff—although, thinking of where he intended to steer this conversation now that he had the facts, perhaps he could have used something stronger.

"What if we could offer her a solution that would be suitable for both of us?" he asked, snatching up a gorgeous piece of raw octopus from his salad. By the time he'd popped it in his mouth and savored it, Cole appeared to have recovered from his funk.

"Such as?"

"Polyamory."

"For *fuck's* sake, Finn."

"No, no, listen"—he held up a hand to stifle Cole's indignation—"because clearly she's upset over this. I think it has a little to do with your, well, ridiculous inability to express yourself, but also because she's realized she has feelings for both of us—"

"Because you know her so well, right?" Cole pushed some fries around, though Finn wasn't sure he had seen the man take a single bite of his meal yet.

"Who, out of the two of us, has actually spoken with her in the last twenty-four hours? Hell, the last *week*?" Finn raised his eyebrows, waiting for a response—and ignoring the fact that Skye hadn't responded to his usual good morning text message yet. "Hmm?"

Cole pursed his lips for a moment. "Fair enough."

"What if," he steeled himself, fully aware that this was a long shot, "we present her with the opportunity to date *both* of us? Exclusively." Cole's expression turned skeptical, as expected, but Finn carried on, finally releasing what he'd been mulling over since last night. "You can continue to work knowing that Skye's emotional needs are met by someone, someone who has a shared understanding of the expectations of the relationship. *She* can get over this fear that falling for two people is some sort of mortal sin."

Finn had always had an open mind to the full spectrum of sexual proclivities that the world had to offer. Sex parties. Bi-curiosity. Multiple partners. The rest of his family had been appalled when he shared his philosophy of healthy sexuality with them back in his twenties, and he hadn't broached the subject since. Besides, it wasn't that he frequently found himself in open relationships where he or his partner dated other people. In fact, all of his past relationships had been unfulfilling and painfully ordinary. He was just *open* to the possibility of *more* than what society dictated. He'd never wanted to attempt such a complex affair with anyone either—until Skye and Cole.

Finn wanted to be with Skye. Cole was one of his best friends. Finn was seldom the jealous type, and Cole had never struck him as such either. The likelihood for success here was high if everyone gave it a fighting chance.

"This way, I don't have to sever ties with either of you. For Christ's sake, Cole, I can fly her out to wherever you are in the world when you're missing each other." He paused to catch his breath, then offered what he suspected Cole truly desired out of all this. "And you two can finally eliminate this ridiculous contract and just *be* with each other without you worrying you're going to lose your business... or her."

"That..." Cole licked his lips, and Finn stilled, noting that he looked like he was considering it. However, a quick headshake and scoff dashed all his hopes in an instant. "That sounds positively mad. Absolutely insane."

"Does it? We've shared before."

"Skye isn't a one-night fuckfest in Istanbul, Finn," Cole said pointedly. "Sharing a girl for a night is, is... *easy*. What you're talking about is sharing an entire relationship."

"Obviously we'll need to figure a few things out," Finn argued, "with Skye's input, of course."

"Why would you even want this?" Cole sat back in his chair, appraising Finn with the same calculating gleam in his eye that he used on rivals in the boardroom. "Why not just let her and me crash and burn, then swoop in and get the girl all to yourself?"

Finn frowned. "What in the history of our friendship suggests that I would want that for either of us?"

"Perhaps I'm just failing to see what you get out of this proposed ménage à trois. I know you've slept with her, but what other interactions have you had? Why the sudden interest?"

Finn shook his head, smiling. "You wouldn't believe me if I told you."

He had asked Skye if she believed in love at first sight the first time he showed up at her apartment with edible roses. Naturally, both had laughed the absurd notion off—but, when Finn had thought about it after seeing her last night, love at first sight was the only thing that made sense.

"Just know that my offer is genuine," he told a somewhat skeptical looking Cole, hoping that years of trust and friendship would validate him, "as is my affection for her. I mean, she's not just a beautiful face with a body designed to be made into marble statues. She's... *challenging*. Witty. Bright. Engaging. When you talk to her, she seems to listen and process and respond with thought and care I've never experienced before. Most of all, she seems to have no interest in changing me or reining me in. She doesn't *want* anything. She makes me work, but not in some childish game for her attention. You know my past relationships. You know they wanted my money, or my family name, or a chance to further their careers. Skye hasn't asked for anything. In fact, she seems rather taken with me just as I am. I... I..."

Holy fucking Christ. Finn swallowed hard, then grabbed his drink and downed the rest of it in a single gulp. He had been trying to figure out what it was about Skye that he was so infatuated with. Love at first sight had seemed like an easy theory. One needed no rhyme or reason there. It just *happened*. But in trying to convince Cole that he was serious about this, about *her*, Finn had spelled it all out for himself. Plain as anything. Skye didn't want to change him. She put up with his oddities and quirks with a smile and a laugh, genuine and open in her interest of *him*—Finn, not Finn Rai, inheritor of the Rai's Sweets empire.

Finn had never experienced that sort of affection from a woman before. It had always been models and actresses and party girls interested in squandering his money on alcohol and private booths at exclusive clubs. Skye just wanted to talk. She asked questions. She confided in him about her day, her fears, her career aspirations, everything. They watched TV together, in separate homes, just to have a laugh over the phone. *Of course* Finn was falling in love with her a few weeks after meeting her. How could he have been so thick as to not piece it together before?

He set his glass down and realized his mouth was hanging open slightly. When he looked up, he knew he wore the expression of a bewildered, love-struck man, and to his surprise, Cole's mouth twitched into a little smile. They stared at one another for a few moments, then Cole's whole being seemed to relax as he finally dug into his meal. Knowing the conversation was nowhere near complete, Finn returned to his own meal, deep in thought, and polished off his rolls before slowly working through his salad. He watched the waves roll in, a few birds divebombing the water, and studied the other diners around him. By the time Cole next spoke, Finn had nearly finished eating, yet Cole was perhaps a tenth of the way through his basket of deep-fried fish.

"If we take her aside and propose this, we'll scare her off," he stated. "I can't risk that."

"We could let her choose," Finn offered, the idea distasteful. "Tell her we'll honor and respect whatever decision she makes."

"I won't risk that either—"

"Well, you have to make a decision, Cole." Finn had been trying not to veer into the lecturing tone he had once used, eons ago. Unfortunately, he couldn't help himself—

and from the look on his friend's face, perhaps that was the tone needed here. If it woke Cole up to the dangerous realities of their situation, so be it. Skye's heart was worth a bit of lecturing. "You have to fight for her at some point. You can't keep paying her rent and buying her clothes and believing that amounts to what either of you really want... or need."

Cole's lips parted. Finn tensed. A lesser man might have blown a fuse, stormed off, given up. Instead, Cole straightened in his seat, cracked his neck from side to side, and nodded.

"I choose option number one," he said carefully, and Finn detected a slight tremor in his hands as he spoke. "I think it has merit. It will need to be discussed more thoroughly, of course"—he eyed Finn, whose head bobbed quickly in agreement—"but it's the best chance I have to... to... *love* her as I can right now." His breath hitched in his throat, but he shook it off. "We'll propose it to her together."

Grinning, Finn offered his outstretched hand halfway across the table. "Agreed."

They shook on it as gentlemen, and finished the remainder of their meal as friends.

13

DONE DEAL

"Oh... shit." Skye's eyes widened as her teller computer screen jumped suddenly to a page she hadn't visited yet, leaving her scrambling to correct it before this ridiculous system did something that would make her seem like a complete moron. New job. Day one. It was hard *not* to feel like a moron, especially since she hadn't technically worked anywhere in four years. Still, it was Wednesday at noon. Skye worked at a sex museum. Thus far her day hadn't exactly been jam-packed with eager patrons of the arts desperate for a peek inside Gallery Sens.

There had been the little old couple who showed up shortly after opening. Back then, Hans had walked her through the step-by-step process of museum admissions. The pair of them were regulars and came to see the new weekly instalment religiously. They had more know-how about the front desk computer system than Skye did, and she spent much of the transaction beet-red and fumbling.

After that, it was radio silence—excluding the family of German tourists who had ripped her a new one for not allowing them in. Skye didn't make the rules: no one under eighteen permitted, parental consent or not. She had just stood there, deer-in-headlights, behind the two feet of desk separating her from the general public. Nod and smile. Apologize. Explain the rules. Do it again. Smile. Apologize *again*. Customer service was still customer service, even in a museum. After they had left in a huff, she had a few traumatic memories of her fast food days flash before her eyes, where getting screamed at by a customer was a daily occurrence. While it had left her rattled, at least she was still standing—and no one had demanded to speak with a manager.

She decided she'd take that as a day one success story. Otherwise, she'd go home miserable. While issuing regular admissions was fairly straightforward, the computer system was convoluted, slow, and had ten steps to get from Point A to Point B when two would suffice. Illogical. Frustrating. Tedious. There were special days, special prices, special discounts—all of which she had to memorize as soon as possible. Skye was the first point of contact. She had to sell the museum confidently and speak knowledgeably.

Now, four hours into her first shift, she wanted to rip her hair out, cry in frustration, *and* celebrate the fact that she had a real grown-up job at last, with real grown-up possibilities in her future. It was a veritable clusterfuck of feelings, and she couldn't wait to curl up on the couch with Oz and distract herself from her first day fumbles with a bottle of wine. Brynn had already asked if she wanted to hit up a bar after her shift, but Skye needed the solo time to decompress. Getting shit-faced surrounded by strangers just wouldn't cut it today.

"Just play around," her new boss had told her before he'd left her to her own devices. "No one expects you to know everything by the end of the day. Take your time. My extension number is written on the phone if you have questions."

With the number literally taped to the top of the multi-line front desk phone, Skye could, in theory, ring up old Hans Timmons if she found herself struggling. But she hadn't. Skye wanted to prove that she was better than that. She had spent so many years getting her degree. She was probably older than all the other applicants who had applied for this position. She could do this, damn it. First day jitters would *not* get her down.

Now, if only this stupid, terrible, time-consuming system would go back to the inventory page like she wanted... Why have a touchscreen system if you could only use it when ringing up an order?

Suddenly, the GUESTS ARRIVING box at the top of the screen flashed. Hooked up to the main doors, its purpose was to alert her, discreetly, that she had someone to pander to. Squaring her shoulders, she ran through a mental checklist of everything she should say, do, and prompt, then looked up with a bright smile.

One that vanished instantly when she realized who had just waltzed in like they owned the place.

Cole and Finn.

Together.

At her new job. On her first day.

Heat flooded her cheeks, and Skye could feel herself wilting as they approached. It had been about a week and a half since Finn had driven her home from her night of drinking, dancing, and belligerently gossiping with college friends. A week and a half since she'd kissed him and admitted to herself that she was in love with Cole—while also falling for Finn. A week and a half to realize that this wouldn't work, for any of them, and it was time to be an adult and end this charade.

Only Skye was a coward. She'd simply stopped responding to messages from both men and buried herself in job prep, apartment hunting, and reconnecting with visiting friends. After all, if she was going to end this for the good of everyone's heart involved, she needed to cut ties with her sugar daddy. Which meant no more gorgeous, expensive apartment. No more spending without thinking of her bank account. No more financial security.

And no more Cole *and* Finn. When she wasn't staring blankly at apartment ads, halfheartedly reading her job contracts, and forcing a smile with her friends, she was mourning the loss to come. A brave person would have severed ties already. A brave person didn't need *days* to build up the courage to do it. A brave person wouldn't have forced these two men, these friends, to seek her out at work. Whatever was headed her way in the form of two perfect specimens in fitted suits, Skye only had herself to blame.

The thought of ending it...

Well, it broke her.

But that didn't matter. In the long run, it made sense. Right now, it was devastating, and she could barely look at them as they sauntered up to her new front desk kingdom. A huge square with the middle cut out, Skye's station was the only thing in the main entryway. A few tasteful nude portraits, steeped in shadow and intrigue, hung on the walls, but otherwise it was just her, the front desk cube, the tile, and the walls. Behind her, there was an entrance and an exit door, where patrons would start and finish their tour of the displays inside.

"Skye." Finn tipped his head, sidling right up to her

station and leaning against it. "Look at you. All delicious in your little outfit—"

"What are you guys doing here?" she demanded, smoothing a hand down the black collared shirt Hans had given her that morning. This wasn't the time or the place for *any* of what she had in mind to go down. Her gaze flitted nervously to Cole, who wore an annoyingly unreadable expression. To his credit, his phone was nowhere to be seen.

"We've been discussing our situation," Finn told her, "and, since you've been rather pointedly avoiding us, we figured it was time to come to you."

"Congratulations," Cole offered as he scanned the room, his voice soft and familiar, "on the job. I... I should have said something sooner."

Skye exhaled sharply, eyes darting between the two men before her. One whom she had been falling hopelessly in love with and *pining* after for years. The other who had reignited her spirit, who challenged her—who was both shamelessly uncomplicated and drenched in potential heartache.

"Today really isn't a good day to do this," she protested, crossing her arms when Finn stared pointedly around the empty room.

"We can wait until the crowd dies down."

Cole shot his friend a narrowed look, and Skye braced herself when his lips parted, but, as usual, he had nothing to say. Fine. If they were determined to do this right this second, Skye could get onboard. Never mind that this was her first day. Never mind that her nerves were frayed and her head was full of fog. If they wanted to show up and demand to talk, then she would let them have it.

"Fine." On wobbly legs, she stalked to the back of her little cube, struggled with the tricky door latch, and then motioned for them to follow her outside. No way was she recording the shattering of her heart on the security camera.

She stopped at the curb just outside the main doors, her arms crossed, if only to hide the way her hands shook. All Skye really wanted to do in that moment was hug Cole and kiss Finn—but that was part of the problem. She couldn't have her cake and eat it too. That wasn't the way the world worked. As desperate as she was to lose herself in Cole's arms, to forget the spat they'd had and sweep it under the rug like always, she couldn't. And as much as she wanted to kiss Finn's smirking mouth, run her hand over his rock-hard body and feel *alive* again, she definitely couldn't.

"Cole and I have been talking," Finn started with a quick glance to Cole, who nodded, "and we're all on the same page here about what's been happening since my soiree last month."

"Okay." Skye could already hear what they were going to say. If they were angry that she had slept with both of them, they had every right to be. If they were hurt that she loved one while still managing to save a piece of her heart for the other, she couldn't blame them. So, she figured she might as well save them some time. "But let me go first."

"Skye—"

"No," she said firmly, holding up a hand to stop Cole, "I need to say this."

The pair exchanged looks, Cole seeming more hesitant than Finn, but he eventually gestured for her to proceed. Skye sucked in a soft breath, briefly entertaining the idea of zipping across the street to the loitering cab in front of the hotel. No. She had been running and hiding from this for long enough.

"First of all, I never wanted to come between two friends," she told them, the rehearsed words flying out with more speed than intended. "I'd never want to ruin something, or put pressure or tension between you guys, and I'm really sorry if I did. It wasn't my intention."

Cole shook his head and stepped toward her. "No, you didn't... Skye—"

"But," she said firmly, "it's helped me realize what I need to do. We need to end things. We have to cut ties, because I c-can't keep doing this." Difficult as it was, Skye ignored the panicked expression on Cole's face, followed by the swift frown on Finn's. "Now that I'm working and done with school, I think it'll be best that we end our, uhm, contract as well. It's too hard for me to keep on doing what we've been doing." Her eyes darted to Finn. "Every time we talk, it's just a reminder that I'm putting a wedge between two people I care a lot about. And... I... Both of you..."

Damn it. She blinked back her tears. She had *practiced* this, although she had never intended to say it in front of both of them—but maybe that was for the best. Just rip the band-aid off. Get it over with.

"Skye, you don't have to do this," Cole insisted, his tone gentle as he moved in, perhaps to take her hand, but she stepped back and shook her head.

"I do. I do have to do this. I refuse to put you two in a situation where you or I have to choose."

Finn cleared his throat. "That's not what we're—"

"This hurts me too much," she blurted, her eyes watery and her words tight. She swallowed hard and looked away. "I'm sorry. I made a mistake, and I... I should pay the price for it."

"No, Skye—"

"You don't have to—"

"But that's the decision I've made," she told them. "It's what I deserve."

"Oh Skye, don't be so dramatic," Finn said with a slight eye roll. "We can talk about this."

Mercifully, Hans took that moment to poke his head out the main doors, eyebrows up.

"Is everything okay out here?" he asked, ignoring Finn and Cole, his gaze fixed on Skye. She offered a frantic nod, mortified that all this had played out at her new job, potentially in front of the man who could make or break her fledging museum career.

"Fine," she told him, clearing her throat as she beelined for the door. "I'm so sorry. I'll be right back inside. This... This can count as my break."

"Hardly," her new boss remarked, finally looking Finn and Cole over. "This doesn't seem all that relaxing. Gentlemen, are you here for a tour?"

"No, they were just leaving," Skye insisted, her hand on the door. "Again, I'm so sorry. For everything."

Hans shot her one of those looks that said they'd discuss this later, but it didn't contain the same kind of malice she'd seen with former employers. More like mild curiosity. When he disappeared inside, she lingered in the doorway for a moment.

"That's my solution to our problem," she muttered, unable to look at them—the ultimate coward. "If you want to talk more, we can, but I'm not going to change my mind."

Knowing her resolve would shatter if either one of them tried to stop her, she forced herself back into the lobby, legs like stilts as she shuffled over to her new kingdom. After assuring Hans that everything was fine and apologizing a few more times, she plopped herself down in front of that troublesome computer system, determined to figure it out before the end of the day.

Briefly, her eyes darted up to the main doors. Through

the tinted glass, she thought she would see Finn and Cole standing there—but they were gone.

And rightly so.

Skye wouldn't have stuck around either after that disaster.

Her lips quivered and the screen blurred, and there, alone in the lobby, Skye Summers finally let her tears fall.

"Well, that was an absolute trainwreck."

Finn ordered two coffees before the waitress could even reach their table, knowing full well that no one deserved the dejected wrath of Cole so shortly after, well, what had happened. She nodded and skirted back to the hotel bar. Sighing, Finn unbuttoned his suit jacket, then settled on the rather hard wooden bench on the opposite side of their booth. Through the window beside them, they had a perfect view of Gallery Sens, and in it, the woman they had made cry.

"It did not go according to plan, no," Finn agreed stiffly, grabbing a packet of sugar and fiddling with it as Cole scowled down at the table, seeming to be forcing himself to take deep, even breaths. "I didn't want to appear presumptuous and, well, *pushy* by speaking over her, but perhaps I could have done something to steer the conversation."

"She'd already made up her mind before we got there," his friend noted. "I don't think anything we said today could have changed that, and I seriously doubt our proposal would have gone over well."

"Perhaps ambushing her on her first day at a new job wasn't ideal either."

Cole's jaw clenched briefly before he glanced out the window. "Well. No. I suppose we could have used more tact." He huffed. "I need a cigarette."

"Like I'd let you spiral into that filthy habit." Finn smiled at the waitress as she dropped off two mugs and a bowl of creamers. Seconds later, she set a pot of cold milk down, but was then out of their hair. All around them, the Seashell View Hotel and Suites buzzed with activity, as it was around the standard check-in time and tourists flocked to Coral Bay's charming downtown and relatively open, uncluttered public beaches. Finn and Cole, meanwhile, sat in that damn booth with a veritable storm cloud hanging overhead, one that threatened to burst at any moment.

"Well," Finn muttered as he layered up his coffee with cream and sugar, "we'll just have to get her back."

"How?" Cole shook his head. "Skye can be very stubborn when she wants to, and I have no interest in steamrolling over her like her voice doesn't matter."

"So, you're done? You're giving up on her?" He couldn't keep the bite out of his voice. While Cole had more to lose with Skye's decision, Finn, too, wanted to pout and sulk and throw a tantrum. This wasn't what he wanted. He and Cole had spent time devising the perfect strategy to make *everyone* happy. Their relationships with Skye would be separate entities, yet one wouldn't stand above the other. Equal. A partnership in love. They had agreed not to let their friendship suffer. Logistics had been discussed at length. The only thing they hadn't accounted for was Skye bolting before they could even put the offer on the table.

He should have realized she was so distraught over all this. He should have pushed harder when she stopped answering his calls and texts. He shouldn't have been so damn cocky in his belief that by the end of the day, it would be all sunshine and roses and naked Skye as far as the eye could see.

"Of course I'm not giving up on her," Cole snapped. "She's... I can't imagine my life without her. But what can we do?"

"We'll show her that this can *work*," Finn said, more determined than ever. "We'll show her that she doesn't need to choose, that we can all be happy together. We'll give her time to collect herself after today, and then..."

Cole's eyebrows shot up. "And then?"

"And then..." He cleared his throat, mind blank. Finn had no idea. He had been so certain before, with all his ideas and plans, and then, just like that, he had lost her. "I don't know."

Slowly, Cole's expression softened, as though just realizing that he wasn't the only one hurting here. "We'll figure it out," he said. "I'm not done fighting for her. I feel like I haven't even started, honestly."

Finn cocked his head to the side, pleased that his friend had finally seen the light. "What an astute assessment."

"Fuck off, Finn."

They grinned at one another, then shifted gears into work mode, armed with an unlimited supply of caffeine and an unfettered view of the woman they both adored.

Operation Win Back Skye was officially a go.

SKYE

Skye Summers: A sugar baby no more.

14

REGRETS ABOUND

"Is that the last of them?" Skye Summers watched the herd of former high schoolers—according to their IDs—push through the main doors of Gallery Sens, chatting just as animatedly as they had when they first arrived. However, when they had strolled into the sex museum two hours earlier, full of giggles and whispers, they'd been *much* more intolerable. Now that they'd had a chance to see what was inside, their tune had changed for the better.

In her first month as the front desk and museum admissions attendant, Skye had realized that was the case with most. Sex was still such a taboo topic, even in the age of free porn and celebrity sex tapes. Most visitors under the age of forty arrived all aquiver, like they were doing something naughty by visiting Coral Bay's infamous sex show.

However, once they went through the exhibits and realized this was a place to learn and appreciate the history of human sexuality, they usually left with the same energy as those high schoolers: subdued but interested.

Hans Timmons, museum/gallery owner and boss extraordinaire, nodded at her question without looking up. He was rather particular about how the brochures were arranged at the back of the front desk cube, and even though Skye had a month of experience under her belt, apparently she still couldn't get them right.

"They were quite loud, weren't they?" he muttered as he shuffled a few stacks of brochures around, then straightened up with a smile. "But we're done for the day. Why don't you count down? I'm sure you have somewhere more exciting to be."

"One can dare to dream," she said with a chuckle. Skye had nothing waiting for her after her eight-hour shift but a certain fluffy white cat and leftovers from yesterday's dinner. Oh, and *Fear Factor*. The TV gods had revived the program, which she had watched religiously as a kid, and lately Skye had a thing for reality shows featuring people who were more of a mess than she was.

After balancing her cash till, chatting amicably with Hans as she worked, Skye stepped aside and let him confirm her numbers. When he finished, the pair tidied up the front desk area, and she ended her day by sweeping the lobby. There weren't many big bosses out there who would take the time to help their lowliest employees clean their station, but Hans did. Every day, without fail, he usually hung around for the last ten minutes of her shift. At first Skye had thought he was micromanaging—until she learned he did it with every employee, and used the time to find out how their day had gone. It was why the fifteen employees who staffed the museum had staggered clock-out times—and any work problems were addressed almost immediately.

Even if selling tickets and giving information to tourists and lookie-loos wasn't what Skye had envisioned as her first postgrad job, she had never been happier at work. For the first time in her life, she didn't dread the start of each day, nor did she lay in bed fantasizing about elaborate, awesome ways to quit as her alarm shrieked unchecked on her nightstand.

And she needed that, considering every other part of her life was a fucking disaster.

Just after Skye put her cleaning supplies away in the small, nondescript storage closet near the museum exit door, a bright-eyed college-aged woman strolled into the lobby, dressed to the nines with a folder tucked under her arm. Before Skye had a chance to intercede, Hans directed her to carry on through, saying he would be there momentarily.

"I'm considering bringing on another intern," he explained when the woman disappeared through the museum entrance. Skye schooled her features as she nodded. When *she* had applied to work here, she'd been passed over because she lacked experience. That woman couldn't have been older than twenty-one.

"That'll be nice."

"One of the college programs is doing an HR internship," he clarified, as though sensing the shift in her tone. "I'll get additional funding for hiring one of their students."

"Oh." She brightened, then instantly felt ridiculous for having such a sour reaction. After all, who was she to make a face at Hans's hiring procedures? At least she had a job she liked and a boss who liked her. She still had the opportunity to join the back-of-house museum staffers in a few months, at the very least. "That's great. If you need help organizing the interviews, just let me know."

They quickly tidied up the rest of the space, and, just as

she was switching from heels to flip-flops, Hans stopped her.

"One last thing," he said. "There is a museum fair happening next weekend. All the local establishments will have a booth. There will be games, prizes, guest lectures from specialists. We even have a few larger institutions gracing us with their presence, and I was wondering if you would like to help me and Theresa man the booth?"

Skye blinked, taking a few seconds to process the wealth of information, then hastily nodded. "I would love to!"

Anything to show she was committed to being a more hands-on member of the team.

Hans told her he would give her the details tomorrow, then shooed her out, insisting her shift had ended eight minutes ago and she had the whole night ahead of her. Weekdays meant an eleven-to-seven shift, so by *whole night*, he meant dinner and a few hours of TV before crashing in bed. Still, Skye appreciated that he took an interest in their out-of-work lives and was always determined to at least *try* to get everyone out on time. Gossip through the museum circles suggested that other owners, directors, managers and the like were less inclined to believe their employees even had a life outside of work.

She hurried out the main glass doors, waving as Hans locked them behind her, and walked home with an extra bit of pep in her step. However, that pep quickly leeched out of her when she spotted her apartment building—an ever-present reminder of Cole Daniels, and, by association, Finn Rai, two men she had been trying to keep out of her mind since ending things with both them a month ago.

That was always made more difficult, however, when she returned home to find a stack of moving boxes by the front door, still flat and waiting to be put together. Since ending her sugar daddy contract with Cole and cutting ties with the company who had paired them, Skye had been determined to move out of his apartment and find a place of her own. Unfortunately, rent was sky-high in Coral Bay, and after living in an incredibly safe building for the last four years, sketchy suburbs and rundown low-rises on the city outskirts had zero appeal. Cole had insisted she stay until she found something better—but better seemed more and more unlikely with each day Skye spent scouring apartment ads.

"Love of my life," she greeted as Oz weaved his way around the boxes, purring thunderously. She swept him into her arms and snuggled him close, knowing that even if she had lost Cole and Finn, she would always have Oz to keep her warm at night.

In theory, anyway. As soon as the white floof got what he wanted—a quick snuggle and a chin rub—he squirmed out of her arms, circled her legs purr-meowing, and then stuffed his face into her work bag. Rolling her eyes, Skye stepped around the purse-diving expedition and grabbed her pad thai leftovers from the fridge, dumped them in a pot, and set them on the stove. After changing out of her work clothes, she stretched out on the couch, got the TV going, and half watched while she perused her phone's notifications.

A little part of her was always disappointed not to see anything from Finn or Cole—but that was absurd. Of course she wouldn't get anything from them. She had sent them packing firmly and abruptly when they showed up at work on her first day, insisting the jig was up. That had been a month ago, and besides the brief bit of contact she'd had to have with Cole about the apartment, both men had kept a respectable distance.

Did she regret how it all went down? Absolutely.

Was her regret strictly related to how she handled things? No.

Did she regret walking away from *them*? Definitely.

But Skye knew she couldn't change that now. As much as she missed texting all day with Finn or wiping lipstick off Cole's cheek, laughing, nothing could change what had happened. Her decision, while heart-wrenching, would be the best for everyone in the long run. All she could hope was that they were both happy. Because they deserved to be happy.

Skye, on the other hand, accepted her regret, her sadness, and her pain in stride. She had been in the wrong, even if Cole could never communicate properly and Finn probably shouldn't have pursued his friend's sugar baby. It didn't matter now. It was in the past.

So why couldn't she stop thinking about it?

Why did she hope to see their names flashing on the screen whenever her phone rang?

Why had it hit her this hard?

And why, for goodness sake, couldn't she stop thinking about them? *Both* of them. Work offered some reprieve, as she was still learning the ins and outs of the business, but as soon as those heels came off and she was out the door, Cole and Finn managed to wriggle their way to the front of her mind. It was a vicious cycle: missing them, then remembering *she* had severed the connection and this was all her fault, then scolding herself for being upset, followed by a swift game of *what if*. It wasn't healthy, but she couldn't stop it. That fucking cycle was on repeat, and now, a month after everything had happened, Skye still hadn't figured out how to break it.

At the sound of something sizzling on the stove, she tore

herself away from her phone and dashed across the sprawling living space into the kitchen, hastily turning down the burner and stirring her day-old noodles. After a few pitiful meows from Oz, she fed him his dinner a little early, then flopped back down on the couch for a little guilt-free TV time before she dove back into rental listings.

And tried, at least for a few hours, to forget about the man who actually owned her apartment—and the man who had once showed up at its door with chocolate roses.

15

CHOCOLATE KNIGHT

Skye was in a waking nightmare.

All around her, kids aged seven and under screeched at the top of their lungs, running into each other, knocking things over—and no one was coming to save her.

"Guys," she cried as she tried to gently remove gum from a sweet little blonde's very fragile hair. "Come on, let's settle down. We can't start our games if you don't... settle... down..."

Hopeless. The only relatively sane one was the delicate creature whimpering in front of her, tears spilling down her cheeks and a wad of bright pink gum in her hair. The best she'd been able to offer, when Skye asked who had done it, was *a boy*, which was promptly followed by waterworks. And not a parent in sight, of course.

"Almost out, sweetheart," Skye told her, but from the look on the girl's face, she didn't trust Skye's half-crazed smile and frantic eyes. Somewhere behind the multicolored jungle gym playset, someone screamed, the sound followed by laughter and the scattering of a bunch of little shits in superhero shirts. Skye exhaled sharply, wishing she'd had the good sense to tie her hair up before she had stepped into this madness. Sweat trickled down the back of her neck. For an indoor kiddie playroom, it certainly was sweltering as fuck.

Or maybe Skye was just melting into the floor.

She could deal with that. Just dissolve into a puddle of sweat and stress. Puddles didn't have to manage a herd of twenty monsters.

Everyone had done it, apparently. The Central California Museum Togetherness Festival at White Water Point, a midsize city about a half hour inland from Coral Bay, had a children's room inside the convention center where parents could dump their brats. It allowed them to peruse the many booths, displays, and exhibits without worrying their kid might break something, get lost, or cost them extra cash. Museums got a discount on their booth fee if they signed up for an hour of monitoring the playroom. They had all been told that an attendant who handled kids this age for a living would be present. From what Skye had heard from the other museum folk suckered into this gig, it had sounded like an hour of phone time.

When Skye arrived, Janet, the trained attendant, had zipped out immediately, citing the excuse that she hadn't had a break yet during her ten-hour day. So there was Skye. Alone. In a room that *smelled* sticky, with twenty chubby-cheeked munchkins who wouldn't. sit. still.

Had she expected Hans or Theresa to do this? No. Both had seniority over her. Both were more knowledgeable at the booth. But she would have at least preferred there to be a vote. Something. Instead, Hans had clapped a hand on her shoulder about fifteen minutes ago and smiled sadly. Skye had known right then and there that things were about to take a turn for the awful.

"There we go," she said, a victorious cackle slipping out of her mouth when she pried the gum from the little girl's hair. "Free!"

She had expected the tears to cease immediately and the gum's prisoner to rejoin the chaos. Instead, the girl dug her hand into Skye's jeans pocket—hooray for informal attire—and followed her to the garbage can.

Okay. She was going to have a shadow now. The blonde couldn't have been more than four or five, and when Skye crouched down and asked her for her name, she uttered an almost inaudible *Cassandra* before her lip started to quiver again.

"What a pretty name," Skye cooed. "Do you want to be my helper?"

Lip still wobbling, Cassandra nodded, blonde curls bouncing and cheeks a rosy pink. Skye sighed and straightened, trying to figure out the best way to keep Cassandra from bawling *and* wrangle the rest of them into something closer to organized chaos than what it was right now.

"Well, doesn't this look like a barrel of laughs..."

Skye's head snapped in the direction of the door, eyes widening at the sound of an all-too-familiar voice—one she hadn't heard for over a month, but sometimes whispered naughty things in her dreams. Finn Rai. In the flesh. Leaning on the locked swinging gate—which came up to roughly to Skye's waist and was the only thing keeping the beasts from breaking out and ruining the festival. There was an actual door located inside the storage room at the back, of course, if she needed to make an escape to the outside world. It had been singing its siren song for the last ten minutes or so. Suddenly *this* door, however, was much more appealing.

The convention center that had offered to host the museum fair had several rooms just like this. Some were used for choir practice or other musical affairs, given how wonderful the acoustics were. This one, however, sat at the far end of the building, past the bathrooms, the for-rent art studios, and even the food court. Totally round, its walls coated in animal kingdom murals, the day care took place inside during the week. Parents would check their child in at that little gate, which would swing open and lock soundly behind them, and then watch the little hellion dive into the fun from the safety of the other side.

Someone should have been manning said gate. The person who was *paid* to deal with kids should have been manning it, monitoring the sheets of parent names that coordinated with a specific child. Well, no, *Skye* should have been doing that. Fucking *Janet* should be pulling gum out of string-thin hair and wrangling the little monsters.

But she was all by her lonesome.

Cue the entrance of her white knight, just when she least expected him.

No. Her chocolate knight. Skye hadn't touched any Rai's Sweets products since that awful day, and yet there was Finn, grinning down at her before whipping out a packet of her favourites—chocolate balls stuffed with salted caramel. How did he know chocolate was *precisely* what she needed in this exact moment?

Wait—how did he even know she was here? Did he have a secret love child checked into her waking nightmare who was causing everyone a world of misery? Skye stood and swept her hair out of her face, then took a quick count of the kids. All accounted for—and none that resembled a miniature Finn.

"What are you doing here?" she asked, finally striding

toward the door, Cassandra at her heels. The little girl barely gave her an inch of space as she shuffled along after her, grabbing hold of the fold in Skye's jeans when she stopped.

Handsome as ever, Finn's dark eyes swept over her. Skye had missed the way he studied her, like she was a living, breathing work of art that he desperately needed for his private collection. He had a knack for making her feel special, like the only woman in the world, without saying a word. Her cheeks burned at the thought, and she bit them, hard, in an effort to distract herself.

Clearing his throat, he gave a slight shake of his head, as if to refocus, and then leaned over the kiddie gate.

"Well, hello," he crooned down to Cassandra, whose face went beet red as soon as their eyes met. "Who is this charming creature?"

"Finn—"

"Would she possibly be interested in a bit of chocolate?"

"*Finn.*" As soon as the pack of hyenas inside caught wind of chocolate, they'd tear Cassandra apart to get it. Like any of them needed additional sugar.

"All right, all right," he said, straightening with a chuckle. "I brought them for you, anyway, but it's always polite to share."

"And *why*," she said, forcing a smile at the feel of Cassandra's huge round eyes peering up at her, "are you *here*, bringing me chocolate?"

"Oh, get over yourself." Finn picked a nonexistent bit of lint off his navy suit jacket, a garment perfectly tailored to highlight every delicious curve of his muscular, towering frame. "I'm here for the fair. I've invested in six of the museums attending... Figured I'd check on things in a less official capacity."

"Oh. Right. Sorry." Her blush darkened. Of course he was here on business. Both he and Cole had probably slipped right back to their high-class lifestyles in a flash without her. They'd probably already found new women to fill their free time with.

Well. Not Cole. But he could certainly afford to take on a new sugar baby now that Skye had severed ties.

The very idea made her stomach twist, even though she knew it had no right to.

"But," Finn murmured, leaning in just slightly, as though whispering a wicked secret, "I thought you might be here. At the fair. So, really, the chocolates *were* intended for you. I planned ahead."

"Why?" Behind her, the shrieks and laughter had reached a crescendo. She had to get back in there. Skye winced at the sound of something crashing to the floor.

"Consider it a peace offering," Finn told her, albeit somewhat distractedly as he peered over her. "What on earth is happening in there?"

"Chaos," she huffed. "Pure, unbridled chaos. I'm not a nanny, but apparently today I..." Skye pressed her lips together, only *just* processing what he had initially said. "Finn, you don't need to give me a peace offering. I... owe you one, if anything."

"Water under the bridge, darling," he said, still distracted. "Would you like a hand?"

"What?" Skye opened and closed her mouth, but no words of protest came when he shoved the chocolates into her hand, then reached over and unlatched the door. Finn slipped into the room, body no more than a breath from hers, and she tried not to inhale too deeply at the first hint of his intoxicating cologne wafting over her.

"You look like you've lost control," he noted. "Are you all by yourself?"

"I'm just here because we volunteered to help for an hour. The girl who actually captains this sinking ship is on her break."

"Unacceptable."

"Well, it's been a long day—"

"Find a place for this where no one will touch it with what I suspect are sticky little fingers," Finn instructed, slipping off his jacket and holding it out to her. Bewildered, Skye took it and hung it over her arm, then watched as he unbuttoned the cuffs of his collared dress shirt, rolled the sleeves up to his elbows, and squared his shoulders. A steely glint appeared in his eye as he surveyed the scene. "Fortunately for you, children love me."

He shot Cassandra a quick wink and a dazzling grin, and Skye held back a smile as the little girl hid her flushed face against Skye's leg.

Don't worry. He has that effect on everyone.

"Finn, you really don't have to..."

But he was already off, marching into the eye of the storm, clapping loudly and calling for everyone to meet him by the jungle gym. Much to her surprise, the horde of tiny shits *listened.*

Mystified, Skye watched as Finn settled everyone down, made a few of them giggle, and then explained the nuanced gameplay of *Red Light, Green Light.* Within two minutes, he had all the kids heading to one side of the room, himself included, while a volunteer raced to the other and faced the wall. Her eyebrows shot up when the game went off without a hitch, leaving her biting her cheeks to keep from smiling at the sight of a grown man in notably expensive attire creeping alongside an army of elementary-aged kids, freezing in silly positions when *RED LIGHT* was shrieked from the other side of the room. Anyone who moved on a red light was out. The goal was to make it to the other side and touch the wall without the red-green announcer catching you.

Finn had been right.

Kids loved him.

Skye would kill for that kind of credibility.

He had also introduced an additional callout: *Godzilla*. As soon as the announcer on the other side of the room said it, everyone shrieked and went running back to the wall they'd started on. The kid who'd been tagged took over the announcer's duties, and the game started again.

The first round lasted about two minutes, and at the commencement of the third, a soft, feminine voice called out for Cassandra, who was still glued to Skye's hip.

"Mommy!"

Sure enough, after an ID check and a signature, Cassandra's mother checked her out. Skye recognized the woman as a museum employee from another booth, not a fair visitor, but she didn't stick around long enough to chat. With her shadow gone, Skye gently placed Finn's soft, warm, delicious-smelling jacket on an unused hook by the gate, then started to tidy up the area after the whirling tornadoes had turned it upside down.

"Come on, Skye," Finn called as he charged back to the other side of the room, jogging beside the herd of mad-dash kids. "Join the fun!"

After a chorus of encouragement from the horde who had blatantly ignored her attempt to assert her authority less than ten minutes earlier, Skye slipped off her kitten heels and entered the arena. She purposefully situated herself as far from Finn as she could, still unable to process what the hell was happening, but was soon lost in the game at hand—and found herself enjoying it.

And, as usual, enjoying Finn. Not only was he excellent at wrangling kids, encouraging them, exciting them about the other games he had in mind—he could throw down the gauntlet when challenged, too. When the ringleader of the little boy terrorists pushed a girl and laughed when she fell, Finn marched him right out of the game, sat him down on a comically tiny stool, and had him face the wall for a five-minute time-out. When he'd served his time, his minions had fled and his power was gone, and that was the last bit of trouble they got out of him.

Skye eventually withdrew from an intense game of *Blob Tag*—kids who were tagged held hands and hunted down everyone else as a blob-like unit—when Janet, the attendant who was *supposed* to be minding the madness, finally returned from her break.

"Hey," Skye said breathlessly, noting the way the woman's hawkish eyes assessed the situation over her shoulder. "How was your—"

"Who the hell is *he*?" Janet demanded, her gaze fixed on Finn—and her tone unnecessarily snippy. Skye crossed her arms, incredulous at the unsaid accusation.

"*He* is a friend of mine who stepped in to help with the mess *you* left me," she replied coolly. "I look forward to mentioning that to your supervisor... You know, that you left me alone with—"

"Yeah, whatever," the woman muttered, tossing her purse by the door and sighing. "You think I get paid enough to care? I'll take over if you can handle the check-outs. The fair's closing in a half hour and we're done in ten minutes. Parents'll be here all at once, as usual."

"Fine." Skye's curt tone earned her no response from

the attendant, and she watched the woman charge in, break up the game, and re-introduce unorganized chaos—also known as free time. Within seconds, the screaming, shrieking, and crashing resumed. Oh yeah. Skye would *definitely* be speaking with this woman's supervisor. She wasn't the type to report some poor underpaid employee if they were just trying to do their shitty job, but this was ridiculous.

"Well, she's a peach, isn't she?" Finn muttered after stalking back to Skye's side, watching the scene unfold with crossed arms and a scowl. "Is she the one who was supposed to be watching the children?"

"The very same."

"Right. I have a few choice words for whoever is actually in charge here."

They exchanged glances, Skye's lips twitching into a smile before she forced herself to look away. Now that they didn't have the kids to distract them or change the subject, she couldn't ignore the absurdity of the situation.

"Finn, why are you here?" She gestured toward the madness, trying not to roll her eyes when the attendant pulled out her phone as kids ran haywire around her. "Why did you... stay to help?"

"Because I saw a damsel in distress," he remarked with a shrug. "There were an awful lot of dragons to slay by yourself." When she opened her mouth to argue, he held up a hand. "Look, I'm not trying to be slick with you. My sister did the whole scout-troop-leader charade with both of her kids when they were younger. I've been roped into similar situations before, and I like it. I just thought you could use a hand, that's all."

Skye swallowed hard as all the time she had spent agonizing over whether she had made the right decision a month ago, if it had been right to cut Cole and Finn loose cold turkey, came flooding back to her. Right now, as Finn stood watching the madness, his body exuding its own gravitational pull that Skye was still fighting with every fiber of her being, she wasn't so sure it *had* been the right thing to do. Long-term, yes. Or maybe no. Should she have just tried her luck with Finn?

No. That would never work. She couldn't look at him without some little voice at the back of her mind bringing up Cole, and then she'd remember how much she cared about him too.

"Finn..." She touched his arm, an electrical current racing along her skin from her fingertips to her shoulder, then straight to her heart. When he looked down at her, eyebrows up, she lost her nerve. "You don't have to stay. I think we've got it under control."

The muscle in his jaw flickered slightly, but just when his lips parted, someone cleared their throat from the other side of the gate. As Janet had bemoaned moments earlier, parents were starting to line up, and Skye had no choice but to busy herself with the checkout procedures. Finn could leave. There was no reason for him to stay.

But, of course, he did. Because Finn wasn't that kind of man. Instead, he was the kind to pull kids out of the chaos and walk them back to the door, their little faces red and smiling. He did it for each and every checkout, exchanging some back-and-forth with the parents for good measure as Skye handled the paperwork.

And each time he returned to her side, charming everyone within a five-mile radius, she found herself edging closer to the realization that she had, in fact, made a mistake.

A mistake of epic proportions.

One that was probably too late to correct, whether she wanted to or not.

So, for now, she contented herself with the smell of his cologne, the sound of his voice, and the barely-there caress of his talented fingers on the small of her back whenever he stood beside her.

Knowing it was probably the best she could hope for, that she shouldn't *want* more.

But deep down... she did.

16

CLIMACTIC REUNIONS

"Absolutely ridiculous," Finn grumbled as he stacked a pile of teeny-tiny chairs on top of each other to make them easier to carry. "She ought to be getting fired, not given a *stern talking to.*"

"I think you're being a little hard on her," Skye told him. "I mean, yeah, it was shitty to leave me here by myself, but I don't think it's a fireable offense."

"That paired with her horrible attitude ought to at least be worthy of a suspension."

Honestly, that awful cow worked with *children*. If she was really so blasé about her duties, she ought to seek employment elsewhere. Finn scowled at the mere memory of his conversation with the day care's supervisor, who had seemed just as nonplussed by the incident as her employee had. Although he'd been assured the issue would be addressed, he had serious doubts anything would come of it—and he planned to check with the weekday staff to ensure this wasn't a common occurrence. Parents put their *trust* in these people. It was a good thing Skye wasn't the type to sit around on her phone and let chaos reign, or someone could have gotten hurt.

Never mind the fact that the woman's absence had all but ruined his plan to reconnect with Skye in a meaningful, perhaps more salacious way. He closed his eyes and took a deep breath, realizing that *that* was primary reason for his frustration—and now he was taking a snippy tone with Skye because of it. Exhaling, he pushed his ire to the side; it ought to be unleashed on the appropriate person, after all, and not the woman he was falling in love with.

"Regardless of all that, I hardly think it was your responsibility to offer to stay and clean while she's being reprimanded," he said, straightening up to stretch his lower back. It had been some time since he entertained children under the age of ten. He'd forgotten what a strain it put on his body—a body he considered in rather fit shape at that. Not that he minded the achy twinges: Finn had enjoyed horsing around with the little ones, even if they cut into the time reserved for winning back Skye.

"Well, she's had a long day, and I feel bad that it'll be even longer because we tattled on her," she insisted as she piled a bunch of inch-thick mats on top of each other, then hoisted them up. "*You* don't have to stay. I mean, I'm getting paid to be here."

"Like I would let you undertake this mess by yourself." Finn grabbed the two piles of stacked plastic chairs, one in each hand, and shot her a grin. "Besides, your company is payment enough."

Something in his chest tightened at the way her cheeks flushed, and he cleared his throat, trying his damnedest to play it *cool*.

No matter what he had told her earlier, Finn was here with the express purpose of talking to Skye. He and Cole had spent the last month working like madmen to allow themselves the time off to pursue her again. After all, as much as they would have liked to spend all their waking hours in Skye Mode, they both had jobs. Cole, as usual, buried himself in work; Finn had hardly seen him, though they were in virtual contact almost every day.

Finn had been in LA for much of the month, preparing for the launch of the customizable edible chocolate creations line his father had charged him with, along with opening a brick-and-mortar location in Beverly Hills. Things were on schedule and running smoothly, but mostly because Finn knew how to hire the right people for the right job. Cole, meanwhile, had every iron in every fire, and Finn could never understand *why*. Sure, the man was a workaholic, but that didn't justify the insane hours he put in on a daily, weekly, monthly basis.

All those crazy hours, however, had allowed both men to take a full two weeks off now—no shop talk, no conference calls, no factory inspections. Cole was down to a single phone. Finn had told his people not to bother him unless something was literally on fire.

They had given Skye a month to cool off after her decision to sever things, and hopefully, now that some of the more taxing emotions had settled, Finn and Cole could start to rebuild. Slowly. Neither wanted to frighten her off by being too bold, too presumptuous—Finn had had a *lot* of other ideas that fit both adjectives perfectly, but Cole had nixed them before they even got off the ground. They wanted to assure Skye that her opinion was respected, but also show her that her fears were unnecessary.

A relationship between the three of them could work.

He and Cole had hammered out the details.

Now all they needed was to bring the lovely Miss

Summers into the fold—and not scare her off in the process. She had already bolted once. Her reasons for doing so, while frustratingly inaccurate to the situation, were valid. She hadn't wanted to hurt either of them, not realizing that they had no intention of making her choose *or* allowing her to sully the friendship between them. Both he and Cole admired her for what she had done, even if it had, at the time, felt like he'd stepped on an active landmine.

Both of them had needed to find ways to *casually* run into her, the plan falling in line with their don't-make-her-run-again theme. Having learned from their mistakes, they had decided her workplace was off-limits. Cole had something rather secretive up his sleeve, and given how excited he was about it, Finn hadn't the heart to demand all the details. If Cole was throwing himself into something *other* than work, Finn wasn't about to stop him.

Unfortunately, that had meant he needed his own way to casually "happen" upon Skye out in the real world. Bars were no good; she'd be with friends and more likely to seek shelter in them. Work was out. Cole had already used the "oh, *you* take yoga classes here too?" excuse. When Finn had learned from a social peer that today's museum event was taking place, he had looked up the details immediately. Pleased to find Gallery Sens in attendance, Finn had brought Skye's favourite chocolates and wandered around aimlessly all day hoping that he might bump into her. It had been Skye's boss who eventually sent him in the direction of the children's day care.

The building around them had gone quiet now, with vendors in the midst of packing up, all the visitors gone for the day. Skye had volunteered to stay behind to tidy a little, which meant Finn was *also* tidying up. Just the two of them. Alone in this bizarre, circular room that smelled like apple juice. Just him and her—Finn and Skye, who was wearing the perfect pair of dark-wash jeans, the kind that hugged her sinfully tight little backside to the point of being a major distraction. Skye, with her thick red hair billowing around her in messy beach waves, sexier than if some stylist had tried to create it for her. Skye, whose freckles he wanted to trace with his tongue. Skye, whose hazel eyes Finn could stare into for—

"Are you even listening to me?"

"What?" Finn snapped out of his daydreaming and realized he had just been standing there, staring at Skye and her adorable little blush—holding an obscene number of stacked tiny neon chairs in each hand. "Sorry. I was just a bit distracted."

Her eyebrows furrowed slightly, a pile of squishy multicolored mats hugged tight to her delightfully toned frame. Beneath those jeans and that purple chiffon blouse was a masterpiece. Finn blinked hard, not wanting to lose himself again, and nodded toward the nearly invisible doorway at the back of the room.

"I take it all of these go in there?"

"Apparently they're worried about people stealing them," she said with a roll of her eyes. "Thank you... for staying to help. And for wrangling the kids. And for speaking to that woman's supervisor." She paused, drawing a soft breath. "Thank you for being here."

Not wanting her to notice that her thanks was like catnip to him, Finn shrugged. "It's all just a happy coincidence, I promise."

"Well, you didn't have to stay, but you did. So. Thank you."

"Anytime, Skye."

They studied one another in a weighted silence, before

she turned and marched straight for the concealed door. Finn followed at a safe distance, allowing his gaze to drop, just for a moment, to her pert arse.

It was positively sinful how fantastic those jeans made it look.

All he wanted to do was trail his hand over that generous curve, then slide it between her thighs, listening to the gasp that was sure to follow, and...

No. He shook his head and hurried after her. Carnal desires, no matter how strong, belonged on the backburner while Finn convinced Skye neither he nor Cole—collectively—were a threat to her heart.

But then again, he was only a man. A living, breathing, human man. It would take the resolve of a god not to succumb to the wiles of Skye Summers.

Apparently, all that time apart had made him even more susceptible to distraction around her than ever. Not good. Skye reduced him to nothing more than a horny teen who had never been alone with a woman before. Not good at all. *Focus, you prat. Remember the bigger picture.*

He followed her through the doorway to the storage room, but came to a sudden stop at the sight of the nightmare inside.

"Good lord."

Everything was... everywhere. The room was quite expansive, surprisingly so, but it appeared as though some giant, brightly colored beast had vomited everywhere. Toys. Chairs. Mats. Three-wheeled bicycles. Books. It was sheer, unadulterated chaos, even more so than the actual children had been. Not wanting to contribute to it, Finn merely set his load of plastic chairs to the side of the door, then slowly closed said door to give them a bit of privacy.

"Yeah, those were my thoughts exactly," Skye said as

she looked around the room. "I'm not cleaning this up. I said we'd put some stuff away... That's it."

"I wouldn't touch this mess with a ten-foot pole." Finn wrinkled his nose as he surveyed the storage room. Everyone had seemingly done the same thing: walked in, seen the mess, tossed their armful of *whatever* wherever, then closed the door behind them. To the day care's credit, at least it smelled clean. The room that housed the children was another story. It wouldn't surprise him if employees retreated in here periodically throughout their day to scream into a pillow.

"If they really wanted our help, they should have put us museum folks in *here* all day," she said, hands on her hips as she slowly turned on the spot to face him. "Can you imagine how meticulous this would be if a few archival techs got their hands on it? We were wasted on those kids." Skye laughed, her blush rising from the dead when their eyes met.

"Oh, I don't know." He risked a step toward her, then another when she didn't flee. "I think you fared rather well out there."

"Because of you."

Another step. "Possibly."

With nothing more than a foot of space between them, Finn cocked his head to the side, holding her gaze for a moment before allowing his to wander freely. Her freckles really were delightful. At the sight of her swallowing hard, her head bowed slightly, Finn threw caution to the wind—and tucked a bit of sunset-red hair behind her ear.

She looked up sharply at the contact, and Finn made no apologies for the way his fingers trailed over the shell of her ear, then ghosted down the column of her neck. If he grazed her pulse point, would he feel it racing?

She inhaled sharply, her eyes fixed on a point over his shoulder. "Finn."

"Skye."

A flicker of something passed across her face—desire, concern, interest, perhaps a combination of the three. Although his name might have been meant to come across as a warning, Finn focused on the slight tremor, the whispery quality of her voice. It emboldened him. He had always been a fearless man, facing life and all it had to offer without batting an eye.

Skye made him afraid—afraid to lose her for good, afraid to fuck it all up.

But the way she said his name, half warning, half plea...

Finn wasn't afraid anymore.

His hand curved around her neck before sliding down to the base of her throat. He felt her gulp, and tipped her head up with a thumb under her chin. Slowly, cautiously, her eyes lifted to his, hazel to ebony. He hadn't come here for this. Finn had just wanted to talk to her and eventually steer the conversation toward a reunion. But here they were. Alone. Her pulse pounding beneath his fingertips, her eyes asking a thousand questions.

Questions for which there was only one answer.

Tightening his hold on her, Finn leaned down and captured her lips in a curious, gentle kiss. Her hand shot to his elbow, clutching it lightly, and he caught the way her eyelashes fluttered—as though she fought to keep them open. Her lips, soft and pliant and deliciously kissable, trembled beneath his, before she pushed against his chest, retreating.

"I'm sorry," Finn said quickly, clearing his throat and dragging his hands away. "I didn't mean to do—"

He was so worried that he'd taken things too fast that he

missed the signs of her surrender; the way her eyes darted to his lips, the twitch in her fingers as her hand hovered between them, the barely audible breath catching in her throat. With all the speed of a cracking whip, she grabbed the untucked hem of his shirt, half yanking him back to her and half using the momentum to fling herself onto him. Their mouths met in a frenzied storm of tongue, teeth, and swollen, sensitive lips.

Even if this wasn't what Finn had intended to do when he and Skye first saw each other again, there was no stopping it now. They were in a free fall. The only way to stop was to crash, and Finn had no intention of letting that happen.

Grasping at her messy red waves, he walked them both back, turning just in time to press her up against the closed door. She whimpered softly, her body arching beneath him, molding to his in a synchronicity Finn had never experienced before. A perfect fit. Two puzzle pieces slating together—if only she realized that a third piece would make them whole. It didn't need to be one, the other, or nothing at all, because from the way she kissed him, the way her hungry hands tugged at his clothing and clumsily yanked open his belt, nothing at all wasn't working for her either.

He swallowed his groan when she brushed over his achingly hard cock, so desperate for her that all it took was a little hot and heavy petting and he was at full mast. While Finn preferred a slow, tortuous approach to lovemaking, always eager to work his lover into a panting, dripping, whimpering *mess* before unleashing a volcanic eruption of pleasure, he feared they might not have the time for their usual song and dance. He yearned to taste Skye again, to fuck her with his tongue, to suck at her clit until she screamed his name. He'd had fantasies of tethering her delicate wrists to his bedposts and having his way with her for hours, watching her climax over and over again until he couldn't *stand* the thought of not being buried balls deep in her. Unfortunately, today might not be the day for that.

Luckily for both of them, Finn was adaptive. If slow, agonizingly sweet lovemaking was out the window today, hard and desperate fucking would be an apt placeholder.

Dragging himself away from their frantic kiss, he scraped his teeth along her jaw, reveling in the way she twisted and arced beneath him, her hands fumbling as they delved into his briefs. While he wanted nothing more than to truly *feel* what those hands could do, what torment they'd wreak on his painfully erect shaft, there wasn't time for that either. Finn retreated slightly, his body palpably mourning the distance from hers, then ripped open Skye's jeans, yanking the zipper down hurriedly.

Her panting encouraged him, aroused him, *demanded* his speed. Never one to leave a woman wanting, Finn unceremoniously dragged those dark jeans down her lovely legs, fighting the urge to stop halfway and bury his face between her thighs. She helped once he reached the ankles, an unsteady hand resting on his shoulder as she stepped out of the tight pants, remaining there until he'd tugged her silken black panties down too.

He hadn't kept the last pair—a regret he'd realized only after, when awareness struck him at just how badly he had fallen for Skye in so short a time. This pair found a home in his pocket, and when he glanced up, he caught her watching with heavy lidded eyes and delectably pouty lips —and not once protesting the thievery.

Finn grinned, slowly sliding his hand along her inner thigh as he stood. Much to his surprise—and delight—he found her wet and wanting when he cupped her sex, so much so that he couldn't resist probing between her folds. Eyes fixed on her face, he watched her shudder under his leisurely exploration, then forced himself to keep quiet when he slipped two fingers into her unhindered. Her eyes shot open in surprise, back arching and stance widening. Unable to help himself, Finn swooped down and caught her lower lip, sucking as his fingers pumped in and out of her below.

As if tumbling out of her stupor, Skye responded vigorously, edging up onto her tiptoes to take back the power in their kiss, her hips bucking against his hand.

"Finn," she whimpered, but before he could respond, a teasing limerick about patience on the tip of his tongue, she wrenched his briefs down further and nipped at his lip. Only a fool would mistake what she needed—and Finn had never fancied himself a fool.

Your wish is my command. He said the words with his eyes, with the way he deepened the kiss, the way his slick fingers circled her little bud before he withdrew. She squirmed against him, hands scrambling for purchase along his arms before finally knotting together behind his neck. Hooking his own hands beneath her knees, he hoisted her up with ease as his mouth trailed down her neck, where he stopped and sucked again, hoping he'd leave a mark for at least a day or two. Skye cried out, her heels digging into the small of his back, urging their bodies together.

Slow, torturous teasing be damned. He hadn't the patience anymore—not after all this time apart. He reached between them and maneuvered his straining cock against her entrance. A quick flicker of his gaze to hers, one last chance to stop this, to turn him away. He wouldn't hold it against her. But she tipped her head back in wild abandon, fingers twining around his hair, her unspoken *yes please* dancing across his skin.

Teeth gritted, Finn pushed into her, eyes clenched shut as her delicious, wet tightness wrapped around him and wouldn't let go.

"*Fuck* me," he hissed against her skin, sinking in until there was no room between them—until finally the distance had truly vanished. Her response, a mix between a moan and a delighted cry, echoed throughout the storage room, and Finn clamped a hand down over her mouth. If someone found them because she couldn't control herself... Well, Finn would be rather proud, but also incredibly fucking *annoyed* with whoever dared open the door and force an abrupt end to their perfect reunion. She murmured something weakly against his palm, eyes fluttering closed when he swirled his hips against hers.

He had missed the moment where he took her, the moment he always savored with a lover, but as Finn slowly thrust in and out of her, he decided there would be *many* opportunities in the future to make up for that. There had to be.

With Skye in mind, he kept his thrusts short yet firm, hoping to graze her inner and outer pleasure sensors each time. From the way she tugged at his hair, the little jerks of pain blending seamlessly with the blissful tightening of his body, Finn suspected he had succeeded. Her muffled squeaks were nearly his undoing, forced out each time his cock pounded into her, and Finn distracted himself with a study of her features—the lovely red flush on her cheeks, the smattering of freckles over her nose, the length of her eyelashes.

She really was beautiful, but it wasn't her beauty he had missed over the last month. An added bonus, surely, but

Finn had longed for her wit, for her banter, for the way she laughed at his ridiculous puns. Skye was the first woman who hadn't tried to immediately change him, to mold him to her liking, and *she* was the only woman Finn hadn't wished were just *slightly* different in one way or another. Strengths, flaws—he wanted to learn them all. He wanted to watch her grow, and he wanted her to keep him grounded.

Thank goodness he had kept his hand over her mouth, because when she came with a muffled cry, her sex clenching around him so tight that he saw stars, the whole building would have been alerted to the scandal. As her fingers finally started to loosen in his hair, as the redness began to fade from her cheeks, Finn slowly removed his hand, kissed her gently, then buried his face against her neck and took her. Hard. Fast. Pistoning in and out until he found his own blessed release. He groaned her name, hands pinching her thighs as he spilled himself into her.

He had seen stars before, but climaxing now dragged galaxies across his field of view, and he found himself sagging, totally spent, against her. Finn blinked rapidly, trying to eschew the visions, worried he might be crushing her—until Skye wrapped her arms around him in a hug and kissed his cheek ever so sweetly.

Eyes closed, he stood there, breathing her in, with no intention of releasing her. Not until she made him.

What on *earth* had she been thinking?

Skye had worked so hard over the last month to push Finn Rai and Cole Daniels out of her mind—no easy task, given that she lived in Cole's apartment and still had the remnants of one of Finn's chocolate bouquets in her freezer. She might have been miserable suppressing her feelings. She might have hated not speaking to either one of them. She might have spent about five minutes in the bathroom mirror every morning giving herself a pep talk, but damn it, she was *trying*. Usually failing, too, but never mind that.

And now Finn had strolled back into her life, seemingly out of nowhere, playing the dashing hero and the orgasm king simultaneously—and all her hard work went right out the window.

If only she were stronger. If only she hadn't walked into that storage closet. Maybe she should have made him carry everything while she supervised from a safe distance. Maybe, if she only had some fucking willpower, she would have pushed him away when he kissed her instead of flocking to him like a moth to a flame—

"You *really* need to stop that," Finn said, his voice shocking her out of her thoughts. Blushing, Skye went for her purse, rooting through the enormous thing to dig out her sunglasses.

"What? Walking quietly, keeping my thoughts to myself?" When had they arrived at the parking lot? Had she been so lost in her head that she hadn't even noticed them navigate the convention center and go *outside*?! Good grief. After their hasty lovemafucking in the day care storage room, they had cleaned up, dressed, and snuck out of there like a couple of guilty teens. It was only then, as they strolled through the now quiet, half-lit hallways, that Skye had realized what a colossal error she had made, and she'd been chiding herself ever since.

"The walking part is fine," Finn told her as they neared the curb, the parking lot ahead of them only a tenth of the way full now. "It's the keeping your thoughts to yourself part. I don't think you realize how plainly they read on your face."

"Oh." She touched her cheek, swallowing hard, then slipped her sunglasses on. "Sorry. I was just... thinking."

Finn sighed and slid his hands into his pockets. "Yes, that's been established. Might I offer a penny for those thoughts?"

"I don't think you'd want to know," she said. There was no point in lying to him. Skye had made her feelings about Finn and Cole clear the day they showed up at work and forced her into *that* conversation.

"Skye..."

She braced herself, expecting him to dredge everything back up. Instead, he turned and stared straight into her eyes, that near-black gaze penetrating through her aviators. "I really think you need to give yourself a break."

Her eyebrows shot up. "W-what?"

"I know you've been feeling guilty for what happened between you, Cole, and myself," he remarked, and her stomach twisted into a painfully tight knot. Finn, however, showed not even the slightest bit of discomfort. "I want you to stop. It's unnecessary."

"But—"

"We understand your concerns, your fears, and your reservations," he pressed on, buttoning his jacket and peering around the parking lot. "But I really hope that you'll give us a chance to change your mind. That's what I wanted to talk to you about today. A chance. Some of your time and patience to hear us out. What do you think?"

She shook her head slightly, then flinched when her phone buzzed from the depths of her purse. Feeling a little waterlogged with information, her mind slowly processing what he'd said, she dug into her purse again and fished out her phone. Theresa. Curator's senior assistant. She had offered to give Skye a lift back to Coral Bay as long as Skye helped her shop for a swanky party she was throwing for her husband's law firm partners tomorrow night. After all, Skye had a bit of experience with the rich and petulant.

"I... I..." She stared at Theresa's text message. The woman was sitting in her car near the service entrance. Was Skye ready to go? No. Not really.

"You need time to consider it," Finn offered. "That's fine. Do you have a ride home?"

"Yes," she answered automatically, her hand falling by her side as she tried to figure out what was happening with this conversation. "Thanks."

Nodding, he pressed a quick kiss to her cheek, then flashed a breathtaking smile before sauntering into the parking lot. She watched him go, numb, until the realization hit her.

"Wait... Give *us* a chance?"

What was he talking about? Her phone buzzed again, and she headed in Theresa's direction on unsteady legs, trying to put the pieces together—and coming up short.

17

MEDDLING MEDDLER

"Mr. Cocksman will be with you in a moment. Can I get you a coffee or tea while you wait?"

Skye shook her head, smiling politely. "No, thank you. I'm fine."

Mr. Cocksman. Yikes. What an unfortunate name to say out loud. She wasn't sure how his secretary managed to keep a straight face, but the woman in the red pantsuit did so unflinchingly. Clearing her throat, Skye reached into her purse at the foot of her chair and dug out her phone. As subtly as she could, she checked her hair and makeup, pleased that the ungodly winds outside hadn't ruined either, then did a quick time check. She had arrived fifteen minutes early, and with five minutes to go, she was no less confused as to why the hell she had been summoned here in the first place.

Sunday, no more than twelve hours after running into and fucking Finn at the fair, she found herself seated in the management building of another museum. These offices managed a whole chain of popular museum locations that operated throughout the state, focusing on frontier-era history, with a special emphasis on the gold rush. They'd been pretty successful with their historical reenactments, frontier cottage camping retreats, gold digs and washes for kids, *and* spectacular in-house exhibits. This location was about a twenty-five-minute drive from Coral Bay and was one of the first places she'd applied to. Skye had sent her résumé to almost every department, despite having never performed a historical reenactment in her life—not even a grade school theater production. Her logic at the time was that there was opportunity for growth since the chains were plentiful with a *lot* of on-site staff, and she had been disappointed when she received a form letter rejection shortly after her submission.

Imagine her surprise, then, when she got a call at nine this morning asking her to meet with the guy who ran *everything*. Not just the owner of one location, but the head honcho of the whole operation. His secretary hadn't been very specific on the phone, nor had she provided much more information since Skye arrived at the office. All Skye had been told was that she'd been invited to meet with Quintin Cocksman, and, oh, sorry it's such short notice. Out of sheer curiosity, Skye had dressed up as if attending yet another interview, taken a cab out to the location, and sat in the waiting room—all the while clueless as to why she was even there. It couldn't be for an interview, as she'd been outright rejected already.

So, there she was—guessing. Fidgety. A bit uncomfortable under the intense blasts of AC.

Mercifully, she wasn't left waiting for long. About two minutes before her two o'clock appointment, the secretary cleared her throat and nodded to the big black door across the room.

"Mr. Cocksman will see you now."

Right. Skye grabbed her purse and stood, smoothing a hand down her high-waisted skirt and fluffing out her beige blouse so that it wouldn't stick to her. With her hair up in a sleek ballerina bun, she padded across the curiously modern reception area—everywhere else *screamed* eighteenth-century colonial chic—and opened the door.

"Ah, Miss Summers. Please come in."

Resisting her face's need to twist with confusion, she slipped inside and closed the door, noting that the hard lines, neutral tones, and subdued wall décor had continued in from the reception area. There, behind a thin glass desk, sat Quintin Cocksman, a man in his late forties by Skye's best estimate, with a pencil-thin black mustache and enormous designer frames—with no glass in them. While there was nothing wrong with trying to prove you were not your brand, this was a little ridiculous. She crossed the room with her hand outstretched, smiling when he rose to shake it. Slim and narrow-shouldered, he wore a fitted grey suit, a white dress shirt, and the emblem for the New England Patriots on his cuffs.

The only reason she even *knew* the emblem of any NFL team was because Cole had briefly entertained the idea of purchasing one about three years ago. Eager for a billionaire to own their team, marketing departments from across the country had flooded his beach bungalow with merchandise. Skye held back a smile at the memory: she and Cole had spent a whole weekend sorting through NFL crap, putting it into piles and researching teams, only for Cole to realize it'd be a poor fit. He ended up scrapping the whole thing, donating the gear to children's hospitals and charities, and treating her to a spa day for wasting her time.

Back then, she hadn't thought it was a waste of time.

Even though she had been drowning in homework, being with Cole, just the two of them in sweats surrounded by mountains of NFL swag, sushi takeout for just about every meal, had been Skye's idea of a perfect weekend.

Quintin Cocksman's almost too-hard handshake brought her firmly back to reality, and her smile faltered. If she wanted to get over Cole, reminiscing had to be off the table.

Screwing Finn should also be off the table, but Skye had already dropped the ball on that one.

"Please, have a seat," Quintin insisted, gesturing to a pair of black and silver chairs in front of his desk. Neither had an inch of padding anywhere, and once she settled into one, Skye could confirm that sitting on a boulder would probably be more comfortable.

And better for her back.

Years of wearing convincing fake smiles for Cole's social circle had prepared her for instances like this, and she managed to effortlessly hide her discomfort.

"Now, I'm sure you're wondering what you're doing here," Quintin said after he took a seat behind his sleek glass desk, hands folded on top of it.

"Well, a little." Skye hoped her smile continued to look natural, rather than showing the strain she was starting to feel. "Your secretary wasn't very specific on the phone."

"We've had another look at your résumé," he told her. "First, thank you for submitting it. The cover letter was very thoughtful."

She bit the insides of her cheeks: all her cover letters had been the same, minus a few tweaked sentences to make them *seem* unique to the specific job in question. "Thank you."

"We've decided to go ahead and offer you a position here with us at this location," he said, "in management."

For a few long seconds, all Skye heard was a high-pitched whine, the world fading in and out of focus until she blinked. Had she heard him right? She was being offered a job somewhere she hadn't formally interviewed at—after they had already rejected her?

"I'm sorry," she said, her laugh sounding mildly maniacal. "You're going to have to repeat that. I don't...understand."

"I just think you'd be a good fit for our corporate environment," he insisted, though Skye didn't believe him—and she wasn't sure why. The lack of enthusiasm in his voice? His dark, dead eyes? Something felt off.

"But... I haven't interviewed." She shook her head, all pretenses of fake smiling gone. "Your hiring manager rejected my application almost immediately."

"We get so many applications," he said, motioning toward the huge window behind him. Below, out among the pines and cedars, was where most of the historical reenactments took place. "A lot of actors looking for work... The hiring department gets swamped sometimes. I do apologize."

Again, Skye didn't believe him. "Okay."

"The position would entail managing the interns and assistants at this location," Quintin explained without missing a beat, his head cocked to one side as he studied her—perhaps searching for something beyond Skye's bewildered expression. "You'll manage day-to-day operations of the exhibits, which the interns and assistants run, and ensure our guest needs are met in the gift shop, the washing stations, and the colonial village. Does that sound like something you would be interested in?"

Skye stared at him, finally deciding that he was serious, and answered honestly. "No. Not really."

Ten brutally awkward seconds later, she cleared her throat, realizing she might come across as disrespectful.

"No, I'm sorry." She forced her smile back up. "It's just... I've accepted a position elsewhere and I'm not interested in leaving."

Was it glamorous to sell tickets at Gallery Sens? No, but Skye had the opportunity to establish herself, learn a lot, and work her way up. Managing a whole team of people at an enormous museum facility was totally out of her realm of experience right now. Skye couldn't imagine being responsible for *anything* beyond her little kingdom. She had been upset about it when she was first hired, considering she was older than most of the other candidates *and* had a university degree. However, the more time she spent at her new job, the more she realized she *wasn't* qualified for much else. Classroom knowledge translated somewhat to the real world, but there was still a lot to learn otherwise.

And Skye wanted to prove she *could* work her way up from the bottom. She wanted to get to the top knowing she had insider knowledge and experience of *every* position below.

"Ah. Well." Quintin leaned back in his chair. "That's perfectly fine. No harm done."

Skye tried not to frown at him; couldn't this conversation have happened over the phone—or an email? Had she really needed to waste money on a cab, and lose a huge chunk of her day off, driving out here?

"Thank you," she said, resisting the urge to sprint the hell out of the building, "for the offer. It's very generous, but I wouldn't feel right taking it when I've just started working elsewhere. I also don't think I'm qualified for it, honestly."

He grinned, seeming more relaxed. "I appreciate your candor. Please tell Mr. Daniels that an offer was, at the very least, extended—"

"Wait," she said, leaning forward and pressing a hand down on his desk. "*What* did you just say?"

For a few long seconds, he looked at her like she was crazy—or that this was a practical joke of some kind. "Er, Cole Daniels? You two are, uh..." He gestured between Skye and himself, as if that explained what he meant. "He and I are both creative arts patrons. We met at a fundraiser about three weeks ago and he wouldn't let me leave until I promised to find you a position. He said you'd be the best person for the job and that I was a fool if I didn't at least sit down with you. I'm sorry it took me so long to follow up, I've just been busy with..."

Tuning out his reasoning, Skye fell back in her chair and winced at the way the backrest cut into her back just under her shoulder blades. Cole had done *what*? A flood of emotions ripped through her all at once: appreciation, rage, discomfort, nostalgia, irritation, love... The list went on, and Skye could feel her cheeks heating up as each one made itself known across her body.

"I'm so sorry that Mr. Daniels wasted your time, Mr. Cox," she said stiffly as she stood, unsure if she had cut him off or not. "And thank you for the offer."

They shook hands again, with Quintin staring up at her warily like she was a bomb about to go off, and Skye marched out of his office with her hands in fists. The high-pitched ringing in her ears returned as she stalked through the management building, unable to think coherently until she reached the roundabout loop at the main doors where her cab had dropped her off.

It was quite peaceful out there now that the wind had

died down, surrounded by thick forest, birds twittering in the distance. The visitor portion of the museum was on the other side of the management lodge; here, just for a moment, she was totally alone. Nothing but her and early-August greenery as far as the eye could see.

Her gaze darted from tree to tree, unable to think, to process, to *grasp*, that Cole had meddled in her professional career. Their sugar daddy contract had been severed. Skye no longer had any affiliation with the agency that had matched them four years ago. For all intents and purposes, she and Cole were broken up—yet he still thought he had a right to stick his nose in her business. Sure, this job was a marked improvement from her current position, but that wasn't the point. Knowing Cole, he had her best interests in mind, but again—that wasn't the fucking point.

Jaw clenched, she retrieved her phone and called for another cab. When the operator asked if she would be returning to the location they had originally picked her up at—her apartment...*Cole's* apartment—Skye hesitated.

"No," she said thickly, her voice catching. "I have a new destination in mind, actually..."

18

YOU FUCKING TWAT

"Garrett Jones will be a good fit," Cole insisted as he took the long, winding bend leading up to his Coral Bay vacation home. His eyes flickered to the mirror—not a soul behind him—then down to the built-in touch screen on his dash. The call had been in progress for the last twenty minutes, but he felt like he'd been going on and on about this for hours. "See that the salary is higher than average... Significantly."

Marta Jensen, his tech empire's CFO, sighed into the phone. "You can't keep doing this with every new person we hire."

"I can and I will." He clicked the remote for his front gate when it came into view, nestled between large cement walls. "Marta, I want to step *back* from things, and I need to know the people I'm delegating to will take the job seriously."

"That's why we're offering them the position," she argued, "because after an exhaustive interview process, they've proved that they will. Cole, you're driving me up the wall."

He grinned, slowing his navy Bugatti Veyron as the gate swung open. "I know. I appreciate it. You know how I am."

"That I do." Marta had been with him from the beginning. At almost fifteen years his senior, with immense experience in the industry, she was an invaluable asset. Without her and a few of the other top-tier personnel, Cole wouldn't have been able to get to where he was today. His fortune would have gone to someone else, and he probably would have been writing code for them in a dingy cubicle. Or on some ridiculous communal bean bag chair. Skill and ingenuity got you far in the ever-growing tech and cyber security industry, but you needed a whole crew of people with vastly different, and sometimes superior, skill sets if you wanted to dominate the market.

Which Cole had.

And the thought of handing off a sizeable percentage of his usual responsibilities, responsibilities most other CEOs wouldn't be caught dead doing, had been giving him heart palpitations all month. Literally. His private physician was about ten seconds away from medicating him if Cole didn't get his anxiety back under control. He knew, logically, that easing away only *slightly* and passing off *some* of his workload to capable, competent people was the right thing to do. He worked himself to death just about every year, and Coral Bay—with Skye Summers nearby—had been his medically-mandated retreat where he forced himself to recoup and refocus to get through the rest of the year.

But if he wanted to pursue a relationship with the woman he loved, all that needed to stop. He could still work, of course, but as he and Finn had agreed, Cole needed to do so significantly less. So, here he was, managing interviews from his car even though he had promised Finn he'd take the next two weeks off to really concentrate on the task ahead. He couldn't help himself—and it didn't hurt anyone if he could efficiently multitask. The trunk of his newest car was full of cat toys, bedding, food, and litter for Oz's upcoming birthday. He had spent most of the day bouncing between specialty pet boutiques, and afterward he hadn't seen any harm in checking up on things with Marta on the drive home. Once he was parked, he'd hang up and get to wrapping.

Maybe. Maybe he'd stay on the phone a little while longer to find out about a few of the other corporate positions they were trying to fill. His assistant had been rather deft at fielding calls from the office this week, which meant Cole was out of the loop and panicking. Being out of the loop meant being out of control. He didn't know what was happening with his company, or to his employees, and that only made his anxiety worse.

But he had to do it. For Skye, he *would* do it.

Speaking of Skye... Cole swallowed hard when he spotted an unexpected yet gorgeously familiar figure sitting on his front stoop, her arms crossed, her coppery waves caught in the wind, and her face pinched in annoyance.

"Marta, I'll have to call you back. Just move forward with salary negotiations," Cole said quickly as Skye stood, her hands in fists. "Remember to offer significantly higher than—"

"Industry standard, I know," his CFO muttered, and Cole disconnected the line with a quick tap, tap, tap around the custom built-in screen. Feeling his palms starting to sweat, he parked the car on the far side of the driveway near the path down to the beach, needing a bit of a buffer between himself and Skye—if only to get his panic under control.

She looked upset. Angry, more like. Cole would

probably only need one guess as to what had her in a tizzy, but he'd rather her come right out and say it.

God, she was beautiful, even when she was angry. He'd always thought so, from the second he saw her picture on that dreadful sugar daddy website all those years ago, right up until now. Stunning in every sense of the word. He wasn't sure what he'd done in a past life to have her feature so prominently in this one, but he must have been some kind of saint or something.

Taking a few deep breaths to calm his racing heart, he popped his sunglasses on his head, cut the car engine, and hurried out. By the time he closed the door, Skye was about five feet from him.

Do not leer at her. No matter what kinds of wonderful things that skirt does for her hips, do. not. leer.

"Skye," he said as he slid his clammy hands into his pockets. "This is a pleasant surprise."

Cole did his best to sound calm, cool, and collected, but he hadn't felt any of those things since the night of Finn's sex party. There had always been a much-needed, much-cherished sense of comfort between him and Skye; it was something Cole found himself craving whenever they were apart, sometimes longing for it so desperately it physically hurt. However, ever since that night, and all the fuckery he'd wrought upon their relationship after, the comfort was gone. Something had shifted between them. Something had changed.

Change was good. People said it all the time. But change was hard, and Cole had never been very good at it. Not as a highly anxious, socially inept child, and not now, as a less anxious, still somewhat socially inept man who had learned to fake his confidence when necessary.

Things had always been easy with her. His best friend.

The woman he felt most at ease with, no matter the situation. She bolstered his confidence—she made him brave, even if she didn't know it. All the racing thoughts, the fears, the stress, it all disappeared when they were together. Skye Summers and writing his own code: two of the best forms of anxiety medication he'd ever known, besides his *actual* medication. Now, however, it seemed every little thing he did in an effort to repair his previous fuck-ups just made the distance between them even greater.

Being so close to her in that moment, not able to touch her, to smile at her as he once did, made his stomach knot so tightly that he almost doubled over.

"Stop," she said, raising a hand to silence him, a fury burning in those hazel eyes he'd never seen before. "Just answer honestly."

"Always." The word slipped out before he could stop it. Cole mentally kicked himself when her gaze narrowed.

"Did you, or did you not, force Quintin Cocksman to *give* me a job?"

He shook his head. "I wouldn't say *force*—"

"Cole!"

She'd yelled at him. Skye had never yelled at him before. Cole stared at her for a moment, from the red in her cheeks to the fire in her eyes. Somewhere in the back of his mind, a snide little voice commented that in all their history, Skye had been his sugar baby. She owed her university degree, her home, and her financial standing to *him*. Perhaps that had kept her from ever yelling before. He raised his chin, unsure if that theory had any validity, and squared his shoulders.

"I didn't *force* anyone to do anything," he told her—and that was the truth. Yes, he had heavily suggested that Quintin Cocksman, a pompous asshole who had spent the whole fundraiser they were at sneering rude things about the wait staff, offer Skye a position worthy of her within his vast museum empire. "I spoke with Cocksman about you and your hard work and expressed what a good fit you would be in his organization. Skye..." He took a soft breath, noting the way one of her hands had uncurled. "The job you have now is *beneath* you. You are capable of so much more, and I was just trying to—"

"I like my job!" She threw her hands in the air and started pacing. "Is it everything I could have hoped for and more? No, but it's *mine*."

His anxiety retreated into the recesses of his person, allowing the frustration he'd been feeling *for* her to come to the forefront. "Skye, you are more intelligent, more capable, and certainly more qualified than selling tickets."

"That might be your opinion—"

"It's fact."

"But it's not your decision to make!" She rounded back on him, angrily brushing her loose red waves from her face. "It's *my* life. It's *my* job, *my* career, and I got it on my own. You had no right to meddle like that. We're not even..." The colour drained from her face, and she crossed her arms, her gaze lifting skyward. "Cole, we're not together anymore. You don't get to have a hand in how I manage my career. The choice to be there is mine. I earned it."

He opened his mouth, ready and able to counter with a few thoughts of his own, but thought better of it. Head bowed, he stared at the stone pattern of his driveway, suddenly feeling rather foolish—not an uncommon thing these days.

Because she was right. Skye had done the work to acquire her degree. He had seen her during various exam seasons. Hell, he had cooked her meals and hired a maid service to clean her apartment for a whole month one year because she was so stressed with everything. He had even cancelled work duties to help her, paying for it the following month by working night and day to make up for his absence. And now here she was, finding her way in the world, and he thought he had a right to steer her in the direction of his choosing.

"Skye... I'm sorry."

She was also right in that they weren't together anymore. Nothing had stung more than when the sugar daddy agency informed him that Skye had gracefully exited their contract.

He knew he had to fight for her—*actually* fight for her. In the past, circumstance had always brought them back together. Now that they were both free agents, Cole needed to roll up his sleeves and get his hands dirty. Metaphorically, of course. Dirty with feelings and messy emotions he'd tried to avoid for years, worried about what said feelings and emotions might do to their safe, easy relationship.

"I should have considered that there is merit in starting from the bottom," Cole admitted quietly in the silence that followed his apology. "I... I thought you were settling. I thought that by taking another position, you'd have a chance to excel, not realizing you were already doing it on your own. It was, well, rather..."

"Presumptuous of you?" she offered, head tilted slightly to one side. While the fire was gone from her eyes, her entire being looked stiff. Tense. "Yes, it was. You had no right to do what you did. I'm not qualified for the job you told him to give me. I wouldn't have done well there."

He scoffed. "You don't know that."

"I do, actually," she snapped, her curtness forcing him to

look up. "It might come as a surprise to you, but I know a little something about *my* industry. And maybe I'm a bit overqualified for *this* job, but I wasn't ready for anything else. I had no experience. I *want* to learn it all, and you don't get to take that away from me by using your influence to hoist me to the top of the ladder. That's not fair."

Cole blinked rapidly, his brain briefly short-circuiting before a quick reboot showed him *exactly* where he had made a mistake. A huge one. It was a wonder she bothered to come down here at all.

You fucking twat.

"I didn't think about it like that," he said, "and I should have."

When he had, admittedly, bullied that pretentious ass into offering Skye a job, Cole had thought he was doing something that would skyrocket her into a job she *loved*. Even if his and Finn's plan failed and he was never able to hold her again, if she could never know just how much he loved her, then Cole wanted Skye to at least be *happy*. He didn't want to see all that hard work and sacrifice go to waste while she hawked tickets at a sex museum forty hours a week.

But she was right, of course. It hadn't been his call to make. Skye needed to learn the ups and downs of her industry. She needed to put in the hard work. She needed to fall on her face and she needed to soar through the ranks respectively. No one could do it for her, least of all Cole.

"Again," he said, swallowing down the hard lump in his throat, "I'm sorry. Sincerely."

He expected her to stomp off and call a cab, but she just stood there, her eyes misty and her cheeks flushed. When she caught him staring, she turned her head away, biting down on a wobbly lower lip and sniffling. Trying to read the complicated air between them, Cole flexed his hands in and out of fists, a nervous habit that had once been effective in combating the anxious thoughts. Keep moving. One step ahead of the fear. Seeing her so upset, however, did the trick too. He'd never wanted to make her cry, and seeing it with his own two eyes beat the creeping feelings of inadequacy and terror back. He squared his shoulders and clenched his jaw, brow furrowed.

She needs you to be brave, just this once, you bloody coward.

"Skye, I..." He risked a step forward, but his throat clenched up, choking the words before they could roll off his tongue. Cole swallowed hard, breathing through the tightness of his chest; after all, she hadn't retreated. That had to mean something. He wrenched his stiff arm away from his side, forcing his fist to open, and ignored the flood of adrenaline coursing through his system. Instead, he concentrated on her, on the tears in her eyes, the heartache on her face—knowing he was the one who'd put it there—and gently cupped her elbow. "I've missed you."

She continued to avoid his gaze, and he moved from her elbow to her hair when the wind dragged a few thick tresses across her face. Before he could sweep them back, Skye caught him, the physical contact sending a shockwave straight to his heart. Rather than throw his hand away, however, she merely held it, her misty hazel eyes darting to meet his gaze. Then, slowly, she threaded her fingers through his, and they lowered their clasped hands between them.

God, he really had missed her. Cole had been trying to ignore just how *much* he missed her over this last month. Sure, they only ever saw each other in person a few times a year, generally during the busier "social" seasons, but they used to speak at length at least once a week via some device or other. No matter what his mental state, she had always managed to brighten his *life*—not just his mood, his whole fucking world.

How could he have let her go?

But was he making a mistake now? Taking soft, controlled breaths, he did his best to gauge her reaction, searching for signs in her face to tell him what to do. Let go. Move closer. Say something. Say nothing.

Her grip tightened around his hand. Cole inched closer, wanting nothing more than to bury his nose in her hair and breathe her in. To kiss her into sweet oblivion. But he couldn't quiet the fear. In that moment, they stood in silence, nothing but the wind and the distant crashing waves to serenade their reunion. However, his head was the loudest it had been in weeks, conflicting voices shouting for him to let her go, to drag her against him, to apologize again and again until he was blue in the face, to stop being such a colossal fucking idiot—

She leaned in and brushed her lips over his—and suddenly, there were just the waves, the wind, and Skye.

Cole had never felt more at peace in his life.

19

SPILL YOUR GUTS, SIR

They stumbled through the front door in constant contact, as if the universe would swallow them up should they dare let go. Hands fisted in his shirt, Skye dragged Cole into the mercifully air-conditioned beach house, her eyes ablaze with a different sort of fire, and he found himself fumbling over the jingling keys stuck in the lock. In the end, he left them behind, slamming the door and surrendering to the kiss, to the feel of her hot mouth over his, the tentative sweep of her tongue across his lower lip. A growl escaped him, his arm snapped around her waist, and he dragged her closer, using her gasp to plunder her mouth.

It really was a crime that they hadn't kissed sooner. Skye had always made him brave, but kissing her—it was like she made him superhuman. Her lips, plump and supple, were made for every kind of kiss: stolen, fleeting, passionate, desperate. Cole had wanted to try all of them for the last four years. Sometimes, he'd find himself staring at those lips while she talked, while she laughed, so hopelessly in love that it frightened him. And it had. The sheer *weight* of his love for her had startled him from the beginning.

But Skye had needed to focus on school. She didn't need sex and love to distract her, so Cole had settled instead for a wonderful friendship. If all he could ever have was her friendship, he'd still die a happy man. Yet now that he could touch her again, drag her lithe, toned figure so impossibly close to him again, he knew he couldn't settle. Not anymore. And from the way she kissed him, sucking at his lower lip, mouth lifted in that stunning sort of smile he had come to worship, Cole wondered if she felt it too. The pull between them. The gravity. He had always thought they fit so perfectly together, whether they were standing before a wall of screaming press at a movie premiere or seated on opposite ends of the couch reading, their toes touching in the middle, they just *fit*.

Holding her now... It felt like coming home.

Much to his surprise, Skye went for his clothing first, slipping her delicate fingers under the belted waistline of his trousers and tugging. Her intent was clear; even if he couldn't see the inferno in her eyes, he felt it in the way she moved. Her courage emboldened him, and he felt himself come alive at her touch.

Groaning, he tore his mouth from hers and trailed it along her jaw, relishing her taste, her smell—if he wasn't mistaken, she was wearing the Chanel perfume he'd bought her last Christmas. A hint of teeth over the edge of her jawline, catching the delicate skin by surprise and making her gasp. Gently, carefully, he raked those teeth down the column of her throat, savoring the way she shuddered, her hands fumbling over his belt briefly before she regained control and yanked it open.

Cole returned the favor by undoing the stylishly loose

satin bow at the neckline of her blouse with his teeth, then unceremoniously dragging the garment over her head. Her coppery waves fluttered down around her, the flyaways like a halo. Skye Eloise Summers. A veritable angel in his eyes, tinged with a sultry side that made his knees weak and his cock hard. Suddenly shy, she brushed her hair out of her face, cheeks pink and eyes downcast—but the slight quirk of her lips suggested she wasn't the doting submissive she appeared to be.

He watched, curious, as she went for his pants again, this time grazing his steadily hardening shaft as she unzipped them and yanked them down. With trembling fingers, she unbuttoned his dress shirt too, her stare wandering the broad expanse of his relatively hairless chest with blatant interest. Cole rolled his shoulders back when she pushed the shirt off, exposing himself, shedding the armor of business attire.

And that was precisely what it had always been to him. He purchased the finest pieces, tailored them to perfection, spared no expense, because he wore them to battle each and every day. They not only protected him from the so-called sharks of his world, but they trapped his fears inside. True and valuable *armor*. Yet with Skye, they belonged on the floor, forgotten.

With Skye, Cole never needed them.

His eyes flitted down to her skirt briefly, an unspoken request passing between them. Slowly, Skye twisted around and undid the zipper at the back, instantly loosening the waistline. She then pinched the fabric around her hips and slowly, teasingly, wiggled side to side until the skirt was nothing but a puddle of fabric around her feet. A mischievous gleam twinkled in her eye, but as she reached for the now impossible-to-ignore tent in his briefs, Cole caught her wrist and dragged her toward him, holding his captured prize between them.

Molten desire replaced the mischief in those hazel orbs, and he delighted in her soft, shuddering breath as their eyes met, his lidded and controlled, hers bright and wide. The tremor in her lip. Her racing pulse. It put him at ease, just as it had the first time they made love, that his brand of fucking didn't frighten her.

Despite his anxiety, his fears, Cole had always been a bit bossy in bed—but only with the right woman. Years ago, a psychiatrist had deduced that it stemmed from his need to aggressively *give* affection after years of it being denied to him in his childhood. Being in control was an effective tactic to manage his anxiety too, and the psychiatrist had suggested that this, paired with his obsessive need to ensure other people were comfortable and cared for, led to his sexual preferences.

Cole hadn't given much thought to the theory. He liked what he liked, but he would never force it on anyone. After all, it took him being extremely comfortable with the woman in question for that side to come out and play. The few one-night stands he'd had over the years had resulted in pretty standard, vanilla sex. With Skye, Cole knew how he wanted to worship her—like a goddess who deserved nothing but pleasure.

Still gripping her wrist, he took a step forward, and she countered with a measured step back. Their little dance carried them across the small foyer, until Skye reached the four steps that led up to the rest of the house. He thought she'd remember, but her heel caught on the first step and down she went—until Cole caught her.

"Oh!" she giggled, one hand braced on his shoulder while the other covered her mouth. Grinning, Cole slowly lowered her to the small tiled staircase, then nudged her hand aside and captured her lips once more. A soft moan caught in her throat, and she arched up to greet him as he slowly eased down to join her. Only he had no intention of sitting on the stairs, taking her right then and there—as much as he might have wanted to. Instead, he lifted her up two more steps, then snagged her panties and dragged them down her legs. Skye watched, transfixed, her lower lip caught between her teeth, until the cotton passed her ankles and disappeared over Cole's shoulder.

He waited a moment, hands smoothing up her legs and curling under her knees, to give her a chance to catch up. To pull away. To put a gentle stop to where this was headed. But she didn't. Instead, Skye leaned back, her elbows propped up on the step behind her, and cocked her head to the side in the most stunning display of *come hither* Cole had ever seen.

Not needing to be told twice, Cole kissed each knee, then showered her freckled thighs with affection. Tongue. Teeth. Lips. Leave no stone unturned. When he reached the crest of her sex, he found her glistening. Trembling only a little.

He swallowed hard, his eyes darting up to hers as he swept his tongue over her folds. She hissed his name, her head tipping back with palpable delight, and he knew he had to up the ante. Smirking, he circled her swollen bud, then engulfed it with his hot mouth, savoring each moan, each whimper, each spasm of the woman before him.

Worried that this position might put strain on her back, Cole hoisted her legs over his shoulders and took the brunt of her weight. When she started to protest, her hand threading through his hair, he returned to the task at hand: making her scream.

If Cole was forced to compliment himself, he would praise his attention to detail and his thoroughness in getting the job done *right*. While some men may have been content to simply get the task over with, Cole wanted, *needed*, perfection. Skye deserved that much after everything he had put her through. So, he listened to when her breath hitched, when she moaned, when she whispered his name. He learned by how hard she tugged at his hair, the way her legs shifted about on his shoulders so that he could taste her deeper. He adapted his technique, perfecting it slowly but meticulously through trial and error, making a quick study of how Skye liked to be pampered. She preferred her clit to be circled, not pressed on or swept over. He wanted this down to a science for next time, so that when she climaxed then, it would be better, faster, and more potent than today.

She came shortly after he switched things around, circling her clit with his tongue and massaging her inner walls with two fingers. The position let him watch her come undone, let him savor every nuance as she quivered and cried out breathlessly, her body tightening around him and his slowly thrusting fingers until she sagged down. A sheen of perspiration coated her figure, and she blushed from her cheekbones down to the valley of her breasts. Carefully, Cole eased away from her, masking his wince; his cock was ready to explode at this point, so desperate for her that it was suddenly difficult to think straight.

"Thank you," she murmured, a hand on her forehead as she stared down at him. In that light, she appeared utterly relaxed, totally at ease, and Cole rocked back on his heels, grinning.

"Anytime."

They appraised one another briefly, the easy comfort shifting the longer they sat there to something more urgent.

He noticed it in the way her breath quickened, in the embers pulsing where her fire had once been, the flames doused, perhaps, but certainly not extinguished. Swallowing hard, committing her taste to memory, Cole stood and offered a hand. Skye accepted, sliding her elegant hand into his and grasping it with more conviction than he had expected. He helped her upright, steadying her for a moment, then, with what he hoped was an easy smile of his own, he ducked down and hoisted her over his shoulder.

"Cole!" she scream-giggled, swatting at his back as he straightened out. "Put me down!"

"No, not yet," he told her, brightening at the sound of her happiness—even if only temporary, given everything else. But that was all happening outside. As soon as he had shut the door behind them, their problems had taken a backseat. For now, he wanted to bask in her, to enjoy her, and, if she let him, Cole just wanted to love her.

Engaging in a little playful back-and-forth, he carried her through his Coral Bay home, straight down to his bedroom overlooking the ocean. She quieted as they crossed the threshold, propping herself up with her hands on the swell of his lower back. Gently, he lowered her onto his meticulously made bed, and as she crawled back, he got rid of those damn restricting briefs and shoes. Skye unclasped her bra and tossed it aside, and he noticed her gulp as he took her in.

Slowly, he clambered onto the bed, and as he crawled forward, she lay back—the beginnings of yet another dance. Cole started at her ankles, kissing his way up her body until he reached her lips, which he claimed with vigor. She sighed beneath him, caressing his cheek, fingertips ghosting across his recently shaven skin. Catching her wrist before it reached his hair, he pinned it to the bed. In turn, she locked her legs behind him, her enticing heat beckoning him closer.

His eyes closed when she grasped his cock with her free hand and steered him into her. Although every fiber of his being wanted to plunge in and just *take* her, Cole practiced patience, filling her slowly. Their kiss weakened as she gasped, their hips colliding with a startling sense of finality that made his chest tight. Ignoring the fear, he cradled her head in one hand, the other still holding her wrist down, and pumped in and out of her slowly. Sweetly. Gently—relishing every second, just in case it was their last.

Breath quickening, Skye wrenched her arm free and wrapped both around his neck. This time, she pulled *him* impossibly close, and Cole buried his face in the nape of her neck, breathing her in, exploring her with every sense at his disposal. Sight—her beauty. Sound—her little moans. Smell—his gift on her neck. Taste—the sensitive skin on the hollow of her throat. Touch—*everything*. They rocked together, Skye bucking up to meet each thrust of his hips, her grip unwavering. Their pace hastened together, steadily gaining speed until he felt her clench around him again, his name tumbling from her lips as a sob.

He let go then, spilling himself into her as a blinding pleasure skyrocketed through his body. As he floated back to earth, overwhelmed but content, Skye rolled them onto their sides, where they remained, holding one another, catching their breath, and forgetting the rest of the world.

Skye hadn't meant to still be crying when Cole emerged from his ensuite bathroom. Frankly, she'd hoped to have her shitstorm of feelings under control by then. It wasn't fair for him to walk back into the room after what they had just done—twice—and find her crying. But that was the situation, and Skye tried to rectify it as quickly as she could. Unfortunately, he had already seen the tears, and there was no taking them back.

"Skye?" Cole crossed the room and perched on the edge of the bed. She noticed and appreciated the distance he put between them, and she offered a watery smile as thanks, still tucked under his covers, naked.

"I'm fine," she told him, though she knew neither of them believed her. "I just... I keep *doing* this."

His eyebrows twitched up before he turned his attention to his tightly clasped hands. Her intention hadn't been to hurt him, but clearly they had already crossed that hurdle. Sighing, she sat back on the mountain of pillows behind her and took a few deep breaths. After they had made love the first time, Skye just couldn't drag herself away from him. Try as she might, it was like she was a magnet and the bed was one giant fridge, holding her exactly where she belonged. They'd showered separately after their second tryst in his bed, and Skye still hadn't found the will to leave just yet.

"When I ended things between us," she started, knowing now was the time for honesty if there ever was one, "*all* of us, I didn't just do it for kicks. It was better for me emotionally to break the contract and get some distance, but as soon as I see you, either of you, I just fall back into the same old routine. And..." Her voice wobbled as she wiped the streaks of tears from her cheeks. "And I have to *stop*. Nothing's changed. You still work too much for the relationship I *need*, and I still can't make a fucking decision between you and Finn, and that's not fair—"

"Skye, stop."

She gulped, lifting her wet, heavy gaze to Cole. His knuckles had gone white, as though he were clenching his hands together so hard that he could break bone. Much to her surprise, however, he unlaced his fingers, crackling his knuckles as he always did, and then crawled up the bed to sit beside her. There was still about a two-foot gap between them, but when his arm fell to his side, Skye reached out and took his hot, slightly clammy hand.

"I've...started to pull back a little at work," he admitted softly. "It's a process, but I'm doing it."

She wasn't sure what to say to that. Admittedly, it was good news, but she had no idea what pulling back "a little" meant to him. It could still mean insane hours, constant travel, and two phones on him at all times.

"Do you know why I work so much?" he asked. When she shook her head, she felt him clicking his nails together, and she held his hand tighter to still the movement. He let out a shaky breath, his brow furrowed. "Ever since I can remember, I've had anxiety. Not just fleeting moments of panic, but, in many ways, crippling feelings. It wasn't until my dad died that my mum was *allowed* to put me in therapy, get me medicated, all that. As a kid, leaving the house, facing other people, *doing* things in public... It was debilitating. Panic attacks. Inconsolable crying. Bed wetting. Racing thoughts and insomnia. I had everything. So, all I did was sit on the computer. At least there, I had a shield. It was habit-forming, and it followed me into my professional career." His voice hitched, but a soft throat clearing seemed to dislodge it. "I've gotten it relatively under control, but I'm afraid some social situations cause it to, er, flare. You in particular, our relationship, have always been a trigger. I-I lost myself a little when things started to change between us, and for that I have to apologize. It isn't an excuse, but..."

He wouldn't meet her eye, but his other hand had started frantically clicking his nails. So, Skye shuffled closer, reached over him, and stilled that one too, bringing them both into her lap and holding tight.

"Why haven't you ever told me any of this?" she asked. They had talked about their respective childhoods over the years. Cole knew Skye's mom had plunged them into debt after her dad left, and her death when Skye was nineteen had forced her to skip college and *work* until all the debt was paid. In turn, Skye knew Cole's dad had been a piece of work, and that his mom now lived in a cushy English cottage that Cole had purchased the first year his company was profitable. Mental illness, meanwhile, had never come up once in their conversations. She'd always known him to need control in his profession life, and she had memorized his physical ticks, but she hadn't ever thought...

"A grown man with anxiety?" He offered a hollow laugh, his cheeks flushed and his eyes wandering around the room—as if searching for an escape. "Not very sexy, is it? When we first met, we agreed to steer the relationship clear of love and sex, but I still wanted you to...to... You know. I wanted to be appealing. This side of me isn't exactly appealing. Medication helps tremendously, but certain issues still," he swallowed hard, "make the world feel so loud, sometimes. I didn't want to burden you with it. You were already doing so much for me."

She shook her head, frowning. While she could understand the thought pattern, it wasn't applicable to their relationship. Not in the slightest. "I like you for you. The whole package, your workaholic tendencies and all. This doesn't change who you are to me. I wish I'd known from the beginning, because I think it makes me understand *you* better."

"I've been ashamed of it," he muttered, "for a long time. My dad... Well, he didn't help."

"Cole." She grabbed him by the chin and forced him to look at her. "You have been my best friend for years. I know it's scary to tell someone about this, but I..."

I love you no matter what. The realization hit her like a freight train. Even now, after a month apart, none of her feelings had disappeared. Try as she might to fight them, to contain them, to forget them, they were still there, ardent as ever. Sighing softly, she sat back against the pillows, withdrawing her hands and knotting them together on her lap.

What the hell was she supposed to do now?

They sat in a weighted silence for what felt like hours, side by side, both looking everywhere but at the other person. Finally, Cole faced her.

"When I was growing up, my dad used to beat the holy hell out of my mum," he admitted, and Skye looked to him sharply, her eyes wide as he nodded. "Having my anxiety and a dad who scared the absolute shit out of me... It wasn't easy. I still struggle with the fact that I wasn't the least bit sad when he had his heart attack, because it meant that Mum and I were finally free. It took me a few years to sort myself out, with her help, but after that, I knew I had to take care of her. I hadn't stepped up before, and I..."

He looked away, his eyes glassy, and Skye reacted without thinking: she pulled him into a tight hug, rubbing his back, her heart aching.

"Cole, I'm so sorry."

"One day, my little internet security company and its apps just...exploded," he told her as they broke apart, their hands still resting on each other's arms. "Suddenly I had hundreds and hundreds of people who worked for me, and I was hit with this *need* to make sure they were taken care of. It kept me up at night, worrying about all of them. I guess my long-winded explanation of why I work so much is that...I want to make sure every single one of them is treated fairly, with respect. I do too much, I know, but I've always felt like I *had* to, after everything."

"You can't save everyone," she murmured. "That's not how the world works, unfortunately."

"Logically, I know." A flicker of a smile crossed his lips before vanishing. "It's made me lose you. And I regret it. I regret pretending that what we had was enough for me, but I can't... I can't give you everything you deserve right now. Not by myself, anyway."

Skye nodded as the fog started to clear from her mind, slowly piecing together the whole picture as she had never been able to before.

"What happened with Finn and I," Cole started, his voice sounding more certain, "I know it upset you. Confused you. But I believe we have a solution to all this, something that will work for all of us."

And, just like that, everything was muddled again.

"I hadn't meant to get into it today without Finn, but—"

"Don't," she said softly, placing a hand on his chest. "I need some time to process everything. Not what you've told me today, just... Time to process us."

"*Us* can include him, you know," Cole told her, then pressed his lips together and leaned back when she shot him a look. "Fine. Sorry. Yes. Take the time you need to get your thoughts together. Are you at least open to sitting down with the both of us?"

"I..." The thought of being in the same room with them

anytime soon made her stomach churn, but her last plan—quitting cold turkey—had only made her miserable. So, she nodded. "Sure. Just give me a couple days to process."

"Of course. Shall I call you a car?"

"Please," Skye said after a brief pause, smiling. "Thank you."

She tugged the covers over her bare chest. While she didn't *want* to leave, she knew she should. Skye needed the distance from both Cole and Finn in order to see her situation clearly. She had to digest her experiences from the last two days, how she felt being with both of them again, and genuinely consider their offer to meet up to talk about this supposed solution. She couldn't do that naked in Cole's bed.

Even once she was dressed and back in her own apartment, sitting in her own bed under her own covers, with a purring Oz in her lap and a glass of wine on the bedside table, untouched, Skye still wasn't sure she could do it.

But she had to.

For the sake of the three hearts involved, Skye knew she had to try.

20

S.O.K. (SAVE OUR KITTY)

At precisely 11:07 PM on Friday night, Cole's personal phone chirped to life from the other side of his enormous kitchen island. He nearly dropped his bamboo spatula into the pan of sizzling ground beef; he had realized fifteen minutes ago that he hadn't had dinner and was starting to see spots, so thawed ground beef and veg would have to fill the void. Oh, and the leftover cold pasta he'd been munching on ever since he strolled into the kitchen, a bit lightheaded, to see to a proper dinner.

His adrenaline spiked. It was around this time he ought to be getting a rather important phone call from London regarding, well, the future of his professional life.

Tossing the spatula aside, he jogged around the counter and scrambled to pick up his phone—only to frown at the sight of Skye's name on the screen.

True to his word, Cole had been giving her time to sort through her thoughts and feelings, and had even managed to persuade a mildly impatient Finn to do the same. Despite personally wrapping each and every one of Oz's birthday presents, he'd had his assistant drop them off at Skye's apartment a few days ago, along with a note that said he missed her, just to show she was still on his mind even if he had no intention of breaking their agreement.

The fight-or-flight feeling he'd been suffering all night, waiting to for news from Marta, only intensified seeing Skye's name; Cole tapped the answer button and brought the phone to his ear. After all, he had finally decided to *fight*. No more running.

"Skye," he said, hoping to sound breezy and *completely* fine after their last conversation about his personal struggles. It had been a heavy talk, but somehow Cole had felt lighter in the days that followed. Sharing his lifelong secret with the woman he loved had lifted the weight off his shoulders, and for the first time, the niggling thoughts at the back of his mind hadn't cruelly insisted he'd given said weight to Skye. It was just...gone. Poof. Vanished. Going forward, he wanted to breathe some of the fun back into their relationship, starting tonight. "This is a nice surprise. What are you—"

"Oz isn't moving," Skye sobbed into the phone. "H-he isn't moving!"

"All right, all right, calm down," Cole murmured, darting around the island again to turn off the stove. "Take a deep breath and tell me what's happening."

"I just got home from w-work," she cried, the sound breaking his heart. "We had an event a-and it ran late. He's been a bit off for a couple of days, but I've been making sure he's okay. He seemed so much better this morning, but..."

She trailed off into a jumble of incoherent wails as Cole darted around the house, grabbing his keys, wallet, and shoes before stumbling out the front door. He had experienced a call like this once with her already: before they had even gone on their "first date" arranged by the agency, she had called him bawling into the phone about her old family cat who had passed away. It was then he had found the perfect meet-and-greet gift: a fluffy white kitten to help mend her heartache. Skye had named him Oz ten seconds after meeting him. Cole had fallen for her shortly after.

"Cole, I don't..." She devolved into more nonsensical cry-babbling, but he was already out the door, unlocking his Bugatti from the front stoop.

"We're going to take him to the emergency vet, sweetheart," he told her, forcing his voice to remain as calm and steady as possible. Inside, his stomach had already started to fold in on itself, and his palms had broken out in a cold sweat. But he could handle this. "Get Ozzy into his carrier. Give him lots of blankets and keep him warm." He missed the keyhole a few times after tossing all his shit in the passenger seat, then finally managed to angle it right and start the ignition. Skye continued to sob on the other end of the phone. "Skye, are you listening?"

"Y-yes."

"Can you do all that for me?" he asked, clicking around on his built-in navigation screen before reversing the hell down his driveway. The wrought iron gate barely made it open in time for him to come barreling through.

"Y-yes," she managed, and he nodded, smiling—if only for her to hear that smile when he spoke.

"Good girl. I'm on my way. When Ozzy is safe and comfortable, look up the directions to the emergency veterinary clinic." He wanted to tell her to get a sample of Ozzy's bowel movements too; Marta had gone through something similar with her dog and she'd needed to bring a stool sample. Cole had heard all about it, in graphic detail, as he and his CFO video-chatted over lunch yesterday. Skye didn't seem in the right frame of mind to comb through Oz's litterbox, however. "I'll be there before you know it. Just have the directions ready, okay?"

"O-okay."

"I'm going to hang up now," he told her, although he really didn't want to. "I'll call you back in two minutes."

She sniffled loudly. "Okay."

"Okay." He disconnected his cell and tapped into the screen's phone app, directing it to call Finn. The man answered on the third ring, drawling about how Cole was missing a *fabulous* gallery opening. His voice lost its teasing edge, however, when Cole snapped that Skye needed them *immediately*, and to stand by for instructions on where to meet.

"Headed for my car now," Finn stated, the dull roar of obnoxious society conversations echoing around him. "Keep me informed."

"Will do." Cole hung up and barked at the car to call Skye. Within seconds he had her back on the phone, his heart aching as she continued to cry. He slammed his foot on the gas pedal, racing toward Coral Bay. "I'll be there before you know it, sweetheart. Try to breathe. Everything's going to be just fine..."

"I don't understand why I can't go back there with him," Skye said miserably, staring at the off-limits door the emergency on-call vet and his technicians had carried Oz through only minutes earlier. "He'll feel better if he knows that I'm there."

"I know, sweetheart." Cole rubbed his hand up and down her back slowly, seated next to her in the vacant waiting room. It was a separate room from the initial check-in area, chairs lining every inch of available wall space and a TV in the corner playing the news on mute. For the insanely high fees Skye was going to pay to have Ozzy cared for, she would have thought the waiting area for anxious owners might have been a little more comforting. Instead, there were white walls, slate tiles, and a few old magazines on the coffee table in the middle of the room.

She bit the insides of her cheeks, staring at the door. Not being able to see what was happening to her little man made her feel more helpless than she already did, but when she tried to stand up, Cole gently nudged her back into her seat.

"They know what they're doing," he told her, his voice kind as he wrapped an arm around her shoulders. "Just let them do their job. You won't be allowed in the x-ray room anyway, and Ozzy might start to stress if he sees you."

Just hearing his name brought tears to her eyes, but she wiped them away hastily; Skye had been enough of a blubbering baby already, but she couldn't help it. Something had been off with Oz for the last few days, but since he had been eating, drinking, and using the litterbox, her vet had told her just to keep an eye on him and don't panic. He had seemed fine when she left for work that morning, and after a ten-hour shift that included an event with a nude art installation that ran late, Skye had just wanted to go home and curl up in bed with him.

But when her little ball of white fluff hadn't been at the door to greet her, she'd known something was wrong. She had eventually found him in the laundry closet, curled up in a corner. His body hung limp when she picked him up, prompting Skye to burst into tears and call Cole.

A half hour later, with a *lot* consoling and sweet-talking on Cole's part to keep her from spiraling into worst-case scenarios, here they were. The emergency veterinary hospital was located on the other side of the Coral Bay suburbs, and because they had been the only ones there at the time, Oz had seen a vet right away. In the exam, Oz had been dubbed dehydrated and lethargic, and the vet seemed to think he had eaten something that didn't agree with him. When they were asked if it was okay to do x-rays, Cole had agreed right away and told Skye he would cover the costs.

"We'll rule out everything," he had insisted. So, there they were, waiting, hoping the veterinarian would find the source of Ozzy's pain. Skye had managed to stop crying by the time they went in for the exam, but Cole had had to check them in at the front desk when they first arrived. Even though she hadn't come to any lasting decisions about what she wanted to do with their relationship, Skye was beyond grateful to have him there beside her, and would remember it forever.

She slumped down in her seat, casting Cole an appreciative look before letting him take her hand.

"I'm sorry I'm such a mess," she muttered, watching his thumb sweep over her skin in slow, even strokes. "I didn't think I would be. I thought I'd know exactly what to do whenever Oz got sick, but..."

"Well, now you'll know for next time," Cole insisted with a little half-smile. "We're all a bit of a disaster the first time we go through a crisis. Don't worry about it now. I'm here to pick up the slack."

She nodded, all the while knowing she'd still be embarrassed tomorrow morning about just how emotional the situation had made her. Still. Skye loved her silly, fluffy, pampered cat. He was family, and he was hurting. She would question herself if she hadn't been an emotional wreck.

The doors from the main reception area flew open suddenly, and both she and Cole's heads snapped in their direction. In strode Finn, dressed in a dapper tuxedo with the bowtie hanging loose and the top buttons of his shirt undone. He swept across the room, headed straight for her, and Skye found she didn't have the emotional energy to get wrapped up in the fact that both Cole and Finn were here together. All of her feelings were compartmentalized for Oz, though she still blushed furiously when Finn swooped down, cupped her face, and kissed her hard on the lips before taking a seat in the chair on the other side of her.

"How are you?" he asked, his hand on her knee, charcoal-black eyes darting from her to Cole and back again. "How is he? Where is he? What's happening?"

"They're taking him for x-rays," Cole replied, perhaps sensing that Skye couldn't. "The vet thinks he ingested a foreign body that's causing his stomach some trouble. They should be back momentarily."

"Oh, Skye, I'm sorry." Finn gave her knee a little squeeze—all the while Cole continued to hold her hand. Skye looked between them, mildly dumbfounded that they were both there for her, offering physical comfort. Other men who had been sleeping with the same woman might have taken a swing at each other first.

"I... I'm just worried about Oz," she managed with a sniffle, and Finn nodded, eyes oozing such open, raw affection that it actually revived her dormant butterflies.

"Of course you are." Finn tucked her hair behind her ear, sighing. "I'm sure he'll be just fine. My sister adopted a kitten for her daughter last month, and the little bugger gets into everything. They're quite resilient."

Cole chuckled. "Siobhan finally caved?"

"She paid two thousand dollars for one of those hypoallergenic breeds, but yes, Odette *finally* has her very own cat."

"Cheeky thing."

"She's been laying on the charm for months."

"That niece of yours..."

"Master manipulator, I agree."

Skye looked between the men on either side of her, brow slightly furrowed, and listened to their easy back-and-forth about Finn's family. Either they were really good actors, or they genuinely had no animosity about the predicament the trio found themselves in. She nibbled her lower lip and inhaled deeply, finding herself relaxing at the sounds of their voices. Somehow, having both of them there felt...*right*?

Clearing her throat, Skye scooted to the edge of her chair, forcing Finn's hand off her knee and releasing Cole's in the process. It shouldn't feel right to be in love with two men; it wasn't fair to either of them, but now wasn't the time to think about it. Her baby was on the other side of that off-limits door, with strangers, feeling like shit. Boy drama could wait. Skye threaded her hands together and rested her chin on them, elbows on her knees, and looked at the door like it might magically open if she stared hard enough.

Cole and Finn's conversation hiccupped briefly when she withdrew, but it picked up moments later, softly, and Skye found herself appreciating the background noise. If she were here alone, in silence, there would be nothing to keep her panicky thoughts at bay.

Ten minutes later, Cole's phone shrieked, piercing the easy quiet so abruptly that Skye jumped. She glanced back and found him fumbling to get it out—only to reject the call and shove it back in his pocket. Their eyes met, and he shook his head when she raised a curious eyebrow.

Huh. That was a first.

His phone rang twice more a few minutes later, after Finn had started massaging the back of Skye's neck, the trio sitting in a companionable silence. Each time, Cole rejected it, but Skye could see the tension in his jaw after the third one. Sitting up, she set a hand on his thigh and told him to just answer it.

"No, it's not important—"

"Cole," she said, meeting his gaze firmly, "it's okay. You can answer if you need to. If it wasn't important, they wouldn't keep calling at..." A quick glance at the clock hanging near the TV made her groan. "Midnight."

"I..." His phone went off again, and Skye managed a genuine smile, one she actually meant.

"Really. Go answer it."

He hesitated a few seconds longer, letting the phone ring on in his hand, before leaning forward and planting a hasty kiss on her cheek. "Thank you. I'll be one minute, I promise."

"It's fine," she told him as he hurried out the room, smothering a tired laugh at the sound of him snapping a *What?!* to whoever was on the other end. If Finn hadn't been there, she might not have been so receptive to him taking a phone call. However, Skye could tell from Cole's body language, from the tightness of his voice, that he didn't *want* to take it. The change from what he might have done a month ago was startling.

"Must be important," Finn commented as he cracked his neck, tossing his head side to side casually. "We're both taking some time off from work this week."

"I'm sure it is." Work always was, after all. She offered

Finn a small smile, her hand on his forearm. "Thank you for being here. You really didn't have to come—"

"Don't be ridiculous," he said brusquely.

"Seriously. Oz isn't your cat. I wouldn't expect you to—"

"I'm here for *you*, Skye." Finn grinned, her butterflies doing big, arcing loops at the sight. "Cole called me while he was driving to your place. There's nowhere else I'd rather be than right here with both of you. Honestly."

Both of you. There it was again—a reference to multiple people, like all three of them were in a relationship. Skye swallowed hard, deftly dodging the implication and tucking it away for later.

"Well, I appreciate it." She drew a breath, about to ask him where he had been when Cole called—based on the tux, it also seemed important—but the reappearance of the vet technician from earlier shut her right up. She stood as the woman in puppy-patterned orange scrubs held the door open, her expression giving Skye hope for good news.

"We're all finished back here," the technician remarked, nodding to the hallway behind her. "Oz did great. Why don't you come and have a chat with the vet?"

Skye hurried forward, only to stop when she realized Cole wasn't back yet. She looked to the door he had stormed through minutes earlier, then shook her head and went on without him. Finn grabbed her hand once she crossed into the sterile-smelling hallway that led to the exam rooms, slowing her frantic pace slightly. However, before they had taken more than five steps , Cole came stumbling through the heavy metal off-limits door, catching it just before it swung closed.

"Is everything okay?" she asked as he marched toward her, then let out a muffled squeal when his lips collided shamelessly with hers. His hand pressed to her lower back, holding her there, and her butterflies turned into fireworks, crackling and spinning about inside.

"Everything's great," he said somewhat breathlessly when he pulled back, nodding. "Perfect. Let's go see our little man, shall we?"

She caught Finn and Cole exchanging quick, unreadable looks over her head, both suddenly grinning like idiots, and then noticed the vet tech gawking at all three of them. Cheeks red, Skye met the woman's eye and cleared her throat, prompting her to resume leading them down the hall to the exam room, where hopefully the vet was waiting with good news about her fluffy furbaby.

21

ALL IN

Skye awoke the following morning feeling like she'd been hit by a truck. Groaning, she rubbed her forehead, her eyes swollen from crying so excessively the night before.

It quickly became apparent that all her discomfort stemmed from the fact that she wasn't sleeping in her bed. Her eyes flew open. No, she had fallen asleep on the couch —with Cole and Finn on either side of her, pressed up against the armrests on each end, both of them snoring softly. She sat up, careful not to jostle either of them. Her head had been resting on Cole's thigh, while her legs were tossed over Finn's hip; both men looked incredibly squished in their current positions, and she knew they'd feel just as shitty as she did when they finally came to.

Unable to ignore the call of the toilet for long, she gingerly extracted herself from the strange sleeping situation, then tiptoed across the apartment to her bedroom. Once there, she stripped out of last night's work clothes— also not conducive for a great sleep—and took care of what she needed to in the bathroom. Teeth brushed. Face washed. Hair combed and thrown up in a bun. Skye grabbed the frilly pink booty shorts she occasionally slept in and slipped those on, followed by the oversized T-shirt of kitten Oz that was hanging on the towel rack. Without a bra beneath it, the old tee was nearly see-through, but she was too wrecked from last night to care.

Studying herself in the mirror, she found a small smile spreading across her lips at the sight of kitten Ozzy staring back at her, a baby blue bow around his neck. Her darling little man was currently recuperating from a bout of acute gastritis at the veterinary hospital. Apparently, the x-ray had showed a bit of ribbon in his stomach, and when the vet told her, Skye had been mortified—because she'd known instantly it was her fault Ozzy was in so much pain.

A few days ago, Cole's assistant had dropped off a mountain of gifts for Oz's birthday, a gesture that Skye had taken seriously to heart regarding her future romantic relationship with the man. Oz had played in the wrapping paper, chased the ribbons around as Skye dragged them across the couch, and turned into a crazy stoner cat after rolling around in all the expensive catnip. When they had finished celebrating, Skye had cleaned up, put all the toys and whatnot away, and that was the end of it.

Oz must have found a ribbon worth eating behind her back, and that had triggered all his issues. Cole had also been horrified, and had immediately blamed himself for using ribbons on the gifts. There had been a bit of back-and-forth between them about who was *more* at fault, each of them blaming themselves as the vet and his technician stood by awkwardly, until Finn shut the whole argument down by stating they both were and weren't to blame for what had happened. It'd been a horrible accident, but Oz was going to be okay. That was all that mattered.

While the vet had insisted she could take Oz home that night, Cole and Finn argued the man into a corner, insisting Ozzy be kept for observation with the *finest* care available. Skye watched, hugging her baby with his little IV to her chest, as both men pushed for all the upgrades, top-dollar charges—*whatever* was necessary to ensure that Oz had someone constantly watching him for the next two days, or until the ribbon safely passed. While the situation had been a bit tense with all of Cole and Finn's demands, it was clear the vet technicians assigned to Oz would take great care of her baby. In the morning, they'd planned to call her actual veterinarian and get him up to speed on things.

So, after all those tears, Oz was going to be fine. Still, Skye couldn't resist contacting both her vet and the emergency hospital after she got changed. Padding back out to the living room, she saw Cole rubbing his eyes, head flung over the armrest of the couch, and Finn sitting up and stretching his neck. Skye quietly dug her phone out of her purse and barricaded herself in the guest room to make all the necessary calls.

Fifteen minutes later, she had spoken to everyone she needed to. Skye had given her permission for Oz to be transferred to her normal veterinary clinic, where he would be staying in a "deluxe suite," whatever that was, for the next two days. Apparently he was eating well this morning, and her vet assured her they would call if he was ready to go home early. At no point did anyone suggest they were monitoring him for anything life-threatening, and when Skye hung up, she let out a long, much-needed sigh of relief. Phone cradled in her hands, she glanced at the closed guest room door, listening to the faint sounds of life on the other side.

Now that Oz was taken care of, she had two other

important men she needed to address. In no way was it acceptable to hide out in here until they gave up and left, so Skye took a deep breath, rolled her shoulders back, and stood. Before things had gone south with Ozzy, she'd been leaning toward listening to what Finn and Cole had to say regarding this *thing* they were all engaged in. After their support last night, she felt she owed it to both of them to at least hear them out.

When she returned to the living room, gripping her phone tightly in one hand, she found Cole filling her kettle and Finn strolling out of her bedroom, presumably having just used her bathroom. No one said a word, the silence heavy when Cole turned off the tap and set the kettle to boil. Wordlessly, the boys headed back to the couch, expressions more guarded than she would have liked, and Skye followed soon after. However, rather than settling in between them as she had last night, she pushed the coffee table out a bit and sat there.

"How's Oz?" Cole asked, the first to break the silence. Skye nodded and smiled.

"Good. He's doing really good. They're going to watch him for the next few days, but the vet thinks I'll be able to pick him up tomorrow, which is good."

"Good."

"Yeah, really good."

"Good," Finn added, smirking. Skye's cheeks warmed.

Ugh. When she thought back to last night, nothing had been awkward or tense. They'd all come back to her apartment, each one exhausted, pizza delivery on the way, and plopped down on the couch. Lacking the energy to talk, Skye had turned on the TV—and that was the last thing she remembered. They all must have fallen asleep at some point together, because they'd been in the same positions when she had woken up that morning, an empty pizza box on her kitchen island.

"Look," she started, knowing she ought to take the lead here. "Thank you for last night. I don't know what I would have done without you, either of you." Her gaze darted between Finn and Cole. "So, thanks. I really do appreciate it."

Finn dipped his head, a hint of dark bags starting to show under his eyes. "Of course. We'd do it all over again if we had to."

There it was again—*we.* Skye nibbled her lower lip, staring them both down for a moment before taking a deep breath and carrying on.

"Right. So, I think that's a good segue into...a less comfortable conversation," she said, setting her phone aside and resting her elbows on her knees. Both men, to their credit, appeared to be trying very hard to keep their eyes on her face, and not the see-through shirt with her nipples poking through or the generous amount of skin her little shorts showed off.

"It doesn't need to be uncomfortable," Finn argued lightly. "We have a proposition for you. All you have to do is hear us out."

Skye could do that. She hadn't exactly been looking forward to baring her soul and sharing just how difficult the last month had been for her without either of them in her life. So, she gestured for someone to start speaking. The pair exchanged looks, color rising in Cole's cheeks, but, much to her surprise, it was Cole who then took the lead.

"Skye," he said, clearing his throat. Her eyes dipped down to his hands, but only one pulsed in and out of a fist. She understood the physical ticks better now after their last conversation, and she tried not to stare too pointedly at it, worried her attention might make him more anxious.

Cole hesitated for a moment, then pressed both palms flat on his thighs. "Skye, I've been in love with you for...for a long time now."

She blinked, her mind clicking to out-of-signal TV static at the news. Heat crawled up her body and pooled in her cheeks, the declaration doing horrible, wonderful things to just about every bodily system. It took everything she had not to jump up and dance around her apartment, screaming gleefully. Because it wasn't just her and Cole in this conversation. Skye shot a panicky look to Finn, worried suddenly for *his* feelings with this new revelation. He stared back, a small smile tugging at his lips, and said nothing. Swallowing hard, she brought her attention back to Cole, still trying to process the words that had just come out of his mouth.

"I..." Skye shook her head. He was in love with her. Cole *loved* her. Skye hadn't just imagined those fleeting moments subtly woven into the strands of their friendship. "You..."

"I couldn't tell you," he admitted, his hands now gripping the fabric of the grey track pants he'd been wearing since last night. "I loved what we had. You made the noise stop, if you get my meaning. You were the only person in my life who calmed me down, made me feel like *me*, and I couldn't risk it."

"But Cole—"

"I worked too much," he told her, shaking his head, his smile surprisingly sad. "We both knew it. I worked constantly, and what little time I could get with you, I wasn't about to complicate. I couldn't give you the time and attention you deserved back then. It wasn't fair to you, and

I'd never forgive myself if I took us out of our comfortable relationship, complicated things, then fucked it all up because I couldn't be there for you. It was selfish of me, and I knew that, so I gave you what I could. Everything I could, even though I knew it wasn't enough."

Overwhelmed and not trusting herself to speak, Skye moved to the couch, back to her old spot between them, and grabbed Cole's hand with both of hers. Her vision blurred as tears surfaced—happy tears, for once.

"And then you met Finn," Cole said softly, and her heart dropped into her stomach. "And he met you. I just knew... I mean, I get it. He's charming as hell. I don't blame you for falling for him." His eyes, blue like the waters after a storm, shifted to Finn for a moment. "I don't blame either of you. My two favourite people *would* fall for each other—"

"What he's trying to say," Finn interjected, his expression hedging on more amused than annoyed, "less eloquently than we practiced, is that neither of us are upset about our current situation. Both of us care for you very deeply. Cole's said it himself: he loves you. And I think I've been falling in love with you ever since I saw you standing there, covered in wine and cursing the high heavens."

Skye's face must have looked like a ripe cherry tomato. She pulled her hands back and pressed them to her cheeks, suddenly feeling so hot she couldn't stand the fact that she was wearing clothes.

"All we want is for you to be happy," Finn told her, his head cocked to the side, lips lifted in that trademark smirk that made her heart skip a beat. "We want to *make* you happy. Together."

Skye wanted to take the time to properly mull over every word in this conversation, but she couldn't get her brain to *work*. She couldn't think. She couldn't process. All she could do was feel. And how she felt—it was oddly wonderful, yet she couldn't trust that feeling. Not yet. Not until her logic caught up with her emotions.

"I don't understand," she stammered, looking between them.

"I've agreed to pull back considerably from the company," Cole said, his voice catching as he did. "I've hired a load of new people to take over some of my responsibilities, but I'll still be working. I'll be traveling frequently, but Finn has decided to make Coral Bay his home base. If you'll have us, together, I think we can have something fantastic here."

"You don't have to make a decision," Finn insisted as the pieces started to finally fall into place in her mind. "You don't have to choose between us. Neither of us want that for you."

"So," Skye said slowly, her eyes narrowing, "I'd be in a relationship with both of you?" When they each nodded, she cleared her throat. "Okay. And you two would be what, exactly, to each other?"

Cole flushed at the question, and Finn burst out laughing.

"Well, we're not dating each other, if that's what you're asking," Finn said, his eyes positively twinkling when they met hers. "We thought of it as you being with each of us individually, but the three of us will have a mutual relationship built on, I don't know, trust, communication, and understanding. All that feel-good stuff. No pettiness between Cole and I, no jealousy."

Skye opened and closed her mouth for a moment, then sat back and crossed her arms. Never in her life had she considered dating *two* men before, much less two men who were somehow a part of, yet distinct, inside one relationship bubble. Her gut reaction was to call it taboo and kick them both out of the apartment, but her heart preached patience. After all, despite her best efforts, she couldn't stop thinking about either of them. That *had* to be love. They had strengths and weaknesses that complemented one another; it wasn't that they each added up to form one perfect man, but that she could see herself being happy with both—*and* making them both happy in return.

"Finn and I have put a lot of thought and discussion into the dynamics of the relationship," Cole told her after the silence dragged on for longer than was comfortable. "Of course, we would want your input."

Her eyebrows shot up. "Oh, really? I get a say? How considerate of you two."

"Naturally," Finn said, smirking from the other end of the couch. "If Cole and I are going to be your harem, your input is essential."

Both men chuckled as her cheeks prickled with heat, and Skye pressed her palms back to her face, a rush of emotions making it difficult to think straight. Embarrassment. Flattery. Confusion. Affection. Desire. She wasn't sure how the conversation made her feel, but she didn't want to run—that had to be a good thing.

The idea of Cole cutting back at work so they could be together was touching, but she didn't want him to give up his passions for the sake of the relationship. And the fact that Finn was so ready to dive into such a unique situation just to be with her made her heart skip a beat; she just couldn't fathom *why* such an eligible guy would throw away the dating scene just for her.

But here they were, dead serious despite their brief bout of the giggles, asking her to give love a chance with *both* of them.

"So, okay." She took a deep breath, filling her lungs and calming her giddy energy as she exhaled slowly. "I think I want to give it a try." Skye ignored the way they grinned at her like she was the Christmas present they'd been waiting their whole lives to unwrap. "It will take some time."

"Of course," Cole remarked.

"Trial and error," Finn added with a nod. Skye licked her lips, still overwhelmed but slowly easing herself into the moment.

"I mean, all the feelings are out on the table," she said, more to herself than to them, "and you're telling me I essentially get to have the cake I love and eat it too?"

Cole shifted closer, stretching his arm out along the back of the couch, their thighs bumping against each other. "That's one way to put it, I suppose."

"Though I object to being referred to as a baked good," Finn said as Skye smiled so wide her cheeks hurt. He picked some cat hair off his stark-white dress shirt. "You couldn't have found a proverb involving chocolate? For fuck's sake, Skye. I expected better from you."

She gave him a good-natured smack on his muscular thigh, then looked to Cole. A part of her still couldn't believe that he would be okay with all this, especially after everything they had been through together. In love for years. Best friends. And he had no qualms sharing her?

Their eyes met, yet she saw nothing but raw openness, honesty, and brazen affection staring back at her. No jaw clench. No nail-clacking. No fists. His smile melted her heart, and, unable to stop herself, she leaned in for a kiss. Gentle innocence tinged with heat. Skye wanted to collapse into that kiss and never resurface. His fingers threaded through her hair after he tugged it out of its messy bun, but just as they started to give in to each other, falling into an easy rhythm, Skye pulled away, a hand on his chest. Beneath her palm, Cole's heart hammered, loud and true, and for the first time, she felt with every ounce of her being that it beat for her.

Skye scrambled to catch her breath, flustered, and turned now to Finn, expecting the worst. However, rather than finding even a flicker of jealousy in those dark eyes, she saw a burning desire that would have knocked her on her ass if they were standing.

He started to close the distance, holding her gaze as he prowled across the couch, the electricity between them making the hairs on her arms stand up. However, just as Finn's supple lips threatened to claim hers, one of those awful bark-laughs slipped out before she could stop it, and Skye buried her face in her hands, mortified.

"I'm so sorry," she moaned. "I don't know how to do this with both of you here..."

"It takes some practice," she heard Cole murmur, his hand on her knee and his words dripping with a husky authority that she had only heard twice from him before—and both times he'd been buried between her thighs. She peeked up, her embarrassment ebbing, and found Finn's smoldering gaze once more. He cupped her cheek, breath hot against her skin, and grinned.

"Not to worry," he purred. "We'll be happy to show you the ropes."

"As many times as you need." Cole's hand wandered along her leg, then slipped between her thighs. "Thoroughly."

"After all," Finn's grin turned positively *scandalous* as Skye gasped, startled by Cole cupping her suddenly aching sex, "practice certainly makes perfect."

His mouth captured hers with a surprising degree of

tenderness, and Skye's eyelashes fluttered somewhat as she closed her eyes, falling headfirst into the kiss. Gone was her shyness, her fear. Finn gave her courage, his tongue sweeping over hers as he deepened the kiss. Leaning back against Cole, his toned body supporting hers like she weighed nothing, Skye found comfort. One hand tentatively touched Finn's forearm, her fingertips grazing his warm skin, while the other reached back and fisted in Cole's shirt. A moan slipped from her lips, contained between her and Finn, when Cole started to massage her sex.

Her body wasn't entirely sure how to react, all her sensors on overdrive as Finn's mouth devoured hers, the tenderness slipping away bit by agonizing bit, replaced with a firestorm that made her toes curl. Meanwhile, a pleasurable tightness knotted in her core, streaks like lightning flashing across her body every time Cole's fingers circled her swollen clit.

For the first time in a long time, she didn't find the moment spoiled by aching thoughts, the kind that sprang up at the least opportune moments—their sole purpose to kill the mood. In fact, as her hand wrapped around Finn's wrist and her hips bucked up against Cole's hand, Skye found she had no thoughts—zero. Her mind was blank, trapped in a haze of pleasurable fog that she never wanted to lift. Skye just *existed*. No past. No future. All that mattered was the present, and she sank deeper into it when Cole pushed the soaked fabric of her little sleep shorts aside and slipped a finger into her with ease.

Skye cried out and tore her mouth from Finn's, eyes clenched shut as Cole pumped in and out of her, massaging her inner walls just as ruthlessly as he'd worked her clit. Teeth raked along her jaw, and she tipped her head back as

Finn nibbled and sucked his way down her exposed throat, his hands paving the path across her body for his mouth to follow.

She whimpered, feeling both hopelessly trapped between both men and wildly aroused at the very idea, and clutched at clothing, hers and theirs, desperate to truly *feel* each of them. Before she could make her demands known, Cole's talented fingers slipped back up to tease her aching bud again, circling around it and gently swiping over it, her body twitching with each brush of his thumb.

Finn, meanwhile, had worked his way down to where he knelt on the floor, and Skye lifted her hips obligingly, cheeks hot, as he grabbed her shorts and tugged them off. Cole's hand finally left her, questing under her shirt to grasp her breast, cupping and kneading it, his breath a soft, dangerous hiss in her ear. Her body spasmed again; the cool air washing over her dripping sex paired with the almost too-exquisite bite of Cole's fingers plucking at her nipple, pearled to a stiff peak.

"*Christ*," Finn groaned, and she dragged her gaze down to watch those onyx eyes blaze a searing-hot trail up her legs and to her center, "you're such a stunning creature..."

"Perfect," Cole agreed, catching Skye under her chin and dragging her back for a fiery kiss just as Finn licked a trail up her inner thigh. She whimpered against Cole's mouth, suddenly a little unsure of where to put her hands—or what to even *do* with them. At the feel of Finn's tongue sweeping over her slick folds, Skye threaded one hand through his hair, and the other lifted to graze Cole's clean-shaven cheek.

Although half her mind refused to be distracted from the torturously slow fucking of Finn's tongue, in and out of her, while he lazily circled her clit with his thumb, Skye couldn't ignore the hardness pressing into her back for much longer. After Finn dragged her hips further over the edge of the couch, adjusting the angle just right so that Skye was squirming and moaning up against his mouth like a cat in heat, she managed to get just enough focus together to reach back and tug Cole's track pants down. While their positioning worked better for Finn, his mouth absolutely ravenous as he plundered her, pushing her closer and closer to the brink of ecstasy, she found it difficult to lose herself in Cole's kiss, the strain on her neck too much. As her hand delved into her former sugar daddy's boxers, he cradled her neck with one hand, allowing her to relax against him, and shifted about for better access to her mouth.

An embarrassing squeak slipped out of Skye's mouth when a pair of Finn's fingers delved into her, picking up where Cole had left off along her inner walls while his mouth focused solely on her clit. Her hand tightened in his hair. Her toes curled. She fumbled with Cole's cock, pumping up and down in uneven strokes as he groaned into her mouth. It was too much. Too much to focus on. Too much pleasure. Skye felt like she was about to both burst and fold in on herself, like a star, simultaneously dying and exploding into a thousand pieces of cosmic matter. She wanted to *give* just as much as she received, but with two men showering her with more affection than she'd ever known, it was downright impossible to keep up.

Determined, she slowed her hand, focusing on the velvety-smooth head of Cole's cock, savoring the way he twitched beneath her, his mouth lifting from hers as he threw his head back.

"Fuck..."

Skye licked her lips; she loved the sound of vulgarity rolling off his tongue. However, before she could lose herself in it, before she could smear the glistening liquid down to the base of his shaft, Finn found the *perfect* spot with those two lovely fingers of his. She lurched forward slightly, and her legs would have flailed about if Finn hadn't kept them thrown over his annoyingly clothed shoulders.

"W-wait," she whimpered, suddenly *too* overwhelmed in the moment, too caught up. "Finn, I..."

Cole threaded his fingers through her hair and dragged her back into a kiss just as the levies burst. The floodgates broke, and a tidal wave of a climax washed over her with such force that she saw spots. Skye lost all control, spiraling out as pleasure pounded her body, leaving a trail of heat fluttering down from her cheeks to her navel. Slowly, both men eased away, Cole allowing her to gasp for air and Finn leaving her trembling and drenched in her own arousal, sitting back on his heels.

"Oh my god." Skye pressed a hand to her forehead, flustered—and bouncing back for more faster than she might have expected. She sat up somewhat, still unsteady, and looked between them. "Okay, I feel like you guys have done this before."

"You've only got a bit of catching up to do," Cole told her, tracing her blush down her cheeks, to her neck, and then fingering the neckline of her T-shirt. Finn smirked, and when he stood, she caught his very prominent erection straining beneath his dress pants.

"Not to worry," he said. "We'll be sure to get you up to speed as soon as possible."

"Arrogant dicks," Skye muttered, laughing when the men—*her* men—exchanged quick looks.

"Oh, you have no idea," Finn purred, leaning down and helping her to her feet. He slowly turned her so that she faced Cole on the couch, his hands planted squarely on her hips, lips brushing her ear as he said, "Do you want to stop?"

She swallowed hard, her heart skipping a beat and her sex clenching with need. "No."

"Good." He lifted her shirt up and over her head, then tossed it aside. "Just what we wanted to hear."

With her lower lip caught between her teeth, she stood there, waiting, struggling to ignore the heat in Cole's eyes as he drank in her naked body. Wordlessly, Finn guided her onto the couch, and Cole followed suit, shuffling back to give them more space. On her knees, she accepted a quick, deep, earthshattering kiss from Finn, feeling like putty in his hands, tasting herself on his tongue, before he had her facing Cole again. With a hand on her lower back, Finn eased her downward, and Skye set to work on freeing Cole from his briefs, his cock straining to get back to her. However, before she could lean down and take the silky-smooth head in her mouth, he caught her by the chin and dragged her into another kiss.

Skye moaned as Cole cupped each breast, every swipe of his thumb over her nipple sending a jolt straight to the crux of her thighs. Behind her, she heard Finn dealing with his belt and zipper, and she pulled away from Cole with a soft shudder at what was to come.

They all moved as if by instinct—a first in Skye's sexual history, but she wasn't about to complain. Even if Cole and Finn *had* done this before with another woman, she still didn't mind. What mattered was that they were there with her now, and that they both cared deeply for her, their feelings mirroring hers with perfect harmony. No wonder this was so easy. With the love there, they couldn't go wrong.

Well, metaphorically, anyway. There was probably still

a learning curve for her to tackle when it came to handling two men, but for the time being, she went on instinct. She didn't think. She just *did*.

Slowly, she trailed her tongue along Cole's solid length, going from top to bottom and back up again to swirl around the tip. He groaned, hands clenching in and out of fists before he threaded one through her hair and rested the other behind his head. Behind her, Finn teased her entrance, first with his fingers, sliding forward to play with her clit just enough to make her squirm, then with the head of his shaft. She moaned as she took Cole in her mouth and arched her hips back, eager, her cheeks warming at the sound of Finn's dark chuckle.

She was just about halfway down Cole's cock, adjusting to the size of him, her hand at its base, when Finn gripped her hips and thrust into her. With her mouth full, her sounds were muffled, and she dug the fingertips of her free hand into Cole's side, eyes clenched shut as Finn filled her. When Finn's hips bumped into her backside, she risked opening her eyes—only to find Cole watching her with a blazing, heavy-lidded stare, lips slightly parted, utterly transfixed.

At Finn's murmured inquiry as to how she was doing, Skye merely nodded, sliding up Cole's cock and gasping for air. Over her shoulder, she caught the bastard grinning, his hands finding their bearings on her hips.

"Good," he purred before almost pulling out completely and pounding back into her. She whimpered his name, watching him take her steadily, firmly, but never harshly. In total control, he pumped in and out of her, each delicious thrust enticing her body back to the brink again, her senses primed for pleasure.

At a slight tug of her hair from Cole, she returned her

attention to his cock, taking him in as much as she could, her fist sliding up and down, their eyes locked together. It was a challenge to maintain her pace, as she found herself getting lost in Finn's skilled handling of her, but Cole managed to keep her as focused as she could be, his hand in her hair, hips bucking slightly to meet her mouth.

As she edged closer to another life-changing orgasm, her men seemed to share an unspoken conversation over the top of her head. Suddenly, Finn pulled out of her, then hoisted her up and respositioned her so that she was sitting on top of Cole. Four hands worked her body, rearranging, lifting, maneuvering, until Skye was sliding down Cole's cock, an incoherent jumble of nonsense rushing from her lips. Cole kept still as she let her body adjust to all the changes, her sex tightening around him, pleasure rippling out from her core with every exquisite clench. Finn, meanwhile, cupped her face and brought it to his almost painfully hard shaft, and she engulfed the tip, adding some pressure behind her lips, without a word. He cursed softly, sliding in and out in shallow strokes, half using her fist at his base, half relying on his own tempo to find his pleasure.

When Skye glanced up, she saw the strain in his neck, his flushed face, his gritted teeth. Within moments, he stiffened and spilled himself into her, and she scrambled to swallow every last bit—because that was *not* dripping onto her couch, thank you very much.

"Sorry," he murmured, stepping away on unsteady legs when he finished, offering an apologetic smile as he stumbled back to the couch. "I'm usually better at giving a bit of a warning..."

"Skye has that effect on men," Cole teased, nipping at her neck as he dragged her back against him. "Haven't you noticed yet?"

"My tutor always said I was a slow learner."

"Ahh, so that's what it is—"

"Oh my god." Skye looked between them, laughing. "Can we *not* with the witty banter right now?"

Finn slumped back into the couch, chuckling, and ran a hand through his hair before letting out a sigh that could only be described as wholly content. Ready with a barb of her own about letting her climax wane, she was about to turn back when Cole curled a hand loosely around her neck, pinning her against him, and started to thrust. Hard. Skye cried out, eyes wide before clenching shut, surrendering to the instant bliss of being truly *taken* by the man she loved.

When his fingers found their way back to her clit, settling in as if coming home, Skye was gone, lost to the pleasure as her second climax hit hard and fast. Warmth bloomed within her core, then radiated out, seeping into every muscle. Unable to kiss Cole as she wanted to, Skye managed to plant a quick nibble on his jaw, and Cole quickened his thrusts, his hand tightening slightly around her throat as his pace stuttered off and he groaned, mouth clamped down on her shoulder.

Panting, they gingerly untwined, Cole's pulsing cock still buried deep inside Skye as he propped her up and massaged the back of her neck. When she found Finn unabashedly watching, his mouth twisted in that scandalous grin again, all she could do was smile shyly back.

"You're beautiful when you come," he told her, words tinted with renewed interest. She swallowed hard when he lifted her chin with the tip of one finger, as if to admiring the hot flush coating her skin.

"And you're sweaty when you come," she said after a moment of letting him have his fill, reaching forward, lingering tendrils of pleasure crawling through her from where she and Cole still joined, to wipe at his slightly shiny forehead. "You're a mess, Finn Rai."

"Suppose we'd better get me cleaned up then." He shuffled to the edge of the couch. "Cole... Is that shower of hers big enough for three people?"

"Five, probably."

"Well, let's not get ahead of ourselves."

"In due time, I suppose."

"Oh my god, *stop*," Skye said, groaning as both of them smirked down at her, a little too pleased with themselves. It couldn't be good for a man's ego to appear quite that smug, but before she could say anything to deflate the look on either of them, they were already moving. Cole scooped her up as he stood, and Finn followed them to the bathroom, his dark gaze promising more than Skye suspected she could handle in a single morning.

But she was certainly willing to try.

THE END

ALL IN TRILOGY: AFTER THE END

Exclusive content for your eyes only! Catch up with the trio after *the end*.

22

PARTY FOUL

"You never manage to get your tie right on the first try, do you?"

Cole lifted his frustrated stare to the bathroom mirror, and it softened when he spied the love of his life leaning in the doorway. Skye Summers cocked her head to the side, lips spread in a smile that always made him feel like he was the only man in the world. Wearing a navy blue A-line dress, shoulders bare and the wavy hem stopping just above her knee, she was an absolute vision—but then again, Skye was also a vision wearing nothing at all, her hair mussed and not a speck of makeup to be found. Tonight, however, her coppery waves had been drawn up in a bouncy ponytail, and her eyelids shimmered with a black smoky-eye look that was *most* alluring. No shoes yet, Cole noted as he turned and openly admired her, but he knew she had a pair of black heels waiting at the front door of what was once his personal, private Coral Bay beach bungalow.

Now, however, it housed not only Cole, but Finn and Skye as well, each with their own bedroom. Oh, and not to mention Ozzy, who had claimed every bookshelf, shelving unit, and window as his own.

And Mason, the labradoodle Skye and Finn had surprised Cole with two months ago after the pair had attended some animal welfare fundraiser. Apparently there had been dogs to adopt, and neither had the willpower to say no. So, what had once been a quiet, peaceful villa overlooking the Pacific was now a chaotic, noise-filled home on a good day.

A year into their polyamorous threesome, Cole wouldn't have it any other way.

"This isn't the first time I've attempted to tie it, no," he agreed, leaning back against the large double-sink-laden countertop. Skye strolled in, hands clasped behind her back, and only stopped when her jutted hips pressed up against his, lips pursed in a deliriously sexy pout.

"Oh, I know," she mused, her hands wandering up his chest, smoothing his pressed dress shirt before gripping the crisp collar. "What is it? Fourth? Fifth? What kind of knot were you even attempting?"

Cole's cheeks warmed as she started to undo the damn thing hanging pathetically around his neck—navy, to match her dress. Finn's was the same.

"It's a Windsor knot," he said weakly, and she snorted, eyes fixed on the task at hand.

"A Windsor it is *not*."

Lower lip caught between her teeth, Skye readjusted the material length, her whole body involved in the act of retying his tie. Cole swallowed hard, unable to stop himself from responding to her little wiggles, their hips fitted snugly together. As she looped one side of the tie around the other, she risked a quick, saucy glance up—then had the audacity to ever so gently grind herself against him.

"Skye..." he warned, but it was too late. Skye had a knack for getting him hard with just a *look*, and that wasn't changing anytime soon.

"What?" she asked with an innocent flutter of her lashes. "Are you okay?"

He bit the insides of his cheeks, a mental image of bending her over the counter, hiking up that dress, and spanking her until she begged him to fuck her flashing across his mind. They'd done it before, much to the satisfaction of both parties involved—and she knew *exactly* what she was doing.

"You..." He closed his eyes when she ground against him once more, this time slowly, sensually, no longer attempting to hide her little game.

"There. Perfect," she whispered, and suddenly her body was gone. Cole's eyes snapped open, and he found her holding the end of his now perfectly knotted tie, her eyes twinkling mischievously. Before he could chastise her, more than capable of taking the *tone* that made her wet and wanting, she slid her hand up the tie, gripped the exceptional Windsor-style knot, and dragged him in for a kiss. Cole went willingly, happily surrendering to the feel of her hot mouth against his, to the way she opened herself for him with the softest, most exquisite little moan. Groaning, he hoisted her up, hands dipping beneath her dress to cup a bare backside.

While he'd already been at half-mast with her previous flirtations, he found himself standing at full salute when he realized she was wearing one of those barely-there pairs of panties. Just a slip in the front, a thin string in the back—perfect for pushing aside or ripping off in the heat of the moment. Both he and Finn had spent a fortune on underwear in the last year because they couldn't stop tearing them off her.

He set Skye down on the counter, his hand locking around the base of her ponytail as he dragged her closer, their kiss deepening so that he could properly *devour* her. It didn't matter that they were expected, dressed and proper, for some function in half an hour. Cole would skip every party, every gala, to spend an evening in bed with Skye.

A growl vibrated in his chest when she nipped at his lower lip—*hard*, the misbehaving little minx—and pulled away. Breathless, she leaned back against the mirror, her pointed toes wandering up and down the backs of his thighs.

"I was only visiting to tell you the car will be here in five minutes," she admitted with a smirk, her cheeks flushed the same rosy pink that always made his heart melt. "And now I have to redo my makeup. How *dare* you..."

Cole watched, dumbstruck, as she slid off the counter, cheekily licking his chin along the way, and then stroked his painfully erect cock.

"You should probably do something about that," she told him, her grin turned wicked. "We don't want to cause a scandal, do we?"

Cole gritted his teeth as she slunk by, wanting to yank her back and properly discipline her for the whole show, but knowing she was right. Cole and Finn had pledged a lot of money to the heart and stroke research center being honored tonight, especially after Finn's father had had his first heart attack earlier this year. He couldn't bail on it—not because he wanted to fuck Skye well into the night, anyway. Not *quite* a valid reason.

Still. Her little stunt had been downright *cruel*.

"*You* should do something about that," he growled at her

retreating form, and she scampered out of his en-suite bathroom with a giggle. Exhaling sharply, Cole stared down at his tented trousers. Well, he wasn't about to rub one out less than five minutes before their ride showed up. So, grumbling to himself, Cole focused on deep breathing and as many non-sexy thoughts as he could, hands on the counter and head hanging. By the time he was finished, his little problem had *mostly* disappeared, but he wouldn't forget it. Skye needed to be *dealt* with. And soon.

After a quick mirror check, his hair in place and face clean-shaven, he re-tucked his dress shirt into his trousers, then stalked out of the bathroom, catching the light switch on the way. Mason, six years old and adorably large, lay sprawled out across Cole's bed, his favourite place in the whole house. As soon as Cole looked at the labradoodle, that huge tail started thumping, and he couldn't resist going in for a cuddle.

"Did you see what your mummy did, Mason?" Cole cooed, crawling across the bed and giving the dog a thorough ruffling. Mason rolled onto his back, tongue lolling out as his tail continued to wag. "Isn't she cruel? Yes, we'll need to deal with her, won't we? Won't we?"

He glanced back at the door and cleared his throat. Finn was merciless about the way Cole babied Mason, especially after he'd made such a stink about not being consulted when Finn and Skye brought him home. Now, however, he couldn't imagine their lives without the loveable oaf.

"Car's here." Finn's voice echoed from somewhere, likely the front door, and Cole dragged himself away from the dog with another soft sigh. After quickly dusting his pants off, he grabbed his wallet, phone, and, just in case, two condoms from his bedside stash.

As he'd suspected, he found Finn standing in the foyer,

lint-rolling his pants as Ozzy continued to wind himself around his legs.

"I just did that leg," the man grumbled, gently pushing the cat away before hastily rolling off the white fur. The cat's tail flicked from side to side before he plopped down by Finn's feet, belly up.

"Well, that's a trap if I've ever seen one," Cole said, chuckling. The giant fluffball rolled over to face him, offering him the same temptation, but Cole merely rubbed the cat's head in passing. "No one's falling for that, Oz."

"We've all learned our lesson. Never again," Finn added as he straightened and tossed the lint roller into the wicker basket Skye had added to the foyer's new table-of-crap. Keys, mail, collars, poop bags, and a whiteboard for salacious note-writing had all somehow migrated into Cole's once spotless, nearly empty front entryway. Now, his coat closet overflowed with jackets and shoes, and Skye had even ordered a new teal rug to fill the space.

He'd never lived in such a cluttered, messy house before —though neither of his partners would acknowledge the clutter *or* the mess.

"What took you so long?" Finn asked as Cole handed him his jacket, which had been hanging off the front closet door. "Thought you'd be ready before me. You started earlier."

"Skye," was Cole's only excuse, and both men slipped into their suit jackets with identical smirks.

"Ah."

"She decided to be a bit distracting."

"Yes, I know the feeling." Finn checked his cuffs, shaking his head. "She was a bit *distracting* while I was in the shower, too. And then *left*. Without finishing."

"A familiar story." Cole crossed his arms, putting the pieces together. "Someone's in a rather teasing mood today."

Finn ran a hand over his perfectly styled hair. "I think she's just excited. You know... First time all three of us are going out together."

"Right." He hadn't forgotten—Cole just hadn't thought it an occasion to celebrate, which had been his mistake. Although they had been navigating the sometimes rocky road of a ménage a trois for over a year now, tonight was the first instance where all three of them would arrive at a function together. They'd pose for press together. They'd navigate the room together. They had collectively agreed to stop hiding their relationship at Skye's somewhat emotional insistence last month, and tonight was the night they made their debut.

Although Finn's house had been larger, they had all initially agreed to move into Cole's about three months into the relationship because it offered more privacy. None of them knew how to handle the new, thrilling, unorthodox situation they'd found themselves in, and had agreed that nosy neighbours only added to the stress. So, Finn had sold his enormous manor in his gated community, stored or donated most of his antiques, and moved in with Cole and Skye. They'd kept the downtown apartment if any of them ever needed space to themselves, but thus far, neither Cole, Finn, nor Skye had made use of it. Instead, they'd decided to redecorate and use it to host family whenever they were in town.

Not wanting the press to have a field day at the start of something delicate and new, they had all agreed to keep things neutral in the public eye. Skye went out with both Cole and Finn, usually separately, and there was a collective pact to keep public displays of affection at a minimum. For some time, it had made their home life even more exciting, but both men had seen the effect it was having on Skye. She was a snuggly creature by nature, wanting to hold their hands and cuddle no matter where they were, public or private, and to be denied over and over again for the sake of "appearances" had been hard on her.

Last month, all three agreed *to hell with it*. Let the press write whatever they wanted. Let the society circles whisper. Cole was in love with her. Finn too. If she wanted to hold *both* of their hands in public, or kiss them whenever the urge struck, who were they to deny her anymore?

So, tonight was their coming out party, in a way. Cole should have realized and made more of a big deal about it. All he and Finn had done was match their suits and ties to the dress Skye had shown them earlier in the week. He frowned. This should have been a more lavish affair. Limousine. Champagne. A huge, beautiful dinner beforehand—rather than yesterday's leftovers gobbled down around the kitchen island, the three of them in sweats, chatting and laughing about their respective work days before the stylist arrived to do Skye's hair and makeup.

"I know what you're thinking," Finn told him, his tone kind. "I think she's fine with how today's gone... I think she's *frisky* because she's excited, that's all. I'm still a bit wound up myself, actually."

"Same here. Perhaps we ought to do something about it," Cole said, an idea sparking to life as he adjusted his still somewhat-snug trousers. When he heard Skye baby-talking Mason from down the hall and the dog barking back happily, Cole moved closer to Finn, his voice low. "It's a bit risky, but hear me out..."

~

Tonight, Skye's smile could outshine the sun.

Finn stood back, watching her chat with a cluster of Coral Bay's social elite like she had been born to do it. So carefree, so easy. She entertained, beguiled, and charmed everyone within a ten-foot radius of her, but no one could have her. No one but him and Cole. Holding two glasses of bubbly, Finn cast a glance across the huge hall that the organizers of tonight's event had reserved at The Starlight Inn, Coral Bay's premiere hotel for tourists without a budget. Cole had also recently been sequestered by a group of society fiends, but he looked noticeably less comfortable than Skye, a glass of untouched red wine clutched in his hand, a tense, forced smile on his lips.

If only their little ball of sunshine were standing beside him—*then* he would be at ease. As it was, they still had more work to do to make Cole a breezy society man. He'd get there. Some people really started to shine in their thirties.

Still, despite the man's stiffness at being cornered by a group of individuals Finn knew for a fact he couldn't stand, Cole was a great deal calmer now than he had been a year ago. As he'd predicted, Cole had been thrilled to finally lay all his feelings for Skye on the line. Their relationship with her was a good thing, for all three of them, but in order to make the most of it, Cole had needed to pull back from his company.

That had proved easier said than done. For the first four months of their now yearlong affair, Cole had been a bit of a disaster. Once he'd let Finn in on his anxiety issues, both Finn and Skye were able to help him transition better, but such monumental changes to his status quo had been a challenge. Luckily, there were two people who had his back through thick and thin, and he'd come out of the turbulence a better man.

Shortly after that, Finn's father had had a heart attack, and suddenly it had been Cole and Skye holding *him* up through the whole ordeal. While his father had made a swift recovery, the incident had shaken Finn to his core, and he made it a goal to visit his parents in the UK at least every other month. All that flying meant Skye was occasionally without both of her men in their shared ocean-side home, but she had been *more* than understanding—with everything, honestly. Skye had been a dream through all the ups and downs of the last year, from learning the ropes of this new dynamic, to Cole's professional crisis, to Finn's father's health scare. She had been sublime.

So, there had hardly been a discussion between Cole and Finn when she'd broken down about a month ago about the lack of public affection between the threesome. In order to keep their blossoming new relationship out of the tabloids, they had all kept their distance until they figured things out. It had damn well nearly *killed* Finn not to touch Skye in public. He could hardly keep his hands off her at home, but at the time he had understood the necessity of not bringing undue stress into the new relationships—the threesome *and* his personal relationship with Skye.

It had made him love her more when she'd eventually expressed her dismay at the whole situation. It was then all three had agreed to flip a collective middle finger to society and just *be*. So, tonight, their first official social outing as a threesome was rather important.

And seeing Skye smile that thousand-watt smile, her energy infectious and her flirtations both frustrating and endearing—Finn was over the moon. He didn't give a damn what people thought, nor would he give two shits about what the tabloids wrote regarding all three of them posing together for the event photographers when they arrived in matching navy blue attire, Skye sandwiched between Cole and Finn.

And, really, that was the norm these days. The trio had a refreshingly active sex life a year into the relationship, with Skye alternating between Cole and Finn—though mostly it was all three together. For the first time in his life, Finn had zero complaints about his sex life with a significant other.

Others. Even if he and Cole weren't romantically entangled in all this, the man was still very much a part of the relationship for Finn.

Usually he welcomed Skye taking the initiative, but the minx had gotten him all hot and bothered in the shower earlier—and hadn't *finished* what she'd started, practically bouncing off the walls because of tonight's outing. It didn't take a genius to read her moods, though he suspected Cole still struggled a bit. As adorable as her excitement was, she had been *far* too handsy before they'd left the house.

And there needed to be *consequences* for being a saucy little tease. Finn took a quick sip from his champagne flute, his grin shifting from smitten to wicked as he crossed the hall toward her.

"So sorry," he murmured as he edged into the gathering of socialites around Skye. Finn handed over her drink, which she took with a brilliant but *cheeky* little smile of her own. Clearing his throat, he raised his voice a little to catch the attention of the group as he said, "I'm afraid I need to steal her away for a moment. Excuse us..."

Hand gently cupping her elbow, Finn steered her away from the crowd, pleased to have her all to himself again. As Skye sampled the champagne, practically purring with delight, he pulled his phone out of his pocket and sent a quick, discrete text to Cole. With the message delivered, he had about ten minutes to get her exactly where they wanted her.

"Where are we going?" she asked when he guided her out of the reception hall, away from the bright lights and red décor. He had already scoped out the first floor of the hotel, but Finn merely shrugged as if to suggest he was making this up as he went along.

"Somewhere private," he rumbled as his arm snaked around her waist and tugged her against him. She giggled, champagne climbing either side of the flute, and he seized the opportunity to swoop down and press a kiss to her neck, teeth grazing the delicate skin ever so slightly.

"*Finn*," she gasped, eyes wide and cheeks red. "We *can't*."

"I won't keep you for long," he assured her, taking a sharp left toward the first-floor conference rooms. He'd already asked an attendant to unlock Conference Room C, which had a view of the pool area and the beach beyond. When the man hesitated, Finn had slipped him a fifty and promised to compensate him at the end of the night too if no one disturbed them. Money was, after all, the universal language.

When they reached the conference room in question, Skye turned and pressed herself back against the door. "Finn—"

"Just a taste," he whispered, his voice dropping to that raspy timbre he knew always drove her wild. His love's eyes sparkled with delight, lips twisting into a suggestive smirk.

"Well. I guess there's nothing wrong with a *taste*." She bit her lower lip as she fumbled behind her for the door handle, crying out in surprise when the door opened without a hitch. She stumbled back with it, and Finn moved in after her, ever the hunter, dark eyes fixed on his delectable prey.

"I think someone's a little drunk," he teased as she found her footing, closing the door gently behind them. As he'd requested, the lighting remained low, only the inner circle of pod lights over the large oval table in the center of the room lit. With the heavy tint on the windows, they were able to see the spectacular view of the gardens and the outdoor pool, twinkling strands of white lights strung up around the space like starlight—but no one could see *them*. Beyond the spectacular manmade view outside, the Pacific lapped at the empty shoreline, the hotel beach off-limits after sunset.

"Well, isn't *this* fancy?" Skye mused. She set her champagne on the table and ran a hand over the back of a leather-backed chair. She then glanced over her shoulder at him, an eyebrow arched. "I almost think you planned this, Mr. Rai."

"On the contrary, Miss Summers..." He sauntered toward her, taking slow, calculated steps—otherwise he would mount her like some savage. Although he was more than a little eager to taste her, wanting nothing more than to pop her up on the table and bury his face between her thighs, his and Cole's plan required tact. Patience. Restraint. He could adeptly switch on those qualities in just about every other area of his life when he needed to—*except* when it came to Skye Eloise Summers. He stopped within a foot of her, then pinched her chin between thumb and forefinger, enjoying the way she inhaled sharply. "I just wanted you all to myself for a few minutes. Wearing *that*, can you blame me?"

She plucked the drink from his hand and set it next to

its twin on the table. He waited, absolutely still, until she grabbed his tie and tugged him toward her.

"I suppose I can spare a few minutes," she murmured, tilting her face up toward his, the heat of her breath dancing across his lips. "Are you sure that's enough time?"

"Miss Summers, how utterly *salacious* of you." Before she could whisper something else, something that might just be his undoing, Finn hooked an arm around her waist and dragged her up against him. She giggled, the sound music to his ears, and opened herself up to him like a flower in bloom, lips parting as soon as his claimed them. Her moan made his cock stir, and it took every ounce of Finn's restraint not to throw her on the table and just have his way with her. Fuck the plan. Cole could join in if he wanted...

No. He caught her lower lip with his teeth and tugged, savoring the way her hands fisted in the material of his suit jacket. They had already worked this out. Skye didn't get to have her cake and eat it too—not today, anyway. Still, he ought to win some kind of award for his fortitude, especially when she arched against him, ground her hips up and sighed contentedly as she sought her own pleasure.

Unable to help himself, Finn found his hand delving under her dress and trailing upward to cup her, groaning when he felt her hot and wet already. As her tongue stroked his, coaxing it into her mouth, he slipped a finger under her panties, quickly realizing she had chosen a pair that were hardly more than a slip of fabric—fabric damp with her arousal at this point. He tore his mouth from hers, running it down the column of her throat as he hastily lifted the flowy material of her dress—and found a nearly bare ass staring up at him when he peered over her shoulder. He hissed, cupping one pert cheek as his teeth sank ever so slightly into the nape of her neck. Skye moaned again, bucking her hips against him.

"Fuck *me,*" Finn growled, grasping her other cheek and squeezing.

"Mmm, gladly," she purred in his ear, hands dropping to his belt. However, just as she got the buckle undone, the conference room door opened—and in walked Cole.

Just in the nick of time. Finn had to all but throw himself away from her; if the man had taken two minutes longer, he would have walked in on them going at it on the middle of that faux mahogany table.

"Took you long enough," he grumbled, doing his belt up as Cole closed the door behind him.

"Hi, you," Skye crooned, leaning back against a nearby chair, sprawled like a delectable appetizer Finn *needed* to devour. However, when Cole locked the door, her saucy little display faltered somewhat, and Finn smirked as she straightened. "What are you doing?"

"Ensuring we have a bit of privacy," Cole remarked, bright, totally sober blue eyes sweeping over Finn as he marched toward her. As soon as they darted back to Skye, however, Finn caught the change—the dark desire pooling within, the blazing heat that burned for Skye and Skye alone.

"Sounds fun," she said, the teasing edge of her tone vanishing as Cole bore down on her. Finn watched her adjust her dress, her barely-there panties, then swallow hard when Cole snatched her wrist and yanked her away from the chair. He thrust her between them, Finn towering over her even in her heels.

"It isn't going to be *fun,* sweetheart," Cole growled, closing in on her with calculated precision. Skye's body bumped into Finn, and she glanced back, eyes wide, when his full-on, albeit currently restrained, erection nudged her backside. He caught her by the hips, forcing her to face forward, all the while biting his cheeks to keep from smiling. Cole, after all, looked perfectly serious. He was *much* better at this shtick than Finn was—which was why he usually let the man take the lead. After all, sometimes it was just as fun to watch a master at work.

"It isn't?" Skye asked, knitting her fingers together behind her back—subtly arching her chest out in the process. Honestly. Did she not know what she did to them?

"No." Cole grasped her by the chin, his hand sliding to the column of her throat. "You've been an awful tease today, and the worst part is, I think you were perfectly aware of what you were doing...to both of us."

"Me?" Skye's eyebrows twitched up, a soft gasping escaping her when Finn tugged her head back ever so slightly by the base of her ponytail. She nibbled her lower lip for a moment, then shook her head—as much as she could move it, anyway. "I don't know what you're talking about. I haven't done *anything* to you guys today."

"Nothing?" Cole glanced up at Finn, voice calm—noticeably in control. "Well... I suppose this will just be a bit of nothing too then, eh?"

"If that's what we're calling it," Finn agreed, then ran his tongue from the base of Skye's neck to the edge of her ear, fighting back a groan at the way she shivered. "Just a bit of nothing...in retaliation for all that nothing earlier. In the shower."

"In the bathroom," Cole added, eyes narrowing when Skye pressed her lips together—as if hiding a smile. He trailed his thumb along her jaw, then slid it across the seam of her lips. "Yes, I think she knows *exactly* what she's doing."

"Guys, I don't—"

She squealed when Cole's mouth crashed over hers, their lips parting as he plundered her. Finn merely held her in place, knowing she loved every second of Cole's roughness from the way she moaned. With his cock straining painfully against his trousers, Finn ground it against her, just for a few seconds of blissful relief, then straightened—as though he was just as in control as his partner-in-crime—and nodded when Cole pulled away and met his stare. Taking his cue, Finn spun the breathless woman around, then nudged her toward Cole and grinned as the man hoisted her up in one swift motion, an arm around her waist and her back pressed to his chest.

"What are you—*oh!*" Her cheeks flushed bright red when Cole hooked an arm under each knee and dragged her legs open, supporting her weight with surprising ease. He carried her to the table, Finn following as though this were a well-rehearsed dance between the three of them, the most forbidden tango imaginable. However, rather than splaying her across the wood as Finn thought he might, Cole merely kicked a chair aside and leaned back against the table himself, keeping Skye lifted and exposed.

That sliver of underwear may as well have been on the floor. Her slick sex practically swallowed the fabric, her arousal slicking her swollen lips and the cleft of her thighs. Finn grinned. *Perfect* for tasting—but he figured she would enjoy that too much. He had learned how to make her come in about three minutes flat with just his tongue.

Tonight, Skye wasn't going to come at all. Punishment, for her past transgressions. Finn ripped those useless panties off, the strings snapping with the most minimal of efforts. His cock throbbed at the way she gasped and mumbled an incoherent protest; Finn knew she'd get *some* pleasure from all this. Actually, a whole *lot* of pleasure. She just wasn't allowed to climax. That was part of the game, one she had started hours earlier.

He slipped the wet thong into his pocket, then trailed his finger over her sex, circling it around the wet, swollen bud at the helm. She whimpered, shifting about in Cole's arms, yet the man showed no signs of discomfort. He nipped at her neck in response, an unspoken command to keep still, and Finn bit his cheeks to keep from grinning again; this was going to be too fun. They really would have to make it up to her later.

"What if someone walks in?" she managed, her eyes rolling back and fluttering closed as Finn resumed his leisurely circling of her clit. "W-what if someone sees?"

"Tinted windows, love," he mused.

"And a locked door," Cole added, then adjusted his hold on her so that he held her open even wider. It'd be so *easy* to sink into her—to whip out his cock, about two seconds from bursting, and plunge straight into her delicious heat. Finn took a few measured breaths, reminding himself that this wasn't about *his* desires. It was about Skye's—and denying them.

So, he thrust two fingers into her instead, finding almost no resistance as her wet channel took him in. Finn hissed with pleasure at the feel of her, hot and tight, at the way her arousal coated his knuckles, her head thrown back over Cole's shoulder and lips parted.

"How wet is she?" Cole demanded, his voice a gravelly rasp as Finn pumped in and out of her, quickly settling on that tender spot along her inner wall.

"Drenched," he said, adding a faux disappointed sigh, his pace relentless as he worked her over. "I'm not sure we should allow it... This is a *punishment*, after all."

Cole's eyes practically glittered at the word, and he looked pointedly down to his right hand, which held up Skye's left knee. Catching his meaning, they traded off, Finn propping that leg up with his arm, her knee bent over the crook of his elbow. His pace fumbled briefly during the adjustment, and he grinned when Cole clamped his now-free hand over Skye's mouth. She moaned louder when Finn worked her faster, pumping that little spot furiously before sliding out to smother her clit. Her hips bucked against him, grinding, seeking her pleasure, but Cole kept her in check when he latched onto her neck and sucked; Finn knew from experience that, if he took her shoes off in that moment, he'd find her toes curled tightly. At the first sign of that telltale blush working down her face, where it would ooze along her neck and pool between her pert breasts, Finn figured she was close.

He ought to stop. That was the plan, after all. Bring her to the edge, first Finn, then Cole, and leave her a writhing, soaked mess on the table while they went out to rejoin the party.

But Finn couldn't stop. Not now. Not when all he wanted to do was bury himself balls deep inside her and feel her come undone around his cock.

Teeth gritted, he slipped his fingers back inside, working her into such a frenzy that he and Cole had a tough time holding her up.

"Fuck it," he hissed, retracting his fingers and shaking his head at Cole. "I can't do it."

"Condom's in my pocket," the man told him with a smirk. "I knew you'd break first."

Skye gave a hapless moan, the sound muffled by Cole's hand over her mouth. It quickly moved to take her knee as Finn reached around into the man's pocket, accidentally nudging another not entirely unexpected rock-hard shaft. The muscles in Cole's cheek twitched, and Finn pulled away quickly as soon as he found the two condoms, tossing one on the table and ripping the other open with his teeth.

"You *guys*," Skye whined, helpless in Cole's arms, her swollen, positively dripping sex left on display between them. "What are you *doing*?"

"Change of plans," Finn told her as he undid his pants. He let them drop to his ankles, briefs too, and quickly rolled the condom on. Normally they went without; despite the fact that Skye was regularly fucking two men, they were a monogamous little trio. Condoms weren't necessary—unless it was unlikely they would find a shower in the aftermath of what was to come. This was supposed to be a cheeky, fun sort of punishment, but Skye wouldn't be happy if she had to leave the party because they'd soiled her dress.

From the look on her face, however, that was probably the last thing on her mind. She bit her lip, eyebrows knitted as she grabbed Finn's jacket and dragged him back to her. Cole, however, stopped Finn from plunging in and taking her like he wanted with nothing more than a warning look.

"Not until you ask nicely, sweetheart," he rasped in Skye's ear. Finn's jaw clenched, one hand in a fist as the other massaged her clit again. *Cole* always enjoyed Skye begging, but not everyone had that kind of fucking patience.

"Please," she choked, her hips chasing Finn's hand when he eased off on the pressure—then pulled away entirely, using her juices to stroke his cock while he waited.

"Please what?" Cole murmured, a familiar back-and-forth between them. Finn still hadn't tired of it, despite the urgency pounding through his veins. He loved to watch Cole work, each and every time.

"Can one of you just please *fuck me already*," she

snapped. Finn chuckled; that wasn't usually a part of their script.

"Always happy to oblige—"

"Perhaps if you asked *nicer*," Cole warned, but Finn was already committed. He shot the man a frustrated look, one that suggested he was going to explode if he wasn't buried in Skye sometime in the next fifteen seconds. Grasping her thigh with one hand, he used the other to steer his cock into her enticing opening.

Heat enveloped him, pleasure trickling through his system and the urge to spasm out of control ever the more difficult to fight. The sounds of Skye mewling, whimpering, and moaning certainly didn't help, and he took a few moments to regain his composure when his hips knocked against hers. Every fiber of his being screamed *go, go, go*, but he waited, savoring the clench of her tight heat around him, the way her breath came in uneven whispers, and the look of sheer pleasure etched across every detail of her exquisite face.

"This isn't part of the punishment. You'll get what's coming to you...some other time," he told her with some difficulty, rocking his hips so that he caught her clit too—she must be *bursting* to climax. Skye nodded frantically, murmuring something incoherent before Cole captured her mouth in another searing kiss. He watched them for a moment, enjoying the show, then decided he'd been civil enough.

No more waiting.

Smoothing his hands around her thighs, he used them for anchorage as he started rocking against her. Finn took her slowly at first, getting them all adjusted to the position, ensuring Cole could handle both of their weight. When neither protested, Finn thrust harder, withdrawing farther before slamming back into her, searching out his pleasure and hers in equal measure. Skye tore her mouth from Cole's with a cry, clutching at Finn's jacket as he started to lose a bit of that carefully maintained control—until it was finally gone for good. Pounding into her, he did his best to catch her clit whenever he could, but it was steadily becoming difficult to *see* straight, let alone think straight.

A fire engulfed him, the flames lapping up his body, his skin ablaze and his thoughts scattered. Faster than he would have liked, Finn succumbed to the pleasure gods, dragging himself to the brink but refusing to tumble over, losing himself in her—in her cries, in the feel of her tightening around him. He gave in to the scandal of the moment, of fucking the woman he loved in a conference room while just down the hall nearly a hundred people sipped champagne and guffawed in each other's faces. They hadn't done this somewhere so public before.

It was rather thrilling.

Skye came with a breathless sob, throwing her head back, face screwed with pleasure, as she dragged Finn up against her—and Cole, by extension. He slowed his pace, grinding against her to prolong the bittersweet torture of it all, nearly coming undone himself as her sex tightened around him.

He seized his opportunity to finally come undone himself when she started to settle, her body trembling and her mouth ripe for the taking. Finn hastily adjusted his hold on her and lifted her out of Cole's arms, crossed the room in a few quick, awkward strides, pants still around his ankles, and pressed her up against the tinted window. With Skye's arms wrapped around him, their mouths met in a storm of lips and teeth and tongue, her fire not even the slightest bit dampened by her recent orgasm. Finn grinned against her mouth, pounding into her until pleasure exploded through his body, his whole field of vision going white, then stark black, as he buried his face against her neck, riding out the ecstasy. He groaned her name, relishing the way her fingers twined in his hair. She tugged hard in response and pressed her heels into his lower back, forcing him deeper into her as he fought to control his spasming body.

"Here," Cole called through the haze, and Finn looked over his shoulder to find the man had cleared a space at the table, chairs pushed aside and trousers unbuckled. "Bring her here."

While he wasn't even sure his legs could support any sort of walking at the moment, Finn obliged, carrying Skye back across the room and depositing her on the edge of the table. When he pulled away, Skye's flushed face greeted him, her smile enough to get him going again.

However, it wasn't his turn anymore.

Smirking, he stepped aside, watching as Cole marched up and rolled her with practiced ease onto her stomach, bending her over the table. The heels helped keep her balanced, oddly enough, and Finn's eyes caught the way her hands tightened to fists as Cole flipped her dress up onto her back—then thrust into her in one swift motion, filling her completely. She cried out, those fists spread wide and flat on the cool wood as Cole gripped her hips.

Finn settled into a nearby chair, his dark eyes ablaze once more, and tugged off then tied up the condom before buckling his pants with slightly shaky hands. With the best view in the whole hotel, he sat back and watched as Cole had his way with their love, skin slapping against skin as he fucked her hard and fast over the table's edge. It appeared Skye *tried* to contain herself—at first. Lips pressed together, she watched him over her shoulder, whimpering delicately, until Cole's hand slipped southward, no doubt to play with her clit, and then she was *gone*.

She flailed out, the flood of heat across her skin palpable even to Finn as another climax struck. Cole barely managed to clap a hand over her mouth, muffling her ragged cries, his pace unrelenting—until he too finally stilled, thrusting hard up against her, one hand gripping her hip so tight Finn wondered if there'd be bruises tomorrow. Cole choked something incoherent, the sound followed by a few more pumps, until finally he sagged over her, panting.

The three caught their breaths in an easy, comfortable silence, the muted lighting of the room appropriate for the aftermath of it all. When Cole gently eased out of Skye, Finn was by her side to help her up, fixing her dress for her as she trembled—and wore the dreamiest smile he'd ever seen.

"If that's what you guys consider a punishment," she said, smoothing a hand over her mussed hair, "then I think I need to start misbehaving more often."

"The punishment's still to come, sweetheart," Cole remarked before stealing a chaste kiss, then peppering several more along her cheek as she giggled. He pulled back with a grin. "Don't you forget it."

"I won't." Skye's hand gripped Finn's, and he planted a kiss of his own on her neck.

All the while knowing that his face mirrored Cole's lovestruck expression exactly as they studied their girl, their perfect, cheeky, stubborn girl.

Who still needed to be punished for earlier.

He smirked at the thought, cock stirring once more, and his mind raced to figure out precisely what sort of pleasurable torture she deserved—as soon as they got home later tonight.

Who was this sex-crazed woman staring back at her in the mirror?

Skye raised her chin, studying the warm pink afterglow of excellent lovemafucking, and decided she didn't *care* if she'd become a sex-crazed monster—she was *happy*. Happier than she'd ever been, and it all had to do with the two men waiting for her outside the ladies room.

Well, not entirely thanks to Cole and Finn, though they had played a huge part in it. Skye had never wanted to be one of those people who disappeared inside a relationship, disconnecting from friends, so obsessed with it that the rest of the world disappeared. Dating two men made it a little more difficult to juggle her social life *and* a demanding work schedule. Half the time she was exhausted, but Cole and Finn had their own ways of energizing her.

Like tonight. She smoothed her hands over her hair, readjusting the perky ponytail that Cole had held onto as he fucked her mercilessly over the table. All it took was a few seconds of reliving it and Skye's face was as red as a cherry tomato. Grinning, she continued to fix her makeup, using the extra supplies she'd brought in her purse as best she could to mimic what the stylist had done earlier.

She had come prepared, of course. After her little stunts back at the house as everyone was getting ready, she *knew* her boys wouldn't just leave it at that. Skye suspected she'd still be in for a bit of retaliation, and as she reapplied her lipstick, unable to stop smiling, she wondered if they had really believed her scandalized charade. From the way they'd handled her, *fucked* her, their whole plan falling to pieces, Skye suspected she'd been successful.

Tossing her lipstick, eyeliner, and cover-up back in her

purse, she straightened and glanced at the door when someone walked in. The woman nodded at her, and Skye returned the greeting with the same dopey grin she'd been wearing since she floated into the hotel bathroom ten minutes earlier.

It was just so rare that she had the upper hand with the two men she loved. Finn excelled at surprises—in both the romance and sex departments. Skye tended to feel like she was playing catch-up most of the time with him. Cole, on the other hand, was such a masterful lover that she couldn't help but follow his lead—loving every single delicious moment of it, whether she was tied spread-eagle to his bedposts or taken hard and fast over the kitchen counter while dinner cooked on the stove. For once, Skye wanted to call the shots.

And she had.

They just hadn't realized it. Skye had orchestrated the whole thing from the moment they got home from work this afternoon, right up until now, with Finn and Cole standing outside the bathroom waiting for her, smugly pleased with how the night had unfolded. Neither of them could stand being teased. Finn did the teasing. Cole did the ordering around. And Skye knew how to play both of them like a fiddle if it meant everyone got exactly what they wanted.

She ran her hands down the front of her designer dress, which she had bought with her own money from last month's paycheck. The fact that both of them were outside wearing suits and ties to match—well, it made her heart sing. If it was even possible, Skye somehow managed to fall more and more in love with them with each passing day—through good times and bad.

Tonight fell squarely in the former, *far* from the latter.

And it was hardly over yet.

Swallowing hard, Skye washed her hands out of habit, dried them with one of the rolled towels waiting in a basket on the counter, then grabbed her clutch and left at the sound of the other woman's toilet flushing. Just as she suspected, she found Finn and Cole waiting for her outside the bathroom door. Both were still a little flushed, but looking just as smug as she'd predicted. They thought they'd won, but after two spectacular orgasms, who was the real winner here?

She took a moment to adjust both of their ties, glancing up cheekily as her fingers manipulated the expensive fabric. Then, because she was a glutton for both of them, Skye stole a lingering kiss from each. Fiery for Finn. Long and torturous for Cole. When she stepped away, both of their eyes blazed with renewed interest, and she sauntered down the hall with an extra sway to her hips—if only to remind them that Finn still had her torn panties in his pocket.

"Come on, you two," she called, smirking over her shoulder, "or people are going to start to talk..."

23

AND BABY MAKES FOUR

"Mason, no," Skye warned, tugging on the labradoodle's leash slightly when he growled at the paparazzo snapping pictures from his not-so-secret hiding spot down the boardwalk. "He's allowed to invade my privacy...when we're in public."

She said it all with a smile, then waved to the guy, pleased that she was wearing her favourite pair of teal leggings. The T-shirt—classic baby Oz—had seen better days, but the tank underneath was cute. Oh, and the bag full of dog poop swinging from her other hand— très chic. Just the kind of stuff those assholes loved to splash across their tabloids.

The guy lowered his camera a few seconds later, then waved back before checking the shots. Rolling her eyes, she gave one last tug at Mason's leash, then continued on her pre-breakfast walk back to the villa. She'd only been living in Malibu for two months with Finn and Cole, but already it was painfully obvious that there were *far* more paparazzi on the prowl here than in Coral Bay. Two years into her polyamorous relationship and you'd think everyone would be bored of it already, but nope—her tight-knit trio always made at least four gossip rags whenever they were photographed together at events, and she caught someone snapping her picture at least once a day when she was out running errands.

While Skye could just ignore them, Mason wanted to chase each and every one of those invasive dicks down—every time. The dog liked just about everyone else. Cole was his absolute favourite, even if Skye was the one who took care of him the most, and he had a soft spot for kids. But lurking guys with enormous cameras? Nope. They might as well be squirrels.

Tossing the bag full of Mason's morning BM in the beachside trash can, she tightened her hold on the leash and hurried him along. The dog forgot all about the photographer, as he always did, as soon as Skye started cooing at him, her ponytail bouncing about and her flip-flops a noisy clamor for the pre-seven-AM boardwalk crowd. She took the same route she always did, slowing when her mildly nauseated stomach began acting up again. It had started a few days ago and she'd thought she had food poisoning—only there was no vomiting. Finn had expressed some concern over the sushi they'd had for lunch earlier in the week, stating that he felt off too, but he had been fine a few hours later. Skye, meanwhile, had felt her stomach churning, on and off, for days on end.

Thankfully, a good dose of morning ocean air seemed to settle it somewhat. What she wouldn't give to be back at the Coral Bay beach house, with her own private strip of sand and surf for Mason to run on. At least there, if this nausea finally *did* something, she could puke without worrying about it appearing in some trashy magazine tomorrow.

Still, it wasn't like she could *complain*. When they'd

had to relocate for Finn's career for a change—commuting between his LA offices and Coral Bay had started to become a chore, even if he wouldn't admit it—Skye, Finn, and Cole had found a villa on a pristine bit of beachfront property in Malibu. Locals called it billionaire's bay, as just about every other house had a director, CEO, or retired actor living inside. She had a sliver of beach all to herself, but it was open to the general public nowadays, and her neighbours always got *snippy* about Mason's happy morning barks, so she took him for a walk down to the open beach area, usually fairly empty this time of day, where he could be as loud as he wanted.

Normally she stopped and got the coffee order on the way back, but as she paused in front of her usual coffee spot, a hand on her stomach, she realized she might not make it through the long work rush lines today. Swallowing hard, she headed for home instead, Mason bouncing along beside her—until the usual cactus garden four houses down from theirs caught his attention. Unfortunately, she didn't feel like standing around today so he could leisurely sniff at it for the next twenty minutes before finally peeing on the corner. He whined when she tugged at the leash again, those enormous chocolate brown eyes guilting her into waiting a few minutes longer before she all but dragged him away.

She headed for the roadside entrance to the two-storey white and blue villa. Cole and Finn had fond memories of some Greece trip they'd taken *years* ago, and that had sold them. At the time, Skye didn't care what they chose—so long as there were four bedrooms, one for each plus the extra for when they all slept together. Oh, and it needed a lot of window space for Oz and a plot of grass for Mason. Otherwise, she was a happy camper.

Before heading inside, she stopped to quickly wipe Mason's sandy paws off. By then, she could already hear Oz meowing from the other side of the door at the far end of the covered car park.

"Okay, we're *coming*," she called back, rolling her eyes. Mason nosed at the base of the door enthusiastically as Skye put his beach towel, leash, and collar away in the storage unit, then barked when she appeared to be taking too long. Hands on her hips, she stared down at him, unimpressed, until the labradoodle finally sat politely and waited, tail going a mile a minute. Chastisement forgotten, Skye grinned down at him. "You want to see your kitten? Are you excited to see your little kitten?"

Mason yipped, tapping his front paws, whole body quivering. Laughing, Skye finally opened the door and stepped aside, allowing her two boys to reunite in peace. Oz slunk out, stretching, then rubbed up against each of Mason's legs as the dog nosed at him, whining. It really was ridiculous how much they loved each other, considering their rocky beginning—Ozzy had *not* been impressed that he was no longer the center of attention—but most mornings nowadays Skye found her big white floofball curled up somewhere on or around Mason, who always slept at the end of Cole's bed.

"Okay, come on," she muttered as she scooped up a purring Ozzy, cuddling him to her chest as she pushed into the small foyer. Although she still felt blegh, a purring cat could pretty much cure whatever ailed you. Kicking off her flip-flops and tossing her slouchy bag next to the closet, she strolled through the blissfully air-conditioned house, headed straight through to the kitchen. While the upstairs had all the bedrooms, the joint kitchen and living room space was absolutely her favourite. It took up nearly the entire lower level, and one wall was just an enormous window overlooking the small fenced-in deck, then the gorgeous, sprawling Pacific beyond.

She found Finn where she always did when he didn't need to be at the office before noon—seated in the breakfast nook, various newspapers spread out in front of him on the table, and the news playing on the wall-mounted flat-screen across the room. With the TV volume on low, she deposited Ozzy on the couch as she passed by, and the cat quickly followed Mason to his water bowl—where she knew he'd sit and watch the dog drink, then paw at the unsettled water until he got bored.

"How was your walk?" Finn asked as he flipped the page of the LA Times, tapping his mug without looking up. "Meant to tell you I made my own coffee this morning."

"Good, because I didn't get any," she said as she shuffled across the enormous open kitchen, skirting the granite-topped island to grab a glass from the cupboard. Light grey and gold flecked surfaces, white cabinetry, stainless steel appliances. Storage galore. It was her dream kitchen—even if Cole was the one who did most of the cooking.

Which, honestly, made it even better. Dream kitchen, dream man—the two combined made Skye one lucky lady.

"Hmm. How're you feeling? Did the walk help?" She finally felt those onyx eyes of her other dream guy wandering her figure, and she glanced back to find concern etched into just about every feature on Finn's handsome face.

"Not really," Skye admitted with a frown, selecting the filter system on the tap to fill her glass. "I don't know what's going on. I feel so blegh."

"Shall I make an appointment for you?"

"No, I'm okay." Days of nausea wasn't *okay*, but she

didn't need Finn fussing over her and bullying the doctor into doing a whole battery of unnecessary tests. It was probably just a stubborn stomach bug. No need to sound the alarms. "You didn't tell Cole, did you?"

The other love of her life had been in Hong Kong for the last two weeks, with another two weeks to go, for some ultra-elite tech festival. It was invite-only and huge for his company, but she certainly missed having him at home. Although it had been a shitstorm when he first eased away from his regular duties, his anxiety maxed out for a *long* time, he had finally settled into a comfortable routine. Most of his flights were domestic lately, not international, which meant he was only gone for a few days here and there, working remotely from home the rest of the time. Given Skye was still job hunting in LA, it had been a dream.

Having him gone for a month was not. She was already neck-deep in Cole withdrawal two weeks into his trip. She and Finn ate out *way* too often without Cole to ground them. Also, the house was a mess pretty much constantly—dishwasher always full, clothes not quite in the hamper, dog toys everywhere. And she just *missed* him. Finn did too, even if he wouldn't admit it. He sparkled a bit brighter when all three of them were together.

"I'm starting to think I *should* tell him," Finn mused, closing the paper and leaning back in the half-circle booth near the patio door. "This has been going on for a few days. You're usually less inclined to argue with him about this sort of thing."

Skye guzzled down half her water in a single gulp, admiring the way Finn's dark grey bath robe fell open with his repositioning to reveal a sculpted chest beneath. *Yum.* Even if they were two years deep into this relationship, Skye still found her heart pitter-pattering at the sight of

Cole and Finn's bodies. The sex only seemed to get better with time—that probably had something to do with it, why she turned into a horny teenager at the slightest slip of skin.

"Skye?" She found him smirking, as if knowing exactly what had distracted her. "Are you listening?"

"Don't tell Cole," she said, leaning against the island. "He'll just worry, and he doesn't need to while he's so far from home. You know what that will do to him. I'm fine."

"You look a bit pale."

"*You* look a bit pale."

Finn rolled his eyes and grabbed the next paper from his stack. "Fine. Be stubborn. But if you're still feeling like this tomorrow, I'm taking you to see Doctor Hendricks—even if I have to throw you over my shoulder and carry you there."

"Don't make promises you can't keep," she purred back, wiggling her eyebrows as he glanced up again. When he didn't drawl something deliciously sexy in return, she finished the rest of her water and huffed. "*Okay*. Deal."

"Good, I..." Finn trailed off at the sound of his phone beeping, and Skye busied herself with refreshing Mason's water and topping up Oz's kibble. As she strolled back to the pet food bowl area near the hallway, she heard Finn tell her the message was from Cole.

"Oh?"

"He says to turn on your phone," he said with a chuckle, tapping around on the screen. "Or just check your email. He's found a few additional job vacancies you can add to your search."

With a glowing reference from Hans at Gallery Sens, Skye figured she would at least be able to get her foot in the door a little easier this time around. She had worked her way up to curator's assistant and tour guide at the little sex museum before she left Coral Bay. Moving was stressful enough, however, and with two billionaire boyfriends, she didn't feel the need to rush the job search just yet. When something perfect came along, she planned to jump on it. Cole, meanwhile, had been job hunting *for* her before they'd even packed the first box. At first she had tried to stop him, but it seemed to be helping *his* stress levels more than hers, so she let him forward daily job postings and the like her way.

"Give him a kiss for me," she said, drumming her fingers on the island countertop. With her stomach looping, she had no idea what she wanted to eat for breakfast. Maybe some bread to settle things? With the way she was feeling, Skye didn't even want to think about food, but she knew she needed something.

"Where's the fucking kiss emoticon?" she heard Finn grumble, hunched over his phone and tapping at it with his two pointer fingers. He was a hunt and peck texter *and* typer, through and through, and neither Cole nor Skye would ever let him live it down. As the oldest in the trio, he already got the bulk of the senior citizen jokes. Just as she was about to make one, however, he looked up with a dazzling grin that made her cheeks hot. "Could you be a lamb and flip my eggs? I think they're getting too crispy..."

"Can't have that, can we?" She sauntered over to the stove, grabbing the spatula beside it and gripping the pan handle. However, as soon as she flipped one sizzling egg, the extra potent whiff of fried egg finally pushed her over the edge. Slapping a hand over her mouth, she bolted out of the kitchen, barely making it to the main floor guest bathroom before retching her guts out into the toilet.

"Skye?" Bare feet slapped against tile as Finn hurried after her, and she tried to close the door, not wanting him to see her puking up what little she had in her stomach so early in the morning. True to form, he batted her groping hand away and crouched beside her. As another wave of nausea struck, forcing her to dry heave into the porcelain bowl, he rubbed his warm hand up and down her back. With her head spinning and some cold sweats taking hold, Skye didn't want to be touched.

"Finn," she croaked, shrugging him off. "Jus' gimme a sec..."

He sat back on the bathroom floor until she got everything out of her—and then some. Groaning, Skye flushed the mess away and plopped down across from him, face sweaty and flushed. Without a word, he stood and ran a cloth under the tap, and Skye closed her eyes as he wiped around her face, then tossed it somewhere. A few moments later, he had a second cold cloth to press against her forehead, and she realized she was shaking.

"I'm taking you to the doctor," he said firmly. "This morning."

"I'm fine," she argued, eyes closed as she took deep, even breaths. "Whatever it was is all out of me *finally*. I've been nauseous for a few days, now it's gone."

"People don't get nauseous for a few days without a reason—"

"It's been mostly in the morning," Skye argued, finally staring up at him as he loomed overhead, hands on his hips and robe half open. "I'm usually fine the rest of the day. I..."

Wait.

Wait.

Her heart pounded, a high-pitched ring sounding between her ears as she started to piece things together.

"Skye? What is it?"

"I..." She held out a hand and Finn helped her up. Tossing the wet cloth in the sink, she leaned back against the wall, still hot and uncomfortable—and now shifting into panic mode. "I don't remember having my period last month. Do you?"

"I... I..." He scratched at his two-day-old stubble, frowning. "I don't remember."

"I know I messed up my pills with the move, but I thought..." She swallowed hard—then made a face at the gross post-vomit taste. After a quick mouth-rinse in the sink, she pushed by Finn and hurried up the nearby staircase to her bedroom, then into her private bath. Skye went straight for the medicine cabinet, Finn and Mason at her heels, and grabbed her birth control pills, then the little calendar she used to track her cycle. When they'd moved, she'd gotten her days mixed up—all the chaos of moving three people and two pets had really done her in, given the men in her life still had to work in the meantime. And. She'd missed *three* pills. Usually she was so careful. Wordlessly she held up her calendar with the X's marked for the days she had missed, mouth opening and closing like a fish out of water.

"Okay. Okay. Okay," Finn rambled, marching back into her bedroom before reappearing at the bathroom door seconds later. "Okay. Okay, we just... Okay."

"Stop saying okay!"

"I'm making a doctor's appointment," he said, gaze distant—she could practically see the wheels turning. "Then I'm going to the drugstore to pick up some tests. It's fine. We're fine. Do you..." He looked to her sharply. "Do you feel fine?"

"I don't know, Finn!" She threw her hands up, then tossed her pill packs and her calendar on the counter. "I don't feel like throwing up anymore, so I guess that's a plus."

He stalked away, muttering *okay* over and over again under his breath. Mason stayed put in the doorway, looking between them like he was watching a world-class tennis match, and Skye took a deep breath.

Okay.

"I'll make the doctor's appointment," she said gently, catching Finn on his next round of pacing. She took him by the arm, leaned up on her toes, and kissed his cheek. "Go to the drug store. We'll regroup in twenty minutes."

"Okay." He leaned down to kiss her, but Skye turned her head at the last moment so he got cheek instead. He then blitzed out of the bedroom, and Skye just stood there, her mind blank.

"Oh..." She hurried out of her bedroom and leaned over the staircase railing. "Finn, put some clothes on!"

Moments later, he came jogging back up the steps, wearing his bathrobe and his gym shoes.

"Right," he muttered in passing, and she held in a laugh.

Right indeed. Less than a minute later, he ran by again in a pair of navy shorts and a neon-pink T-shirt his niece had decorated with cat paw prints for his birthday. He kissed her again in passing, thundering down the stairs, and was out of the door in record time. When she heard the SUV revving to life outside, she shuffled down the stairs, pausing on the last step, Mason a few paces behind her, and planted her hands on her hips.

Mind still blank—but the high-pitched whine was getting worse.

"Okay," Skye muttered. "One step at a time... Doctor's appointment. Where the hell's my phone? Finn? Can you call my..."

Her cheeks warmed when she spotted it sitting next to the TV, where she'd left it, dead but charging. With a shake of her head, Skye grabbed it, hit the power button, and sat beside the power outlet on the floor, waiting.

"Finn," he heard Cole sigh through the TV, which was currently streaming Skye's laptop as per Cole's technological finagling before he left, "I still can't see you. Sort it out."

"I'm trying," he muttered, clacking away at the laptop as Skye sat beside him on the huge L-shaped couch that took up most of the living side of their villa's open concept first floor. He sounded grumpy, Cole, but then again, it was obscenely early in Hong Kong—though it didn't surprise Finn one bit to learn that the man hadn't adapted to an adjusted schedule yet. The tech convention was supposed to last all month. It was a marathon, not a sprint. He and Skye had drilled that into Cole's thick skull the whole week leading up to his departure, but from the odd hours he'd been getting texts from him, Finn didn't think the message had stuck.

After resetting her webcam connection, Finn cut the video feed and then tried to call again. Moments later, Cole's face popped up on the TV screen, the room dark behind him and the bright white glow of the monitor doing his face no favors.

"Good lord."

"Turn the lights on, you gremlin," Skye ordered, arms crossed so that Cole wouldn't see their surprise. She was doing a decent job of hiding her exuberance, but if Cole had been there with them, he'd likely detect the tremor in her hands, the slightly raised octave of her voice. The woman was aglow—for more reasons than one.

Finn bit the insides of his cheeks to hide the enormous grin threatening to escape; many times over the last two years, the conversation of family had come up between him and Cole. No matter where the conversations had started, they would usually end with a very positive discussion about the prospect of starting a family of their own with Skye. Cole had always been so giddy at the thought, his words coming fast and his hands flying all over the place. Although Finn and Skye were overjoyed and struggling to hide it at the moment, he couldn't wait to see the look on Cole's face when he heard the news. Pregnant. *Confirmed* pregnant as of two hours ago.

He and Cole were going to be dads.

Just the thought threatened to shatter his cool, nonplussed demeanor, and Finn pinched his leg to get himself under control.

"You look like shit, man," Finn insisted, voice steady, then moved the laptop about so it would capture both him and Skye equally. Cole had looked a little tired when they'd video-chatted with him two weeks ago, but this was ridiculous. Those bags under his eyes would very easily pass for bean bag *chairs* at this point.

"You guys need to host this thing outdoors next year," Skye added. She was shaking beside him, positively buzzing about the news, and he had to give her credit for sounding calm, cool, and collected, all the while wondering if it was as difficult for her as it was for him. "At least then you'll get some sun."

"Right, fuck *both* of you." Cole flipped them off as he stood. At the sound of a click, light flooded the screen, showing a meticulously kept bedroom suite behind him—and Cole's shit appearance. He sat down with a huff, rubbing his face. "There. Better?"

"You're going to need some serious TLC when you get back," Skye crooned at him, and that managed to bring a smile to the grumpy sod's face. She nuzzled her head onto Finn's shoulder, eyes fixed to the screen. "We miss you."

"I miss you guys too," he said, his voice catching slightly. "Only a week to go. Have you let the house fall to ruin yet?"

"It's…" Finn pursed his lips, knowing the man would see right through him. "We've already arranged for the cleaning service to come through the day before you get back."

"Good. How're the boys?" Cole's eyes, a paler blue than usual thanks to the glow of his computer screen, followed Oz as the cat slunk along the back of the couch and settled down behind Finn's head. "Where's Mason?"

The dog responded with a hearty *woof*, hopping up on the couch beside Skye. Finn had to physically stop him from traipsing over the both of them on his quest to find Cole after hearing him say his name. When he wouldn't behave, Finn ordered him off the couch entirely, but tilted the laptop so the two could greet each other.

Honestly, you'd never know what a fucking fuss Cole had made when Finn and Skye adopted the dog, given the way the two pined after each other now.

"No, you stay down," Cole ordered when Mason whined and tried to sneak back onto the couch. "Good boy."

Skye pushed the laptop back onto Finn's lap, clearly unable to contain herself a second longer. "Okay, okay, *news*."

"Yes, what on Earth could be so important that I need to be up at this hour?"

A giddy twist in Finn's gut forced him to shift about. The initial pregnancy tests had all been positive, and Finn had been holding that news in for days now, all the while feeling horribly guilty whenever he chatted with Cole via text, a huge secret on the tip of his tongue. But they'd had to sure. This wasn't something you played around with. As of today, *two* precious hours ago with news from the doctor, they knew for certain.

And he'd never had a happier day.

"We..." He looked down at Skye, knowing she was the one who ought to share the news. Grinning, he stretched an arm out on the couch behind her, careful not to knock Oz off, and nodded. "Go on. You tell him."

It was then that he realized Skye wasn't the only one shaking. He flexed his hand in and out of a fist, noting the way it trembled.

"Cole, we..." She opened and closed her mouth, looking from Finn to the laptop, then up to the TV screen. "Cole, I'm pregnant!"

Cole blinked back at them, dumbstruck. "W-what?"

"Yeah, Finn panic-bought thirty thousand pregnancy tests when I realized I was having morning sickness," she said, finally showing the ziplock bag she'd kept all the positive test strips in. She held it up, beaming. Skye had never looked more beautiful—sweats, raggedy bun, faded makeup and all. "We just got the blood test results from the doctor... *Pregnant*. He estimates about five or six weeks..."

Finn let her take the lead in telling the story. She had earned that right after all she'd gone through recently. Days of nausea—it must have been a nightmare. When she had finally gotten physically sick, he'd been at his breaking point, wracked with worry despite her assurances that all was *fine*.

And now, he had a lot of *feelings* about the whole thing. Excitement. Nervousness. Hope. Mostly, Finn was just thrilled that their little trio was going to expand by one in the next nine months. He loved Skye to the moon and back, and this was just the next step in the relationship. Was it planned? No. Did that make it any less exciting? Absolutely not. Finn loved kids. He'd always wanted them, even during his wild-child partying days. The thought of Skye having one, whether it was his or Cole's, had made him moonwalk around his bedroom on the first day after she took all the at-home tests. He'd wanted to get his elation out privately at first, because what had really mattered then was how *Skye* felt. Over the last week, she'd fluctuated between panicked and excited, before finally bursting out in happy tears when the doctor had called today with the news.

So, whether she continued to go through the emotional roller-coaster or not, Finn just wanted to be supportive. He already had ideas about how to turn one of the bedrooms into a playroom, then another into a nursery. They'd have to downsize and start sleeping together more, but that didn't bother him one bit—all they needed was a bigger bed. Skye was notorious for starfishing, Cole was a blanket hog, and Finn usually woke up on the floor whenever they all shared a bed. Something would need to be done about that, because their child deserved his or her own room. And playroom. And so much more.

Skye regaled Cole with the events of the last week, from the initial discover to the tests to the doctor's appointment, then finally the fateful call, her mouth moving a mile a minute, her excitement palpable. She was still shaking, her cheeks flushed and her eyes bright, gesticulating wildly with her hands as Finn tried to keep them both in the webcam's view. However, when he looked to Cole, the man was white as a sheet. He'd also picked up a pen and had been clicking it for god knows how long.

Not good.

Skye was too wrapped up in the moment to see it now, but she would. Finn cleared his throat, shifting from giddy mode to comfort mode, sensing he needed to be on his toes. Should he subtly disconnect the line? Something felt off.

Fuck.

"I mean, I was really thrown at first," Skye said, slightly breathless as she smoothed some coppery flyaways behind her ears. "Both of us were. But I think it's going to be amazing."

Finn tensed, steeling himself when she finally clued into the fact that Cole wasn't reacting anywhere *near* how he suspected she wanted him to—how Finn *thought* he would.

"Cole," Finn said firmly, staring straight into the webcam. "Put the pen down. It's fine. We're in this together, right? How are you—"

"Well, I'm all the way over here, aren't I?" Cole said, his voice cracking. "So, are we really in this together?"

Finn frowned, a ripple of anger washing over him when he caught the way Skye's face fell in the webcam image. "What do you mean? Of course we are."

"Look, I...I need to run." If he clicked that damn pen any faster, the thing would implode. "I'm sorry. I... Thank you for telling me. I just need to...I have some things to take care of before this morning's meeting, and I should probably just... I'm sorry. I love you."

And then the screen went black, the call disconnected. The little nugget of anger inside him exploded into a full-blown storm, but Finn swallowed it when Skye started to cry.

"He doesn't seem very happy," she wailed, hands pressed to her red cheeks as tears streamed down them. Mason whined and slunk off; he always thought he was in trouble whenever one of his humans was upset. Unfortunately, the dog hadn't done anything.

Cole, on the other hand...

Finn took a deep breath and pulled Skye into his arms, quickly setting the laptop and the bag of pregnancy tests aside. He hushed her as she sobbed into his chest, her body shuddering more violently than before. As he'd learned over the last two years, sometimes she just needed to exhaust herself, get all that emotion out, and *then* she'd be ready to talk. So, he waited, biting his tongue, swallowing his frustration over what had just happened, and let her cry. Only when Skye started to settle down did he untangle himself from her. He then scooped a sleeping Oz up and set him on her lap, turned the TV on, and grabbed a glass of water, catching the kettle on the way so he could make them both some tea.

Back at her side, the TV on low, he watched her drink the entire glass, then took it back when she stared numbly ahead. Swollen, bloodshot eyes lifted to him when he wiped the last of the tears away, and Finn sighed, knowing she'd understand his emotional state with that sharp exhale—but also knowing he would need to actually say something too.

"I think he was just overwhelmed," Finn told her softly, nodding when her eyebrows started to furrow. "You know what he's like. Change is big. This is *huge*. We probably should have waited until he got home." He paused, considering the idea for a moment. "Actually, we should have *definitely* waited until he got home."

"Maybe," she admitted in a very quiet, very un-Skye-like voice. "Or maybe..."

"Just watch The Devil's Kitchen with Oz," Finn urged, forcing the remote into her hand as one of their usual shows started up. "I'm going to call Cole and get this all sorted out. I'm sure it was just...a poor reaction. He loves you, Skye. Very much. I can guarantee he isn't angry or, or, I don't know, *upset* by any means at the news, all right?"

Skye nodded mutely, staring at the TV. She remained in a daze until Oz stood up on her lap, stretched a high-arched stretch, and rubbed his face along her chin. Only then did she smile weakly, and Finn left, knowing she was in very capable paws.

Clutching his phone so tight he worried he might break the damn thing, he was nearly at the front door when he heard a low whine from the top of the stairs. Mason stared down at him with those huge, sorrowful brown eyes —cowering.

"You're fine," Finn reassured the dog, but when Mason flopped down and whined again, he realized there were *two* beings who needed comforting. Rolling his eyes, he scaled the staircase taking it two steps at a time. As the TV volume increased from the living room, he charmed Mason back to his happy-go-lucky self, and soon enough the dog was bouncing down the stairs ahead of him, nails clacking on the tile, and making his way back to Skye. Finn watched him go, shaking his head when Skye let him cuddle on the couch, and then stalked out to the car park area, only remembering not to slam the door nanoseconds before he did it.

He tapped around his phone irritably, bringing up Cole's profile and selecting the call button. Each ring only made his blood boil more than it already was, and when Cole answered on the sixth ring, the last before it went to voicemail, Finn held nothing back.

"What the *fuck* was that?" he demanded, forcing himself to march back and forth along the length of the SUV parked in the darkness. Ahead, the highway was quiet aside from the odd car whizzing by.

"Finn—"

"No, no," he said sharply. "You *think* before you answer me. She's crying right now. *Crying*. D'you feel good about yourself?"

"Of course not," Cole snapped back. "Do you think that was my goal?" He huffed into the phone. "You couldn't have given me a fucking heads-up?"

"Skye wanted to surprise you. She thought you'd be excited." Finn shook his head, glaring around the dark corners of the cark park—realizing it needed a bit of a cleaning soon. Sand. It got everywhere. When Cole said nothing, he exhaled, pushing out some of his anger with it. "Cole, we've talked about this, you and I. You said you couldn't wait to have kids with Skye. You wanted one with *us*. Was that a load of shit?"

"No, no, no, I just..." Another shaky breath, followed by a gasp of an inhale. "I'm not *there*, Finn."

"So what? You'll be home soon," Finn countered, already detecting the beginnings of a panic attack. *Fuck*. "Cole, sit down."

"No—"

"Sit the fuck down. Don't make me call Hunter." Cole's assistant had been known, at times, to be moderately helpful in calming Cole down. It was rare that Finn had to rely on him, but there wasn't much he could do from an entirely different continent.

"I-I'm not *there*," Cole said, his breath coming faster with each word. "That's just it, right? Classic fucking Cole. Never there when it matters. Always working. Always—"

"That's a lie and you know it. You're here for pretty much everything these days."

"But not the stuff that really matters." Finn heard a tap running in the background, followed by muffled noises for a few moments as Cole splashed his face down. Part of the routine. When he got back on the line, however, he didn't sound any calmer. "I should have been at the doctor's appointment. I should have been there with you and her. How many other things am I going to miss out on? The delivery? Birthdays? Will you be the only dad at the wedding? I..."

He dragged in a raspy breath, and Finn crouched down with a sigh, the last of his anger, anger that he now realized was uncalled for, seeping out of him. "Cole. Sit down."

"I am f-fucking sitting."

Finn pressed a hand to his forehead. There was nothing to do now but wait. "Head between your knees. Come on. You're all right. We're all right."

"It's always w-work, and I—"

"Cole," Finn said firmly. "You're having a panic attack."

"I'm n-not." The hyperventilating was pretty hard to miss.

"You are. Take a breath. It seems worse than it is right now. Skye and I aren't going anywhere. You're going to be home with us soon. We're going to do this together." He waited for a moment, his voice softer when he spoke next. "I'm going to count. You ready?"

There was a brief pause, until: "Y-yes."

Following the protocol they'd all agreed on should Cole ever have an attack, he instructed the man to take a nice, slow, deep breath. Hold it for four seconds. Slow release. Then again. Over and over, paired with reassurance, until Cole's breathing leveled out. The incident lasted about ten minutes, and when it was over, Cole sounded like he'd just ran a marathon.

"I fucked up," he croaked. "I... It all just hit so fast. I'm sorry. Please tell Skye I'm sorry."

"No, Cole, *I'm* sorry. I should have realized... Look, I'll sort it out," Finn told him, rubbing a hand across his face. "She'll understand. I think it's better we all talk about it in person."

"Agreed."

"Are you okay?"

"Fine," Cole muttered, though Finn knew he'd need at least an hour to decompress after the attack. "I feel like the biggest ass..."

"Well, sometimes you can be." Finn chuckled as a weariness descended upon him. "I don't think you were with this. Not intentionally, anyway."

"I really am excited," he said, sounding just as tired as Finn felt. "Really. I just..."

"I know." Cole didn't need to explain himself—not anymore, at least. Finn's gut reaction to his earlier behavior hadn't been far off; the man wasn't upset or angry, just startled. The news was huge, and he wasn't surprised it had triggered Cole's anxiety. Unfortunately, seeing Skye cry had triggered *Finn's* anger, his protectiveness. He should have realized... He shook his head, sighing. Doesn't matter. It was over and done with now—and no one could change it. They all just needed to make it right going forward. "Listen, I should get back and make sure she's okay. Mason and Oz are keeping her company."

"Fuck, Finn..."

"Everything is going to be fine," he assured him. "Go do what you need to, and please don't let this pull you into a spiral. You don't need to. We'll sort it out."

It took a little extra reassurance to get Cole to hang up, but when he did, Finn immediately rang up his assistant and ordered her to arrange the Rai family's private jet to leave tomorrow morning for Hong Kong out of LAX. Even if Cole had agreed not to let this issue fester, Finn knew it would, and the sooner they were all face-to-face, celebrating this wonderful news as a family, the better.

When all that was said and done, he slipped his phone in his pocket and strolled to the end of their driveway. A warm night breeze billowed over him, and as he stood there, Finn closed his eyes and breathed it in. This would be made right. He'd see to that. But in the meantime...

Tears clung to his thick, dark lashes when he opened his eyes again, his surroundings blurred until he blinked the wetness away.

Skye was *pregnant*. The last week had been so hectic, and today had been such a whirlwind of emotion, that he hadn't really taken a proper second to process it. Barring any complications, they were going to have a *child*. Hands planted on his hips, he looked up at a starry sky and laughed, letting the tears roll down his face unhindered.

Running a hand through his hair, he wiped his cheeks and nodded. They were going to have a baby. Someone was going to call Cole and Finn *dad* soon. Even with the mess that tonight had been, even if he felt drained—Finn had never been happier, or more excited, about anything in his life.

Cole had never been this exhausted in his life—and not just physically. Sure, he was absolutely wrecked after being on the go for almost three straight weeks in a row. Since he had gracefully bowed out of the bulk of his old responsibilities as CEO and started working from home to put more time and attention into his relationship, he'd gotten soft. The thought of doing code marathons with his programmers made him queasy, and he had fallen asleep in the car every night for the last week and a half while some of the others participating in the tech convention carried on partying into the night. He wasn't sure where they got their energy from, but drugs came to mind, and it wouldn't surprise him if many were high out of their minds by midnight most nights. There were more than a few bleary, red-eyed folks at the hotel breakfast bar each morning.

But Cole was exhausted in just about every way possible. He hadn't slept a wink since his conversation with Finn and Skye about the baby. Just thinking back to it, how he'd handled it, threatened to bring on another panic attack. Wracked with anxiety, he had been on the steady and rapid decline for about a day and a half now. Standing in the gold-and-ivory-toned lobby, waiting for the private elevator that would take him up to his rented penthouse, he couldn't even remember what had happened today. Guest speakers. Something about innovations. Internet...security? He groaned and pinched the bridge of his nose, his whole body on fire.

It had been on fire ever since he'd hung up with Finn. Hong Kong itself certainly didn't help his state of mind. Fast-paced. Vibrant. Busy. *Full.* Nothing about it helped his racing thoughts, and he'd already put his assistant on call to remind him to take his medication. Normally it didn't matter if he took it an hour or two late, just as long as he took it. Given how he was feeling now, after what a colossal fuck-up he'd made, Cole knew himself well enough to know he'd spiral if he didn't take those tiny white pills on the exact hour, every day.

The fact that he hadn't heard from Skye since that phone call only made things worse. He'd heard from Finn, but it was all the usual stuff: everything's fine, not to worry, we'll see you soon. Nothing that would quiet the tornado hammering the inside of his skull.

Cole glanced at the screen above the elevator doors—nineteen floors to go before it reached the lobby. Scowling, he dug his phone out of his jacket pocket, tie hanging loosely around his neck, and checked for messages. There were many, of course, but none from the people who mattered.

What had he been *thinking*? Of course he wanted to start a family with Skye. In the moment, however, he'd panicked. He'd shoved his foot so deep in his mouth that there was no hope of recovering it. Worst of all, he had made her cry. The chances of Skye and Finn even being at home next week dwindled with each passing hour. After all, they didn't *need* him. They loved each other. They could easily cut him and his insensitivities out of their life. And he'd deserve it, too.

Cole shook his head. The anxious voices hadn't been kind to him over the last forty-eight hours, and the lack of sleep wasn't helping. As the gold, reflective elevator doors peeled open and he stepped inside, Cole heard the rattle of the sleeping pills he'd picked up from the local pharmacy in his bag. If these couldn't knock him out, he might just go insane.

Pressing the button for his floor, he leaned back against the wall and rubbed his face. There was too much to worry about. Too much with the convention, which, up until yesterday, had been going well. His company had made a few acquisitions, opened up additional trade in the Asian markets, and was currently in the works to partner up with Hong Kong's leading security firm for a joint business venture. And all Cole could think about Skye. And what a major fucking idiot he'd been.

He inhaled deeply, filling his lungs to the brim, and held the air for four counts. As his ears popped and the elevator shot up to the top floor, he continued doing it, over and over again, until things inside of his chest settled somewhat. When the doors finally whooshed open, granting him direct access to his suite, Cole was only slightly less clammy—and the voices had been subdued to a dull, whispery roar.

He stepped into a two-storey suite, pitch-black save for the green, red, and blue dots of light from the various electronics scattered around the foyer. Twin winding stairwells ahead led to the second floor, a landing between them with an ivory and gold railing, the color scheme carrying up from the lobby. Straight ahead were the first-floor eat-in kitchen and living room areas, plus the balcony. Cole wondered if he could even make it up to his bedroom without collapsing.

"Fuck me." He groped around in the darkness for a light switch. He could have sworn he'd left everything on this morning, and the cleaning staff hadn't once adjusted any of the suite settings in three weeks. Mind you, all the blaring lights probably hadn't been good for his state of mind either. After leaving the chaos of the city behind, he should have opted for soothing, natural lighting. Maybe he could put in a request...

"Ah, there you are, you bugger," he grumbled when he finally found the switch, which was in a row of a dozen other switches—more buttons than a fucking airplane dashboard. Seconds later, all the foyer's many pod lights came to life above him—including the line along the floor on either side of the elevator—the sudden rush of light like an assault.

"Surprise!"

Cole whirled around, dropping his laptop carrier bag with a heavy *thud*, at the sight of Finn and Skye standing in his lobby, champagne flutes in hand—and a banner hanging from the railing above.

CONGRATULATIONS, DADDY!

"We made it on the plane ride over here," Skye said as Cole continued to stare at the bright, glittery letters, each one surrounded by hearts. It was clearly Skye's writing—and it said *daddy*. Slowly, he lowered his gaze to both of his people, standing across the foyer, dressed to the nines. Finn in one of his favourite black suits, a half-pink, half-blue bow tie around his neck. Skye, looking beautiful in a floor-length red dress, nipped at the waist, with fluttery short sleeves. Makeup. Her hair tossed up in an elegant updo, coppery curls cascading down her neck. No shoes, he noticed when she padded toward him, her feet bare but her toenails painted to match her dress.

She stopped within a foot of him, then offered a champagne flute.

"We shouldn't have told you over a video call," she told him softly, her extended arm hanging between them, the liquid bubbling within the glass. "I'm sorry. I should have realized it would upset you, learning about it but not being there... I was just excited and I wanted you to know."

He cautiously accepted the flute when she nibbled her lower lip, his hand trembling.

"It's nonalcoholic," Finn commented as he strolled toward them. "You know, since we're all on the same team here. She can't drink, we can't drink—apparently."

"No sushi either." Skye pointed between them, eyes narrowed. "I think that's gonna be the hard one..."

Cole closed his mouth and swallowed hard when he realized he'd just been staring mutely. His eyes wandered up to the banner again, then down to Skye.

"I'm so sorry." He barely heard the words despite uttering them himself, a whirlwind of emotion battering him hard. Frowning, Skye handed her glass to Finn, and before Cole knew it, she was holding him, drawing him into her arms and squeezing tight. Ashamed, he clenched his eyes shut, the levies finally bursting, and buried his face against her neck.

She hushed him sweetly, rubbing his back, and when he tried to pull away, she wouldn't let him.

"Skye, I'm so happy about this," he said, hoping he sounded reassuring even as the words clawed up his tight throat. "I responded poorly. I'm, I'm *elated*. I just..."

"Forgiven," she whispered, "and forgotten. I love you."

Gaze blurred with tears, he hugged her back with everything he had, nonalcoholic champagne threatening to slosh over the edges of the glass. With Skye in his arms again, all the weight he'd been carrying lifted in an instant. The ruthlessly tight knots that had been twisting and twisting and *twisting* finally loosened, and as he eased away from her, he still couldn't fathom what he had done to deserve such a perfect pair of partners in this life—but he had to learn to stop questioning it.

"Thank you," he said, looking to Finn as he wiped under his eyes, "for bringing her here. For being here."

When that one text message had said they would see each other soon, this was the last thing Cole had ever expected.

"It seemed like the right thing to do," his friend insisted with a trademark grin, rocking back and forth in his leather-tipped shoes, hands in his pockets. "Besides, it didn't feel proper, the two of us celebrating without you. We thought it best to bring the party here."

"I don't think you know just how much I needed you," Cole managed, then downed half his drink—only to remember it was nonalcoholic. But Finn was right. If Skye couldn't drink, then neither could they. The gravity of it all, of having a *baby* with the woman he loved, hit him like a freight train, and Finn had to reach out to steady him when his knees gave way ever so slightly. Skye wrapped an arm around him, giggling.

"Come on, there's no booze in there—"

He caught her supple lips in a kiss, lingering there for shorter than he wanted to before resting his forehead against hers. "You're pregnant."

"Thirty thousand tests can't lie," she joked, her cheeks rosy and her eyes bright. "We're having a baby..."

Teary-eyed again, he engulfed her in a hug, only then realizing she was also shaking. When he spied Finn hovering over her shoulder, he grabbed the man's sleeve and dragged him in too, all three holding one another, supporting one another.

Loving one another.

They stayed like that a long while, Skye sandwiched in the middle, until she finally wriggled out and skipped back to the stairwell. As she grabbed the bottle of faux bubbly, Cole nudged Finn and held the man's gaze. He owed him—big time.

"Honestly. I'm so sorry. Thank you for being here."

"Where else would we be?" Finn murmured, smirking when Skye joined them moments later to refill Cole's glass.

"A toast," she insisted, taking her flute back from Finn. Their glasses clinked together, and she laughed, looking effortlessly vibrant—and totally in love. "To having a baby girl… Because I seriously can't put up with another boy in this household."

"To our baby girl," Finn agreed, his eyes watery.

Cole nodded and lifted his glass a little higher. "To our family."

FUN FACTS AND FUTURE TIDBITS

At the beginning of the trilogy, Skye was twenty-nine, Cole was thirty, and Finn was thirty-five.

After agreeing to start seeing both Finn and Cole, Skye had to figure out how to juggle three relationships: one with Cole, who she had been partially involved with for four years already; another with Finn, as they were essentially *just* starting to date; and a third between all three of them. It was a bit hectic at first, but over time the playing field evened out, and Skye felt as though she had one relationship consisting of two men.

Finn tends to assume the role of caregiver. As the eldest in the group, and the oldest sibling in his own family, he generally takes command of stressful situations—but that can sometimes mean his feelings sit on the backburner. Skye and Cole are getting more adept at managing a crisis, along with noticing when Finn isn't being heard. It's a process.

Finn is an extrovert. Cole is an introvert. Skye straddles the line between the two.

Cole's idea of a great Saturday night is all three of them at home, in their comfy clothes, making dinner together after some mind-blowing afternoon sex. They'd then spend the evening snuggled up on the couch watching movies.

Finn's idea of a great Saturday night is either a sex marathon, or treating his two favourite people to some exclusive restaurant or club, where they have a private booth or room to themselves—just in case things get interesting.

Skye's idea of a great Saturday night is being with both her boys. Period.

Cole has been clinically diagnosed with anxiety and takes medication to help manage it. Finn was unaware of that for the duration of their friendship until the events of the trilogy. Both Skye and Finn help Cole manage when he needs them, but it has been a learning curve for everyone.

Everybody fights in a relationship, Cole, Finn, and Skye included. Cole tends to bottle things up and explode. Finn and Skye are more argumentative in the heat of the moment, though that tends to resolve the issue faster.

Finn is the only one with parents who are still married. Skye's mother died of cancer when she was nineteen and her dad bailed on her long before that. She has no interest in reaching out to him. Cole's mother lives in a cute cottage in the English countryside, and his father died of a heart attack in his teens. The trio alternate Christmases between Finn and Cole's family, though try to see both if possible.

In the bedroom, Cole is a dominant, Skye is generally submissive, though she prefers being a bratty submissive when she can, and Finn alternates between the two. The three maintain separate bedrooms to give one another space when necessary, although every house they own has one bedroom with a bed big enough to fit everyone. Skye prefers sleeping with Cole if all three aren't sleeping together, but only because he doesn't complain about her bed-hogging. Finn never lets her hear the end of it.

While both Cole and Skye are heterosexual, Finn would classify himself as bisexual.

They go on to have two children. Mallory, known as Mal to friends and family, takes after her mother with her red hair, though she has Cole's eyes. Sahil, two years younger than his sister, is the spitting image of Finn. Both children call Finn and Cole dad. Mallory goes through a wild-child period, which lasts into her late twenties before she settles down, working in fashion, while Sahil follows in Cole's footsteps with university, post-graduate degrees, and a career in tech.

Ozzy lives to the ripe old age of nineteen, and prefers Finn to Cole. Mason, in contrast, passes at age twelve and is obsessed with Cole. Skye is the ruling authority over both, however. The family goes on to adopt more pets after, and Finn eventually sponsors the opening of a big cat sanctuary in northern California. The sanctuary's first lion cubs are honorarily named Cole and Finn, and a snow leopard rescue is named Skye.

Finn also has Rai's Sweets chocolate products named after Cole, Skye, and both their kids. After his father passes, he takes over the company and moves its headquarters to LA to be close to the family.

Skye ends up working remotely from home maintaining a popular museum's website, blog, and event coverage, with a little help from Cole with the technical things, until both kids are in high school. Afterward, she invests her time in charities, preferring the freedom to be with her family when she wants.

Cole's mother is very supportive of the trio's arrangement. Finn's family remain iffy but are generally accepting.

Skye doesn't legally marry either Finn or Cole. They do have a private ceremony where they exchange rings on their five-year anniversary. In their eyes, they're married—and live a long, happy life before retiring together on the Caribbean island of Bequia.

THANKS FOR READING!

Thank you so much for reading! You're awesome. Seriously. Go treat yo' self for being such a fabulous human being.

If you enjoyed the ALL IN trilogy and want to support Liz in some small way, please consider leaving a review at the retailer of your choice, including Goodreads. Reviews help indie authors thrive. I also use reviews as a way to gauge what series to work on next. If contemporary erotic romance is your thing, let me know!

Best wishes,

Liz

Connect with Liz on social media:

Website
Facebook
Twitter
Goodreads
Tumblr
Pinterest
Instagram

ABOUT THE AUTHOR

Liz is a Canadian author who grew up in the Middle East. She has a degree in Bioarchaeology from Western University, and when she isn't writing about her own snarky characters, she is reading about other people's snarky characters, babying her herb garden, loitering on social media, or taking care of her many animals.

Liz dabbles in both paranormal and contemporary erotic romance. Her paranormals are usually dark and angsty, and her contemporaries are stress-free smutfests, but you'll find both full of feels. Most of all, she loves writing realistic characters in fantastical settings.

More from Liz Meldon:

PARANORMAL ROMANCE

The Hunt – a Demon Romance

Predator (#1)
Prey (#2)
Stalker (#3)
Killer (#4)
The Hunt: Book Bundle #1
The Hunt: Book Bundle #2
The Hunt: The Complete Edition
The Uprising: A Companion Novel

***Dark Days* – a Vampire/Wolf Shifter Romance**

Semester One

Semester Two

***Lovers and Liars: Immortal Wars* – a fantasy and paranormal romance series about the old world gods going to war**

Court of the Phantom Queen (2017) – Book #1 (fantasy romance, novella)

Apollo's Priestess (2017) – Book #2 (shifter paranormal romance, novella)

To the North (TBD) – Book #3 (fantasy romance, novella)

CONTEMPORARY EROTIC ROMANCE

All In Trilogy – Sugar Daddies, Billionaires, and Menages – oh my!

Finn (#1)

Cole (#2)

Skye (#3)

All In Trilogy: Book Bundle + Bonus Content

Unbowed – standalone erotic romances featuring kink escorts the alpha men who love them

Belle: Part 1

Belle: Part 2

Penny: Part 1 (2019)

Penny: Part 2 (2019)

Erotic Short Shorts – an Erotic Short Story Series

Happy Hour (2016)
Holiday Hell (2017)

www.ingramcontent.com/pod-product-compliance
Lightning Source LLC
Chambersburg PA
CBHW030602180626
46816CB00005B/1644

9780993894350